Final Payment

Books by Steven F. Havill

The Posadas County Mysteries
Heartshot
Bitter Recoil
Twice Buried
Before She Dies
Privileged to Kill
Prolonged Exposure
Out of Season
Dead Weight
Bag Limit
Red, Green, or Murder
Scavengers
A Discount for Death
Convenient Disposal
Statute of Limitations
Final Payment
The Fourth Time is Murder
Double Prey

The Dr. Thomas Parks Novels
Race for the Dying
Comes a Time for Burning

Other Novels
The Killer
The Worst Enemy
LeadFire
TimberBlood

Final Payment

A Posadas County Mystery

Steven F. Havill

Poisoned Pen Press

Poisoned Pen Press
6962 E. First Ave., Ste. 103
Scottsdale, AZ 85251
www.poisonedpenpress.com
info@poisonedpenpress.com

Printed in the United States of America

For Kathleen

Acknowledgments

The author would like to extend special thanks to Keith Mangelsdorf.

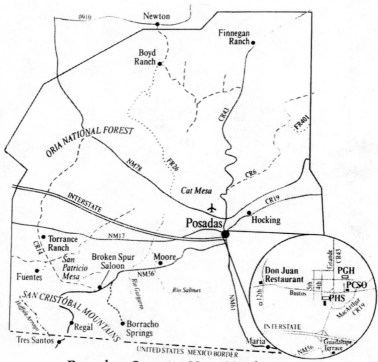

Posadas County, New Mexico

Chapter One

Estelle Reyes-Guzman's passenger leaned forward, enormous blue eyes wide with a mixture of apprehension and excitement.

"Oh my, isn't this something," County Manager Leona Spears whispered. The "something" was a spot where the U.S. Forest Service's two-track meandered close to the formidable, crumbling rim of Cat Mesa. For a few yards, no trees blocked the panoramic view of Posadas County, from the flat, barren reaches of the eastern prairie to the San Cristóbal Mountains to the south and west. The mountains formed a natural barrier with neighboring Mexico. From this spot, Undersheriff Guzman could see the entire southern half of Posadas County, including the village of Posadas, which nestled on the mesa's flank below them.

The road ducked back into the trees again, away from the mesa rim, and almost immediately they saw the flashing lights of the large boxy EMT rescue unit a hundred yards ahead. The ambulance was parked just off the narrow lane, and Estelle pulled her county SUV to a halt a dozen yards behind it.

"And this is only practice," she said. The comment elicited a groan from the county manager. Despite her best efforts, they both knew that there was no way to guarantee safety in a hundred-mile bicycle race through the county's roughest back-country. To the competitors, of course, that was the attraction.

In this instance, the emergency came two days before the race itself, during a casual practice ride.

Estelle could see activity fifty yards ahead through the trees, and she glanced across at the county manager. Leona, with her frilly white blouse, neatly tailored business suit, and stylish low-heeled shoes, was not dressed for the boonies. As if reading the undersheriff's mind, the large woman waved a hand. "You go ahead. I'll wait." That brought a smile from Estelle, who knew Leona's insatiable curiosity.

I'll give you thirty seconds, she thought.

Even as she stepped out and closed the door of the Expedition, Estelle could see the bicycle tracks cut in the dirt. How the injured rider had come to drift so far from the marked race route was still a mystery, unless it was the obvious lure of a "shortcut."

In a moment, as she emerged through the last clump of oak brush, the undersheriff saw that the unlucky cyclist had already been splinted, bandaged, and IV'd, then strapped to a gurney and hoisted to safety. Now, a dozen feet from the mesa edge, three EMTs worked over their patient, ignoring the spectacular abyss behind them. Estelle slipped the small digital camera out of her pocket and took several photos before approaching any closer.

A girl in rainbow-colored spandex, her face pasty white with short red hair plastered to her forehead where her helmet had pressed, sat at the base of a sturdy piñon while a fourth EMT bandaged the girl's bloody knee.

"Hey there, sheriff," the EMT working on the knee said. She had glanced up when she heard the camera. "Not your usual kind of MVA we got this time. What brings you up here?"

"My number came up," Estelle replied cheerfully. The injured girl opened her eyes as Estelle knelt beside her. "What happened?"

"It was his big idea," the girl said, and gulped air. "He said this trail was a shortcut that no one else knew about." She closed her eyes.

"Glad no one else did," EMT Matty Finnegan said sympathetically. She made a diving motion with one hand. "Right over there, Estelle. Looks like he tried to stop when the trail made a turn, but he got crossed up somehow. About a fifteen-foot drop."

"*Ay,*" Estelle said. She touched the girl lightly on the arm. "What's your partner's name?"

The girl grimaced as the EMT snugged the bandage. "Terry Gutierrez. We're from Socorro. I think that dumb butt was looking over his shoulder, to see if I was behind him. Then he didn't have time to stop."

"And your name?"

"April Pritt," she said, gritting her teeth. "Shit, that hurts."

The EMT nodded. "You're a lucky girl, Miss April. Other than the knee," she said to Estelle, "April is okay, sheriff. A nasty laceration. Pretty brave, too. She climbed down over the cliff there to help her friend."

"I lost my balance," April said.

"You sure did. But no fractures." Matty reached out and gently patted the side of her patient's bandaged knee. "No stitches, if she's lucky." She looked critically at one knee, then the other. "Just another scar to keep all the others company."

"How's he?" Estelle turned and watched as one of the EMTs adjusted the huge cervical collar on the injured rider. The young man's eyes were closed, his jaw slack under the oxygen mask.

"Not so lucky," Matty said. "But I think he'll be okay. We'll just have to see. I tell you what, though…thank God for small favors like cell phones."

Stepping so carefully that she appeared to be stalking wild game, the county manager appeared from the oak brush. "Oh my," Leona said, hesitating well back from the mesa edge. The county manager had her own small camera in hand, and Estelle turned to make sure that the enormous woman wasn't planning to step near the rim.

"A bad fall," the undersheriff said to her to make sure she had Leona's attention. "Two competitors from Socorro." The girl with the battered knee looked up at Leona apologetically, even though she had no idea who the enormous woman might be.

"Oh my," Leona said again. She took a reflexive step back when she saw Estelle walk over and stand near the edge of a large block of limestone. The view of the county was spectacular, but Estelle's attention was drawn to the broken juniper limbs below, and the blood swashes on the gray boulders. It made a grim photograph.

As she knelt at the mesa's edge on that warm May afternoon, Estelle leaned forward just enough to trace in her mind's eye the arc of the cyclist's free fall, to imagine the short burst of panic as he realized his mistake. The bicyclist had plunged over the mesa rim, arms flailing, his cry of panic echoing through the canyons. His trajectory ended with a fifteen-foot free flight that smacked into a jumble of jagged boulders capping the long talus slope that formed the mesa's apron. He had hit so hard that his helmet broke open like a coconut shell. The helmet lay next to the mangled bike, and Estelle walked over and picked it up. One deep gash had torn the helmet's brightly colored plastic just above the temple. She grimaced and held it up for Leona to see.

"He's lucky," Leona said.

"We hope so," Estelle replied. The blood on the helmet indicated otherwise. She placed the shattered helmet carefully on the frame of the bike and turned back to the girl.

"You climbed down?" Estelle asked.

"Sort of," April said through clenched teeth. "Not the most graceful thing I've ever done. Is he going to be all right?"

"I think so," Estelle said. She regarded the spot where the eighteen-year-old girl had stopped her bike shy of disaster. No doubt she had seen her boyfriend below, so battered, broken, and lacerated that all he could do was lie in a growing puddle of blood and whimper. There was no easy route down, and her good judgment had been clouded by panic. "You called us from down there?"

"No. I didn't know what to do, so I called 911 first. But then I saw all the blood, and I knew I couldn't wait."

"Brave girl," Estelle said. She turned away from the rim. "Just a wrong turn on an unfamiliar shortcut," Estelle said to Leona. "As simple as that. No shortcuts allowed in the actual race."

"Mercy, I should hope not. You're not climbing down there, are you?"

"No...I don't think I need to." She took another photo, this time zooming in on the blood smear down below as closely as the camera allowed, then zooming back for a panorama.

Eleven miles to the southeast, she could see the village of Posadas where the cyclists had set out on their practice ride as they prepared for the race coming up that weekend. The asphalt ribbon of County Road 43 that wound up the foot of the mesa, first passing the landfill and then the abandoned Consolidated Copper Mine, was the easiest portion of the route. After reaching the old quarry, the race route turned first onto steep Forest Service roads for the ascent up Cat Mesa. Beyond that, it was rough two-tracks, footpaths, streambeds, and worse.

"The Blood and Broken Bones One Hundred," Estelle said, then pointed. The sudden motion made Leona flinch. "You can see more riders coming up the hill."

A handful of specks moved on the paved road, more cyclists taking a final afternoon training ride. No doubt in an hour or so they would stop at this very spot, marveling at their comrade's attempt at unpowered flight.

The undersheriff reached out a hand and rested her palm on the sharp limestone. The gray rock was warm, and with one finger she traced the shape where one of the cyclist's pedal cranks had caught just before he'd launched.

"My, oh my," the Posadas County manager whispered, drawing closer to see the scar on the rock.

"Don't step too close to the edge," Estelle reminded her again. "Some of the rocks are loose," She could imagine the blond, Heidi-braided Brunhilde taking flight, and it wasn't a pretty sight.

"Okay, let's do it," one of the EMTs said, and they picked up the gurney as if the battered and fractured cyclist were weightless. The girl started to get up, but Matty reached out and put a restraining hand on her shoulder.

"No, no," she said. "You don't walk. They'll be back in just a minute with your ride. Just kick back and relax."

"I think I can make it," the girl said.

"I'm sure you can. But you're not going to."

"What about the bikes?" the girl said.

"We'll manage those," Matty said. "Sheriff, can you fit them in your unit?"

"You bet," Estelle said. She knelt by the girl. "They'll be at the sheriff's office on Bustos Avenue in Posadas when you're ready to pick them up, okay? Right now, we need to make sure that Terry's going to be all right."

"We're going to want to X-ray that knee, too," the EMT said. "We'll take care of you guys, then there'll be plenty of time to square things away."

The girl nodded and leaned back against the tree, grateful that she didn't have to move. In a moment, two of the EMTs returned with a second gurney, and the girl was strapped in for her ambulance ride back to Posadas.

Estelle picked up the spectacularly crumpled bike and was immediately surprised at how light it was. The bicycle that Francisco, her seven-year-old son, had just inherited when a neighbor outgrew it weighed more than this one. She looped the shattered helmet's chinstrap around one of the brake levers.

"Let me give you a hand," Leona said. She walked to where the second machine was lying and picked it up, crooking her arm and hoisting the bike to her shoulder for easy walking.

"Do you need any more pictures before we go back?" Estelle asked.

"I don't think so," Leona said. "What we need is a bulldozer to close off this trail so that this doesn't happen again. I can just imagine how much Mr. Iron Man would sue us for if *he* went off here."

Estelle laughed. She knew "Mr. Iron Man" only by name and reputation. Former lieutenant governor Chet Hansen loved bi-, tri-, quad-, or any other flavor of athlons, the more challenging the better. His was the only name on the entry roster that she had recognized, other than a handful of local competitors. The race had attracted a *peletón* from twelve states and three foreign countries.

"A dozer shouldn't be a problem. Maybe you have some folks who still owe you favors," she said, referring to Leona's former life as an engineer with the state highway department.

"Oh, many, many," the county manager said. "But the Forest Service needs to bring theirs in. They're over at Sparkman's Wells, cutting a livestock tank. That's only a mile or two." She shrugged the bike more securely on her shoulder, keeping the oily chain away from her suit. "I'll give them a call when we get back."

It didn't surprise Estelle that the efficient Leona knew exactly where available machinery was working…and the undersheriff was confident that, when the cyclo-cross race burst through this section of the course on the weekend, a fresh berm of dirt would block the rim trail.

In a few minutes, and with some finagling and the removal of front wheels, both bikes were stowed in the back of the Sheriff's Department Expedition.

"How do people manage such things?" Leona said. "For heaven's sakes, when he saw the edge, why didn't he just *stop?*"

"As a dear friend of mine is fond of saying," Estelle said, shifting the bikes for a better fit, "'Events conspire.'"

Leona shivered dramatically. "Is this going to be a problem for us this weekend? Should I be asking that? Do I want to know? Should I worry?"

"You already *are* worrying, Leona," Estelle said. "The race organizers promised that they'll have officials all along the route, and that it'll be prominently marked. Practice sessions are always more dangerous, anyway."

"*Prominently* marked," Leona repeated with emphasis. "*Verrrry* prominently. Otherwise, our first Posadas One Hundred bike race is going to be our last, with a hundred corpses littered about the base of Cat Mesa. What grand publicity for us, especially with the big-city media in town."

"I hope it won't be that bad," Estelle said. "This is just one of those freak things." She knew the race would generate a small splash in the media, perhaps a color photo on page 47 of the *Albuquerque Journal*—and then only because of the former lieutenant governor's efforts. *Former* was usually the first step toward anonymity, amplifying Hansen's term as a *lieutenant* governor—an invisible position to begin with. But Chet Hansen had managed to bike, swim, run, sail, even shoot his way into the press with some regularity.

"Actually, Tomás says that the worst part of the course is further on, where they get into rocks on the west flank of the mesa. The trail that cuts down the west end of the mesa and rejoins the Forest Service road is good for hiking—I can't imagine bikes on it."

Deputy Tom Pasquale, an avid cyclist himself, had ridden the full hundred-mile course half a dozen times during the past year, and parts of it many more times than that. During the early spring, he had played an active role in the race's organization, and his name was included in the list of entrants.

"But he says it's a perfect course," Estelle added. "It's so rugged that in some places the riders have to dismount and carry the bikes." She grimaced. "Apparently that's what makes it perfect. He suggested I take the two boys to see part of the race over on the west side, where all the action will be."

Five-year-old Carlos and his older brother, Francisco, were well beyond training wheels themselves, but their eyes went saucers whenever they saw Tom Pasquale's fancy titanium bike.

"What an odd definition of 'perfect,'" Leona said. "But that's Tomás, of course," she added. "I think I shall take the weekend to go visit my aunt in Kansas City. Let me know when this is all over." She pulled a dainty hanky from her pocket and dabbed her forehead. "And I would, too…but that would mean I'd miss your son's piano recital Saturday night. And my, oh my, I can't wait. How wonderful that's going to be."

"We hope so."

"And he's but seven?"

"Yes."

"That means that in eleven short years, he can enter this foolish race," Leona said, and chuckled. "I could probably have gone all day without reminding you of that."

"Exactly," Estelle said. She paused to look at the mangled bike one more time, then slammed the back door of the Expedition.

"Seriously now," Leona continued, suddenly sounding less fluffy and more official, "this race is a big deal for the county,

Estelle. Is there anything the race organizers need that we haven't provided? And in particular," and she waggled a finger like a first-grade teacher, "is there anything that we haven't thought about that just *might* prevent something like this from happening again?"

"I don't think so," Estelle replied. "And I know they're planning to start the riders at one-minute intervals—it's no big pack thing, where they're all bunched together. No teaming, no girlfrien–boyfriend stuff. That will help, with them running against the clock, rather than pedal to pedal. One a minute, so it'll take a couple hours at the start to get everyone launched. We've agreed to close County Road Forty-three for the start, from Pershing Park in the middle of town all the way to the turnoff by the quarry."

She turned and looked back down the trail through the trees, now thoroughly marked with fresh footprints and tire tracks. "That and a little stretch on the state highway at the end are the only paved roads in the race."

"Joy," Leona said without conviction. "Well, I hope the boy without wings is going to be all right."

"He'll be a spectator, that's for sure," Estelle said.

Leona climbed back into the passenger seat of the Expedition with a sigh of relief. She watched as Estelle went through the ritual of jotting notes in her log. With the EMTs gone, they were the last to leave the scene, and Estelle glanced in the back to make sure the two bikes were secure. As she did so, her cellular phone chirped. She glanced at the caller ID and saw that the call was from Posadas County Sheriff Robert Torrez. Knowing what was coming, she held the phone tight against her ear.

"Guzman."

"Hey," Torrez said, his voice soft almost to the point of inaudibility. "What's your twenty?"

"I'm on the Cat Mesa Forest Service road, about a mile in from Forty-three."

"You finished up there?"

"Yes. Two injured, both transported. One critical with head injuries, maybe more. The other just banged up."

"Okay. Look, I'm going to need you down this way. I'm at the gas company's airstrip on Fourteen. We got us a problem."

Estelle had started the Expedition and she pulled it into gear, backing off the road so she could swing around. The brief hesitation as she did so prompted Torrez to add, "You on the way?"

"Just heading out. It'll be thirty minutes." If he had given it long thought, Robert Torrez would have been hard-pressed to find a spot more removed from his undersheriff's present location and still be within the county.

"Got it. They'll wait. But expedite on down here, all right?"

"What have you got?"

"A triple," Torrez said. "So far, anyway." He clicked off without further explanation.

Estelle's pulse kicked up a notch, and she accelerated harder than she intended, narrowly missing a sturdy piñon with the Expedition's right front fender. She didn't need to ask, *A triple what?* Bicycle riders were still on her mind, though, and she wondered how three riders had managed to kill themselves on a flat dirt road.

Chapter Two

The last hundred yards of the forest road cut through a dusty meadow before reaching the intersection with County Road 43, and Estelle saw a group of three bicyclists heading toward them. Another dozen or more had gathered just off the pavement of the county road for a rest stop, no doubt to let the large ambulance pass.

She turned on the emergency lights and touched the yelp to guarantee their attention. The three cyclists darted off the two-track and stopped. Under other circumstances, the undersheriff would have stopped to chat with the riders, taking the opportunity to emphasize again the need for some small grain of caution on the trail ahead. Instead, as she passed, the cyclists were treated to a voluminous cloud of reddish dust that billowed up behind the Expedition.

One member of the larger group broke away as she approached. He walked out to intercept her, expecting a conversation. She touched the siren again and shot past, tires chirping as she turned onto the asphalt of the county road.

For the past several minutes, the county manager had been the ideal passenger, inquiring about neither the phone call nor the urgency of their departure from the mesa top—choosing instead to let Estelle concentrate on missing trees, boulders, and cyclists. Squared away on the pavement, Estelle glanced at Leona, who sat rigid, one hand holding the panic handle on the door post and the other gripping the top edge of the computer on the center console.

"I can drop you off in town," she said, and braked hard for a tight turn.

"I'm fine," Leona replied. "Don't take the time." She didn't release her grip. "But where are we going?"

"The sheriff has a multiple fatality out by the gas company's airstrip," Estelle explained. "I don't know more than that."

"Oh, my God," Leona said, and readjusted her grip. "That's on the other side of the moon."

"Almost."

They accelerated hard down the hill, passing the last straight stretch along the old quarry before the switchbacks down into town. "Of course, the dead can wait patiently," Leona whispered. She reared back in her seat as Estelle braked hard.

"I don't know what we have," Estelle said, knowing that other bikers would be on the hill, letting the siren serve as conversation. Down past the abandoned mine, past the landfill entrance, they approached the intersection with the state highway that curved out of town, heading west toward the municipal airport. Estelle slowed just enough to have time to check for traffic and then shot through the stop sign, flying down the two-mile straight stretch toward Posadas.

"I thought you said airport," Leona managed.

"No…out past the Broken Spur. The gas company's airstrip? Just south of the Torrance Ranch."

"Oh, my God." Estelle wasn't sure if Leona's reaction was to the distance—nearly thirty miles—or to the remoteness of the spot. By looking southwest with binoculars on a clear day, they could have seen the dash of the airstrip from the mesa top they had just left. "The state planes have used that on more than one occasion," Leona added. "I wonder if…" She left the rest of the sentence unfinished, bracing herself for the dash through town.

The state highway turned into Bustos Avenue, and after a few blocks the undersheriff turned south on Grande. Leaning forward, she turned up the radio. Because of the endless problem with what Sheriff Torrez liked to call "scanner ghouls," they had stopped using the radio when a phone call would do. But the written radio log kept by dispatch still served as an official documentation of times and responses.

With an open street ahead of her, she keyed the mike.

"Three-oh-eight, three-ten is in the village, westbound."

The speaker barked squelch a couple of times for reply.

"Three-oh-eight, ten-fifty-five?"

"That's negative," Torrez said, and he sounded impatient. Had he used the radio earlier, Estelle would have heard it—either in the unit or from the handheld on her belt. "I got a multiple ten-sixty-three. And ten-twenty-one from now on."

Estelle glanced in her rearview at the winking lights that had appeared behind her on Grande just as she guided the Expedition around the curve under the interstate overpass and onto State 56—the long, empty stretch of twenty-six miles between Posadas and the tiny village of Regál at the Mexican border.

"Three-oh-five ETA about eighteen minutes," Sergeant Tom Mears' voice said. No matter how hard Estelle pushed the bulky Expedition, the sergeant's sedan would overtake her before she'd gone a dozen miles. The county coroner—either Dr. Alan Perrone or her husband, Dr. Francis Guzman—would respond to the 10-63 code more sedately. As Leona had already observed, no one was as patient as a corpse.

Holding a steady hundred, Estelle didn't slow until the turnoff to County Road 14, a half mile beyond the Broken Spur Saloon. Tom Mears' patrol car remained a dozen car lengths behind. As they crossed the cattle guard, Leona Spears appeared to relax for the first time, her left hand releasing its grip on the computer.

The wide dirt road swept down to cross a shallow arroyo on a bridge none too wide, then angled up a rise. In a quarter mile, Estelle saw Bob Torrez's again Chevy pickup truck parked on the shoulder of the road. The sheriff leaned against the truck's front fender, arms folded across his chest, one boot crossed over the other—a lounging rancher waiting for a good gab fest.

With no need of lights and siren, Estelle approached slowly. The desert showed no signs of catastrophe. No airplane lay in a smoking heap on the gas company's runway just to the west, no truck pulling an overloaded livestock trailer lay crunched in the bar ditch, no lost tour bus rested on its top...and no mangled cyclists littered the right-of-way.

Torrez pushed himself away from the fender and motioned her away from his side of the road. She stopped, window down.

"You need to park on the other side," he said. He leaned on the Expedition's windowsill and looked across at Leona. The expression on his handsome, dark face asked "Why?" with a raised eyebrow, but he didn't voice it. Estelle had taken the county vehicle that the sheriff normally used because her Crown Victoria would never tackle the rough paths on top of the mesa. Leona's powerful perfume would linger in the Expedition for days, giving the sheriff plenty of reason to complain.

He straightened up and waved for Mears to follow her.

She parked and switched off the truck. "Stay here for a few minutes, all right?" she asked, and Leona nodded.

"How's the kid up on the mesa?" Tom Mears asked as he joined her.

"Badly busted," Estelle replied. Torrez met them in the middle of the county road, his hands thrust in his hip pockets.

"Hey," he greeted. "All the way down at the end. We gotta walk down. There's some stuff you'll want to see."

"What are we looking at?" Estelle asked.

"Three," the sheriff said. "Middle-aged man, middle-aged woman, and a younger guy."

"Migrants?" Mears asked. The jagged mountains to the south formed an effective barrier at this point of the border, and a somewhat less effective border fence had been built just south of Regál, where the official port of entry was manned twelve hours a day.

"No, I don't think so. They aren't dressed like it, and they sure as hell aren't day laborers." He turned and looked back at the Expedition and its occupant. "Tell her that when the coroner shows up, he needs to walk down the right edge of the runway. I don't want any tire tracks in there yet."

Estelle passed the message on to Leona, who brightened instantly. Her interest in law enforcement was keen. Among her various election campaigns—all unsuccessful—was a run for sheriff against Robert Torrez. She had lost in spectacular but good-natured fashion. And now, as an appointed county manager, she had become a powerful voice on behalf of the Sheriff's Department. She frequently indulged herself in ride-alongs with deputies, and had learned when to stay out of the way.

The gas company's access gate was new, solid, and securely locked. The four padlocks, one each for the owners, the Sheriff's Department, the State Police, and the Rural Electric Cooperative, were all intact. Torrez dug out his keys and popped the county lock, swinging the gate just enough for the three of them to enter before dropping the latch. The gravel access road curved fifty yards to the verge of the runway, and they walked it in silence.

Reaching the pavement, Torrez pointed down the runway, a 2,560-foot strip of macadam 26 feet wide with a neat dotted white line down the middle. "All the way down at the other end," he said.

"Well, all right," Tom Mears mused. "Do we get to know how you discovered the bodies without driving in here?" A slender, sandy-haired man an inch shorter than Estelle's five-seven and a full head shorter than Torrez, Mears always seemed completely at ease with his moody boss.

"Damn coyotes," Torrez said, and let that suffice. "Come on." They walked down the right side of the runway for only fifty yards before he held out a hand. The macadam was scrubbed clear in most places, with patches of sand here and there. The prairie vegetation grew right to the edge of the pavement, poised to take over if ignored for more than a season. "Right there," Torrez said. "You can see where the plane landed." Sure enough, two scuff marks about ten feet apart straddled the centerline. "It's the only set I saw," he added. "Most of the time, you can't see 'em. But once in a while, they cross a patch of blow-sand, and it's pretty clear."

They walked on in silence, the half-mile-long runway sloping slightly downhill as it ran from east to west. The afternoon light slanted across the pavement at a perfect angle, picking up the airplane's narrow tire prints every time they ran across a patch of sand. As the end of the runway drew closer, the aircraft had drifted smoothly toward the right, until its right tire ran along the edge of the asphalt. A hundred feet from the end of the runway, the tracks showed that the plane had swung tightly to the left, turning around to face east.

"He went off over there," Torrez said. He pointed without crossing the runway. "Ran the right tire and the nose wheel off the pavement. We'll look at that later. Lemme show you this. And watch where you step."

The first corpse lay partially in a bed of cacti, his right cheek pegged to the fleshy pads by the tough thorns. Estelle bent down and saw the small wound centered just above the collar of the man's dark green work shirt, in the crease between skull and neck—the single shot would have snuffed out the man's life as effectively as an on-off switch kills a light. The wound hadn't bled much, and what blood there was had crusted hard and brown. Without disturbing the body, it was impossible to tell if the bullet had exited the skull. In the past few days, the sun had been harsh, the days hot. The man's shirt stretched taut over his bloating torso.

"No personal possessions? No weapons?" Estelle asked.

"Nothing yet," Torrez said. He stood like a signpost, waiting for her to move, adding no more tracks that later would have to be sorted out.

Moving with great care, Estelle picked her way through the sparse vegetation, aware of Bob Torrez's breathing behind her. The second corpse lay twenty feet from the first, dropped by what appeared to be a single shot just above and behind the right ear. A younger man, perhaps in his early twenties, he lay on his face, hand outstretched as if reaching for the heel of the woman who lay in front of him. She lay curled up in a fetal position as if asleep, exhausted from the grueling trip. The wound through the bridge of her nose had bled a single track to puddle in the sand under her head.

"Just the three?" Estelle whispered.

"So far," Torrez said.

"Looks like they could be mom, pop, and oldest son," Tom Mears said, and Estelle nodded. All three victims were dressed in simple, nondescript clothing, but the older man's fancy leather loafers weren't designed for farm work. The young man wore new running shoes, the woman a neat pair of tan-colored pumps.

She hesitated at the woman's body. Death had not crept up from behind for this one. Perhaps, in the last seconds, she had turned to face her attacker, but there had been no time for a struggle.

"I'd like to run this film backward," Torrez said. "We got somebody out there that knows how to use a gun."

"Ay," she said, and shook her head. "Maybe teamwork. So many questions." She turned in place, trying to picture how a single shooter could so efficiently pop three people, perhaps even in the dark, with them trying desperately to scuttle for cover. Unless it had happened so unexpectedly, so suddenly, that the last victim of the three had had only time to pause and half turn toward her attacker.

"Just a few."

"We don't know if any of this," she turned to frame the three bodies with both hands, "has anything to do with the airstrip, or the plane. We need to establish that."

"Common sense says it does," the sheriff said. County Road 14, passing by the entrance to the small airstrip, was the nearest byway, but it ran north–south, teeing into State 56. That state highway, heading northeast toward Posadas and southwest to the Mexican border of Regál, was a full mile south of this lonely spot in the desert. The border was eight miles by air, eleven by road. "For one thing, nobody's tampered with the gate, near as I can tell. I didn't find any tracks where they walked in across the desert….You can't hide the tracks of three people."

Estelle knew that to be true—as far as Robert Torrez was concerned. Hunting was his passion, whether pronghorn, deer, peccary, coyotes, or people.

"At least four," Estelle corrected. She turned in a complete circle, trying to conjure a scenario in her mind that made sense. "They have nothing with them, though. No water bottles, no extra clothing, no weapons no…nothing."

"Got to be a simple answer," Torrez said.

"I think you're right about the airplane," she said. "That makes sense after a fashion." She stood on her tiptoes, as if adding an extra inch or two would give her the panorama that she needed. "I'd like to have the county's cherry picker down here. An overview might help."

Torrez nodded. He looked at his wristwatch. "It's three fifty-five. It'll take an hour to get the maintenance crew out here with a bucket. In the meantime, I want Perrone to establish a TOD just as quick as he can. I don't think these folks have been camped out here more than a couple of days, three or four at the most. Don't smell like it."

Estelle knelt, looking south. "Why here?" she mused. "Why here?"

"'Cause that's where it was convenient," Torrez said.

"It's like real estate," Estelle said. "Location, location, location."

Chapter Three

Within two hours, the area surrounding the gas company's runway looked like a movie set, complete with a Posadas County utility truck's cherry picker hoisted aloft into the gusty late afternoon sky. Each time she shifted position, Estelle felt the bucket's gentle sway. Her commanding view, with the lift truck parked fifty yards from the end of the runway and the bucket hoisted thirty feet high, told her nothing new. The three bodies lay in pathetic isolation on the prairie, a few tantalizing yards from the spot where they had apparently deplaned.

Sergeant Tom Mears worked with Deputy Tom Pasquale, and the "two Toms," as the sheriff's wife, Gayle Torrez, called them, had established that the pilot had stopped the aircraft just as the right tire sank into the sand, off the macadam and sixty-five feet from the end of the runway. Swinging wide to turn, the pilot had misjudged by mere inches, dropping first a main and then the nose wheel off the pavement. An odd mistake, Estelle thought, for someone who had landed a loaded aircraft on a short runway, most likely in the dead of night.

A night landing made sense to her. The risks of trying to cross the border and then land in this isolated place would escalate in daylight—State 56 was a busy highway, and a plane parked on the airstrip would be in plain view.

With tires precariously in the sandy gravel, it appeared that the pilot had elected to stop the aircraft, perhaps to off-load extra weight. The passengers had deplaned, their feet creating a welter of scuffed prints.

"That's one question answered," Estelle said aloud. Linda Real, the Sheriff's Department's photographer and Deputy Pasquale's roommate, didn't move a muscle. She hung on gamely as the bucket rocked and dipped like a stuck carnival ride.

"Which one?" she asked.

"The trail of shoe prints. I can see them from here." Estelle swept her arm to indicate the route the three victims had apparently taken, and just that small motion bounced the bucket. Linda flinched. The trail was marked with a row of small wire-stemmed surveyor's flags.

"We know—well, we're close to knowing—that they came here by air. We know that in all likelihood they climbed out of the plane right there," and she pointed to where the two Toms worked to pour plaster casts of the vague footprints and the one reasonably clear aircraft tire print. "The trouble is that when the pilot gunned the engine to pull the plane forward out of the sand, the prop wash obliterated most of the prints. That's what I'm thinking right now. We're not going to be able to tell much from the casts. But when he did that, he gave us a sequence of events."

"You mean the footprints first, then gunning the engine to obscure them."

"Exactly. That's a start."

"Are any of the shoe prints clear enough for a comparison?" Linda asked.

"Probably not. Even if we had some notion about what to compare them to. Maybe, maybe. That's what we have right now. A big 'maybe' that they came in by plane, a big nothing beyond that." She rested both forearms on the rim of the bucket, a posture so relaxed that Linda cringed. "So if they got off the plane right there, where was the killer? On the plane? Waiting in the bushes? Why did they do this?" Shifting position slightly, she felt the bucket sway gently under her. "Where were these people from, Linda? And where were they headed?"

"Mexico is an obvious choice," Linda said.

"Sure enough. But they're not migrants, Linda. This isn't just a family headed to Hatch to pick green chile—not in May, anyway. His hands? The roughest thing he's touched in years is a pencil. She hasn't mopped her own floor in decades. I'd bet on it. *Don y doña*. And *hijo*…number-one son. That's what I think. Where would people like that be heading after an illegal entry into the United States in the dead of night?" She looked off toward Posadas, and the slight motion of her turning rocked the bucket again. "And if not Mexico, then where? L.A.? Phoenix?" She turned to look east. "St. Louis? Chicago?"

"I'm betting on the killer being a fourth passenger—or the pilot," Linda said. "It's too complicated to think that he was waiting here. That doesn't make sense to me. For one thing, there are no vehicle tracks other than the airplane's, so we know he wasn't just sitting there in a van, supposedly waiting to pick up a load of illegals. But why would he walk? And all the way to this end of the runway? How did he know this is where the plane would stop?"

"The wind, maybe," Estelle said. She lifted her head and let the soft air play against her face. "What little there is feels like it's from the southwest. If the pilot landed into the wind right now, right this minute, this is where he'd end up. But we don't know what the wind conditions were when this all happened." She thumped the side of the bucket. "If there was no wind, why didn't he land eastbound, so the passengers could get off close to the road?"

"Or turn around and taxi back to the gate," Linda said. "I think the killer was on the plane. For one thing, I don't think someone intent on bumping off three people would walk across the desert for miles and miles, then hope he had the right spot. I think he was on the plane."

"And that leaves us wondering, doesn't it." Estelle looked through the wide-angle lens of her camera again and for a moment watched Sheriff Torrez, Coroner Alan Perrone, and State Police Lieutenant Mark Adams working the area around the third victim. "If the killer did his business and then got back on the plane, was he the pilot?" She turned and looked at Linda. "Were there four on the plane originally, or five? Or more?"

The photographer shrugged carefully. "And if he didn't get back on the plane, where is he now?"

"It's a big desert out there," Estelle said, and she sighed. How large the desert must have seemed for the three victims, how incomprehensible for a few awful minutes. None of this fitted the usual pattern—no plastic bags stuffed with cheap clothing, no plastic water jugs, none of the trappings of a desperate trudge across the desert for migrants seeking American minimum wage, a fortune for them.

"Are there any other angles you want before we go back down?"

"Ah, no," Linda said. "I have the whole thing six ways from Sunday."

Estelle nudged the control and the bucket sank to earth with a faint hydraulic sigh. Bucky Sanchez, the county worker who had driven the bucket truck out to this lonely spot, met them as they stepped off.

"You guys done with me?" he asked hopefully.

"We are," Estelle said. "And thanks, Bucky."

"Anytime," he said, glancing nervously to the west. He managed a weak smile. "And I don't really mean that, either. You think you know what happened out here?"

"No," Estelle said. "But every little bit that we can learn is bound to help."

"Worst thing I ever saw," he said. "When I drive out back to the county road, do you want me to stay over to the side of the runway, same way I came in?"

"Perfect." Estelle nodded. "And if someone asks you what's going on out here, just plead ignorance."

"That ain't hard," Sanchez said. "Why somebody'd do a thing like this is beyond me. *Way* beyond."

She turned at the approach of Tom Mears. "We're finished," she said to the sergeant.

"Inspiration from above?" he asked.

"I don't think so," Estelle said. "But it'll give us some overview pictures to ponder."

Mears looked down at the trowel in his hand as if the answers might lie there. "One of us needs to run out to the airport to talk with Jim Bergin. I'm kinda curious to see if there's a standard wheelbase measurement that's of any use to us." He pointed across the pavement. "We've got a good measurement between the main gear in any number of places. It's right at ninety-seven inches—*más o menos*. It's hard to be exact, but it's a start. By the way, if you look right there," and he pointed at where a small yellow plastic evidence marker rested beside the runway, "you can see where he cranked the nose wheel over when he knew he was getting hung up on the edge of the pavement. I'm guessing that's what happened. That gives us an idea of the distance and geometry between the main gear and the nose gear. Again, nothing exact, but it helps."

"It's interesting that he did that," Estelle said. "And you're right. Jim might have some ideas. He might have seen a plane pass through that didn't mean anything special to him at the time."

"Sure enough. We're not talking a large plane, I'm guessing. The footprint of even a light twin-engine plane would be substantially wider than a single engine, I'd think."

"We have a starting point," she said. "But you know, I'm curious why they walked where they did." She looked off through the brush, her gaze following the trail of yellow flags that had been thrust into the desert. *Why not just fly to Posadas and get off there*, she wondered. Most of the time, Posadas Municipal was untended at night, even deserted. The facility was a comfortable six miles from town, far enough that a conservative landing wouldn't even be heard except by a handful of folks who wouldn't care about casual air traffic in the first place.

"The possibility exists that the three were brought to this spot to be executed," Estelle said. "That simple."

"Interesting," Mears said cryptically. "That's what Bobby thinks, too. And they *were* shot here, not somewhere else and dumped. Execution is the one scenario that explains a lot of what we're seeing. There was no scuffle, no fight. Nothing that left any tracks, anyway." The lift truck started and they watched it trundle back down the runway toward the gate and the county road beyond.

"Tomás, we need the long tape," Mears said, and Pasquale held up the reel. "Let's get some numbers."

He hesitated and turned back to Estelle. "Apropos of nothing, are you ready for Saturday night?"

"I haven't been so nervous in a long, long time." She laughed. Her son's first recital, in which he would be performing along with nearly a dozen other music students, added another dimension to an otherwise already hectic weekend. Tom Mears' fifteen-year-old daughter Melody would also play, but she was a veteran of half a dozen such performances.

"This is a new experience for us," she added.

Sheriff Torrez made his way carefully through the vegetation, walking back to the runway. He greeted them with a heavy sigh, and Estelle didn't know if that was because of the ugly crime, or the nagging pain in his hip irritated by all the walking. During another magic moment two years before, his rump had gotten in the way of a .223 bullet, and the recovery had been long, slow, and painful. "Hey," Torrez said.

Estelle held up her hands in frustration.

"I know what you mean," the sheriff said. "Nothin' except three bodies. All shot one time. Pop, pop, pop. Hey, look—do we need to cancel the race?"

"Cancel the race?" Estelle looked at the sheriff blankly. As if the young man going airborne into the rocks off the mesa rim had been from another lifetime instead of just hours before, Estelle hadn't given the race a moment's thought. In just a few days, 150 cyclists would be pounding down County Road 14 during the second half of the Posadas Cyclo-Cross 100. They would ride as far south on County Road 14 as Bender's Canyon Trail, and turn east, the rough and broken two-track roughly paralleling the state highway. There would be no reason for the cyclists to ride another mile farther south to this remote place.

"I don't think we can do that," she said.

"The hell we can't," Torrez said.

"No, I mean there's no reason to. We'll have someone posted at the intersection of the canyon trail and the county road to make sure no one strays." She glanced across to where Deputy Tom Pasquale was recording numbers from their measurements. "Tom will be one of the cyclists, and that'll give us another set of eyes."

"Bad time to be spread so thin," Torrez said, then held up a plastic evidence bag containing three empty shell casings. "Niners," he said. "I figured as much. It's something, but it ain't much." He turned and waved at Linda Real. "Hey? Needja." He lowered his voice. "Interesting thing is that it looks like the killer didn't move much."

"How so?"

Torrez hefted the bag. "Every empty case we've found was within a fifteen-foot circle. Like he stood in one spot and just pivoted with the target." He hefted the bag thoughtfully, then reached out a hand toward Linda, touching her lightly on the shoulder as if to make sure that she was listening. "I need pictures of the brass locations," he said. "Follow me over."

"Yep," Linda said, and dropped her voice an octave, rending a fair impression of the sheriff. "Pictures."

"Oh," Torrez said, stopping in his tracks. "No belts."

"Belts?"

"None of 'em had belts on."

"Were they tied with them, maybe?"

"No evidence of that. They just weren't wearin' 'em. Maybe they were, at one time. You can see the upset in the loops on their pants. But no belts now. The boy not wearin' a belt don't surprise me. Maybe even dad. But mama's got a little belly.... She's gonna need something. Think on that." He shrugged. "Where you headed now?"

"Sarge is going to swing by the airport to talk with Jim Bergin. Maybe there's a profile of the aircraft we can conjure. I'm going to put together a pack of faces." She gazed across at the bodies. "Someone knows these people, Bobby. They're somebody. You can't just pluck them out of the world and not have somebody notice."

"They ain't wetbacks," the sheriff said. "That's for sure."

"Someone knows them. And that's an advantage for us. The faster I can get a set of faces online, the better."

"See what Naranjo thinks. My money is on Mexico."

"Exactly." Capitán Tomás Naranjo of the Mexican Judiciales could probe far more dark corners south of the border than the Posadas County Sheriff's Department. *Location,* Estelle thought. Did the pilot see the landing strip far below, deserted and inviting? Not at night, he didn't. Did he know beforehand that it was there? If he could read an aeronautical chart, yes.

"I need the faces ASAP, Linda," Estelle called, and the young photographer lifted a hand in acknowledgment. Someone, somewhere, would know who these three people were, and how their lives had tangled to bring them to this empty, lonesome place.

Chapter Four

Cabo primero Emilio Rojas of the district Judiciales, speaking in the clipped, certain tones of command, informed the undersheriff from across the border that Capitán Tomás Naranjo was not available. The *capitán* was busy, doing what only the *capitán* knew, the corporal said.

The border between the United States and Mexico was far more than barbed wire and empty desert, Estelle knew. A great bureaucratic gulf existed, a fundamental difference in approach—to life, to language, and certainly to law enforcement.

She lowered her voice another notch and slipped into the Spanish of her childhood in Tres Santos, speaking differentially, and still making it clear that she was imparting a confidence intended for Rojas' ears only. *"Agente,"* she said, "I'm sending a series of photographs via e-mail. It is important that *el capitán* sees them as soon as possible." She almost added, "within the hour," but knew that *Agente* Rojas wouldn't accept any form of ultimatum from a female. An hour was impossible anyway, if Naranjo was out in the hinterlands riding one of his favorite horses—his preferred prescription for blowing out the cobwebs of the bureaucracy in which he worked.

"Ah," Rojas said in English. "Photographs of what, Sheriff Guzman?"

Before Estelle could elaborate, the phone clicked sharply, and the corporal's stonewall was removed, replaced by a voice so soft and genteel that Estelle had to press the phone tightly to her ear, covering the other with her hand, in order to hear.

"Estelle, how are you?" Captain Tomás Naranjo asked, speaking in faultless English. "I apologize for interrupting, but mention of your name always demands my complete attention."

"Good morning, *mi capitán,*" Estelle said with polite deference. "I hope my call finds you well. And Bianca as well."

"To be sure. What a pleasure to hear from you. It has been too long, you know."

"Yes, it has. I'm calling to ask for your agency's assistance."

"Name it, *señora.*" His seductive avoidance of title wasn't lost on Estelle. She had learned over the years to treat Tomás Naranjo with professional distance, being careful not to open unintended doors.

"I'm sending you an attachment…a series of photographs. We have had an incident that is most puzzling, and I need your help."

"I see." He sounded almost disappointed.

She turned to watch her computer screen. "The first three are morgue photos. The victims came into the country by air—we think. In all likelihood, the plane landed at a private airstrip west of Posadas, and the victims were shot there, apparently by someone else also riding on the airplane. No signs of confrontation or struggle."

"You're referring to the gas company's modest runway west of your town?" Naranjo said, once again demonstrating his complete command of the geography on both sides of the border.

"Exactly," Estelle replied. "Off the west end, half a mile from the county road. There was no identification of any kind found on any of the bodies. The clothing is of quality, but there isn't any labeling that tells us much."

"Everything is made everywhere these days," Naranjo said. "What tells you that they came from Mexico?"

"A hunch. But we're putting the photos through NCIC to hit everyone."

"Ah. Well." And he chuckled softly. "Hunches are important. You have learned to pay attention to those in the past, no?"

"It's just that nothing else makes any *more* sense. The three victims appear to be Hispanic, perhaps even Indian or mestizo. They are not laborers. And the killing was execution style. One neat shot in the head for each."

"Tell me more," Naranjo said.

"Well, I wish I could. It's this simple—we have three victims, dead of gunshot. We *think* they came here by airplane—from where is just a guess."

"And that's the sum total?"

"Nearly so. The murder weapon was a 9mm. We're fairly sure that the killer stood in one spot, like shooting in a gallery. Even in daylight, that's a stunt. If this happened at night, it's even more so."

"But you don't know when it happened."

"No, we don't. And there's this little tidbit. Sheriff Torrez thinks that they might have been wearing belts, but that those belts were removed. Why or when we don't know."

"So interesting. Could it have been robbery, perhaps? Were they wearing money belts, and somehow, someone got wind of that?"

"That's a possibility."

"And of course, we have no witnesses," Naranjo said. "Otherwise we might not be talking at this moment. What did the people at the saloon have to say? Airplanes, shooting… someone must have heard something."

"One of the deputies will follow through with that. In the meantime, I wanted you to see the faces."

There was a pause, and Estelle could hear the clatter of a keyboard in the background. "Ah, I have mail," Naranjo murmured. Estelle waited while the officer opened the photo attachment. "I see," Naranjo said. "An interesting gallery. It would certainly appear to be a family, more or less."

"That may be the case."

"I will see what I can do, but of course, I would prefer to have more to go on."

"Unfortunately…"

"I understand your position," Naranjo said. "But what of the airplane? You said there was evidence that an airplane was involved."

"We have tire tracks. The wheelbase indicates that they're made by a single-engine, most likely."

"But I am confused. How is the airplane tied to the incident? Did you tell me already?"

"An assumption," Estelle said. "There are no vehicle tracks *other* than the airplane's. There's no trail across the prairie from the state highway to the south."

"That's in the neighborhood of a mile, as I remember."

"Exactly so. The sheriff could find no evidence of a trail."

"If he could not, then no one can," Naranjo said. "So…by plane. A plane comes and goes. Someone must have seen it."

"Maybe."

Naranjo drew in a great sigh, and Estelle could hear the rustle of papers. "I assume that time is of the essence? What was the time of death? Have we established that?"

"Not yet. It appears to be days. Perhaps two or three."

"That's not good."

"No, sir."

"And how were the bodies found? That is a remote area… and it's gated off, as I recall."

"The sheriff found them. We're having a bike race here this weekend, and he was down in that area making sure the route to Bender's Canyon Trail was marked. He saw a couple of coyotes playing, and started watching them through binoculars. What they were playing with drew his attention."

"Ah. If you are right—that the victims flew in across the border—I wonder why all the complications to accomplish that. And the risk of unwanted attention. Three bodies dumped in a deserted canyon somewhere in our Mexican wilderness would certainly go unnoticed long enough for those coyotes to clean up the remains, disappearing never to be seen again. But in your backyard? It would seem from all this that the killer is more likely to be in your neighborhood than mine. And the victims as well."

"That may be. I'm trying to cover every avenue, sir. You know so many people from such a wide area, it made sense to call you immediately."

"I appreciate that," Naranjo said, and he leaned on each syllable as if he truly enjoyed the sound of the word. "I will make enquiries, Estelle. You have no names, I am to understand."

"They carried no ID."

"And no other detail beyond what you have told me."

"None. Not yet, anyway."

"And the erstwhile Border Patrol...they have nothing? Nothing on radar, no visuals?"

"Not yet."

"How does the saying go...don't hold your breath? You know," Naranjo said with resignation, "I believe that our border is considerably more...how could we say...*porous* than we like to believe. Human ingenuity and resourcefulness being what they are."

"Perhaps we can talk later today, then," Estelle said, seeking a polite way to cut the conversation short.

"I look forward to that. How's your wonderful mother?"

"She's fine."

"And that talented and fortunate husband of yours?"

"Also fine. Too busy, but fine."

"Yes," Naranjo said quietly. "We are all too busy. You must come down for lunch sometime," and then he promptly added, "the both of you."

"We would enjoy that." She glanced at her watch impatiently, but the captain needed no reminders that time could be of the essence.

"I have both your cell phone and office numbers. I'll be in touch," he said.

Estelle rang off, pleased that she had been able to reach Naranjo on the first try, and disappointed that he hadn't said, *Of course I know these people.* But Mexico was twice the size of New Mexico and Texas combined, and there was no more reason for Naranjo to hit on a random face from a city across the country than for Estelle to know someone mentioned at random from Dallas or Houston.

Homicides were often untidy affairs, exploding in the heat of the moment, with witnesses and weapons and motives. More often than not, the victim was a family member or friend. More often than not, alcohol was the catalyst. But not this time. The bodies found at the airstrip reminded Estelle of a precise, calculated mob hit. A large piece of the nagging puzzle remained Posadas County itself—*location, location, location.*

Chapter Five

"You sure walked into the middle of something," Dr. Alan Perrone observed. The assistant state medical examiner regarded Estelle from across the stainless steel table. The corpse between them had had the worst of the cactus thorns removed from his face, but he looked anything but peaceful. *Startled,* Estelle thought. *Completely and utterly surprised.*

Perrone watched as Estelle examined the skull X-ray. "A 9mm is no hotrod," he said. "But under most circumstances I'd expect more damage than we have here." He reached across, then traced a line with his latex-gloved finger. "It entered low in the back of the skull, didn't veer from the straight and narrow, and stopped just after punching into the back of the orbit. Not a lot of explosive fragmentation. More like a motorized ice pick."

"He could have managed a few steps after being hit?"

Perrone looked skeptical, his thin, aristocratic nose wrinkling. "Ah, I don't think so. Separate the medulla from the system and everything stops, right then. There's enough stippling from hot gas and unburned powder on his neck that I'd guess the gun was just a foot or two behind his head."

"So if the three of them were walking in a line in front of the killer, this one would be right in front of the gun," Estelle said.

"That would make sense."

"The young man was second in line," she said. She looked across at the sheeted figure on the table behind Perrone.

"He turned, then," Perrone said. "Right behind the ear, but the trajectory is more crosswise. That bullet didn't exit, either. Full metal jacket, low velocity. Maybe subsonic. I don't know."

Estelle waved the X-ray that Perrone offered aside. She turned around, looking at the bulky form of the woman.

"Same thing," Perrone said. He moved around the end of the table and flipped the sheet back. The woman had been strikingly handsome, with raven black hair in a tight bun in the old-fashioned style, proud nose, and strong chin. Her mouth was slack, revealing strong, even teeth. For a long time, Estelle stood quietly, letting the image burn itself into her memory. "She turned to face the killer."

Perrone pivoted and pointed at the older man. "Right behind. *Bang.* The son—that's what I guess—he hears the noise, maybe a little gasp, and starts to turn. That positions his skull a little bit sideways, and *bang*. Down he goes. The woman has stopped by this time, and she turns. *Bang.*"

Estelle bent a little to examine the bullet hole through the bridge of the woman's nose. No stippling there, just a nasty, bludgeoning impact as the jacketed slug burst through the thin nasal bones and into her brain.

"The sheriff tells me that no one has a clue where these folks are from," Perrone said. "Just brought here and executed."

"Exactly right."

"I'm not going to be much help," the physician said. "The full autopsy might reveal something, but I doubt it. If I had to *guess*, I'd go with south of the border."

"What makes you think so?"

"Little things. And I could be wrong, too. Whoever their dentist was leaned heavily on gold—and that's not an absolute, you know. But the tendency in this country is toward porcelain now, especially for the teeth that are readily visible in the smile. They've all had good dental care, but even the boy has his share of heavy metal on board." Perrone stepped forward and pulled the sheet far enough down to expose the woman's large torso.

"Not poor folks, either. Whoever did this cesarean was an artist," he said. "The suturing is even, precise—just plain elegant from a medical point of view. No country hack at work." He shrugged. "But that was two decades ago, if this kid," and he jabbed a finger at the sheet-covered body of the young man, "is the child in question."

Estelle reached out and pulled the sheet back in place. "What a sad thing. I hope the twenty years were worth it."

"We never know, do we?" He tidied one corner of the white sheet pensively.

"And speaking of never knowing, did you work on the boy who crashed the bike up on the mesa? Terry Gutierrez, the college kid who went airborne?"

Perrone shook his head. "Glanced in on him, but Francis worked that one up." The crow's-feet around his brilliant blue eyes deepened. He didn't voice the thought, but Estelle understood perfectly.

"I've been too busy turning in pointless circles to talk to anybody, even my own husband," she said. "These three are off to Albuquerque?"

"First thing in the morning. I'm going to be interested in the toxicology, Estelle." He made a face. "I've always wondered what made one human being more tasty to critters than another. What's the attraction?"

"And..." Estelle prompted when he paused.

"There are a few little wounds that are consistent with coyote or dog bites. The really serious work hadn't begun yet, but what little disturbance there was occurred *only* on the father's body, not the others. On the unprotected hand, consistent with him lying on his face, the other arm protected under his body."

"Bobby said that's how he saw the bodies in the first place. He was watching the coyote."

"Right. That's what I understand. I just wonder what makes a coyote choose, that's all."

"That I couldn't begin to guess."

"Nor I. But the question poses itself, and I find that inter-esting." He held up both hands, palms down. "You have two bodies out in the desert. One died with his system so full of booze that you can smell it a mile away. The other died sober. Which one does the scavenger choose?" He waggled his hands. "Marinated or plain?"

"That's grotesque," Estelle said, but she couldn't help laughing. "The alcohol would dissipate, anyway."

"The *flavoring* doesn't, necessarily. It's still a valid question."

"*Por supuesto.* Right now I've got too many of those."

"I'll have the preliminaries to you first thing in the morning. I can't guarantee response from the OMI. Late next week, I imagine. You know the drill."

"I appreciate it."

The disinfectant-rich smell of the room followed her out into the hall, and she pushed open the steel door to the stark, cold stairwell rather than waiting for the elevator. She emerged on the first floor, behind the nurses' station. Karin MacKenzie, one of the RNs, looked up from her computer and offered a broad smile.

"Hi there. You look like you're on the prowl. Of course, if you've been down *there,* small wonder."

"I just spoke with Dr. Perrone," Estelle said.

"Then you know more than I do," Karin replied. "I think your hubby is down by the ICU. You want me to page him?"

"No, no," the undersheriff said quickly. "May I just cruise down that way?"

"You cruise away. Stop back and we'll have a cup of coffee. No...tea. You drink tea, right?"

"I do. Thanks."

Around two corners and down a lengthy hallway, beyond mauve doors labeled for all things expensive, she saw Francis Guzman in conversation with a chubby, balding man whom she recognized as one of the cardiologists from Las Cruces who rotated through the community health system. Francis saw her and reached out a hand to his colleague to hold him in mid-thought as he extended the other hand to Estelle.

"You know Brian Finlan?" Francis said, and the other physician reached out to shake Estelle's hand.

"Yes," she said. "Nice to see you again."

"You're having a busy day," Finlan said sympathetically.

"Yes, we are. A great way to end the week." She turned to Francis. "I need to know where young Gutierrez is," she said. "The mesa head injury?"

"Bike boy is around here somewhere," Francis said. "Try one-oh-nine. Observation overnight, and we'll release him in the morning. His girlfriend was T and R'd, but I would guess she's with him."

"Nothing super serious, then."

"Well, he did a pretty workmanlike job, but all things considered, he's lucky. Right clavicle, right wrist, and nine stitches in his scalp right where it would have killed him if he hadn't been wearing that helmet. And two cracked ribs. No spinal complications."

"Hopefully not a preview," Finlan said. "You know, sheriff, I was looking over the list of competitors for the race, and about a third of them are flatlanders. I even saw our esteemed former lieutenant governor's name—and he wasn't the oldest one in the bunch, believe it or not. So not only flatlanders, but some *old* guys as well. You get all these folks from sea level pushing pedals up on Cat Mesa at eight thousand feet, and there's a lot of things we can expect."

"I know that the race officials were going to include material about that in each competitor's packet," Estelle said. "And they'll talk about it during the prerace meeting, I'm sure. You're staying for the weekend, I hope?"

"Wouldn't miss it."

She noted a certain professional relish in his tone, similar to Alan Perrone's when he spoke of marinated versus plain cooking for coyotes.

"You heading home now, or—," her husband asked.

"In a few minutes. I wanted to drop in on Gutierrez for just a moment. I've got their bikes in the back of the truck." She left the two physicians to their planning and sought out 109, one of the double rooms in the new wing.

The door was ajar, and she could see April Pritt sitting on the edge of the hospital bed, her body leaning over Terry Gutierrez's, supporting herself on her right arm. There might have been a thin piece of hospital gauze's distance between their faces.

Estelle rapped on the door, and April sat upright quickly, but not before Estelle could see that there was nothing wrong with Terry's *left* hand. He maneuvered it back into a more appropriate patient's position on the white sheets.

"You guys doing okay?" Estelle said kindly, although it was clearly obvious that they were. "I just wanted to touch base with you." She stepped into the room, and April rose from the bed. She limped carefully to a straight-backed chair nearby.

"I still have your bikes," Estelle continued. "I haven't been back to the office yet, but that's where I'm headed now. When you are ready to pick them up, just see whoever is sitting dispatch, okay?"

"Thank you *sooo* much," April said. "Everyone has been so kind."

"Well, we're sorry this had to happen," Estelle said. She stepped closer to the bed. "I was just talking to Dr. Guzman. He says battered and bruised, but otherwise okay. How are you feeling?"

The young man shifted a little under the sheet. When he wasn't black and blue, he'd be handsome enough that he didn't need to show off by trying to fly off cliffs. "Awful. Like I got hit by a truck. Thanks, though."

"So, you just took a wrong turn…. Is that what happened?" Estelle gazed at him for a long moment—until his eyes dodged away to his girlfriend.

"That's it," Gutierrez said. He grinned sheepishly. "Trying to cut the course, I guess. Maybe I was showin' off a little."

"A *little*," April said. "Like, try a *lot*, Superman."

"You two go to Tech?" Estelle asked, referring to the university in Socorro.

April nodded. "I'm a senior. He's a *junior.*" She wrinkled her nose at him.

"You'll take care of notifying his folks?"

"We've done that already," she said, as if parents were mere pesky details. "Are you and Dr. Guzman related? I wondered about that."

"He's my husband."

"*Oh.* Well, that's neat. He's a nice guy."

"Yes, he is." Estelle extended a business card to the girl. "The bikes will be at the office. If you need anything else, don't hesitate to call."

"We're fine," April said. "We really are. Thanks again *sooo* much."

Estelle left the hospital room, making sure that the door closed tightly behind her.

Chapter Six

Estelle watched her son's dark face as the music soared, and she found herself wishing that she could share the images that formed in his vivid imagination. She knew that the seven-year-old was excited about the bicycle race on the mountain, and wondered if some of the dashing up and down the piano keys played videos of cyclists in his mind.

Francisco had settled on Mozart's Sonata in F for his recital piece, a lengthy challenge for the little boy. On more than one occasion, Estelle had sat beside her son on the piano bench, reading through the piece with him as he played—even though Francisco himself rarely looked at the music. No musician herself, Estelle knew enough to be able to follow his progress, and she could see that the problem wasn't the sonata's fourteen-page length. The little boy's capacity at the keyboard was far greater than perhaps even the seventeen-year-old Mozart could have imagined when he wrote the challenge of his sonata.

No, the problem was Francisco's agile little mind itself. Something in the sonata's images cracked him up every time he played the piece—not an unusual reaction when he played the piano. He mimicked the motif in variations of his own, he giggled and composed little answers to Mozart's questions and comments, and he sometimes went off hiking on his own, deep into his own musical world.

Estelle understood that, no matter how astonishing her son's talent, he was still bridled by a seven-year-old's healthy lack of discipline. If there was another trail to skip down, another tonal butterfly to chase, another dark canyon to explore, Francisco did so.

Edith Gracie, Francisco's piano instructor, remained unconcerned. "We need not worry," she was fond of saying. *Easily said,* Estelle thought. And on Saturday, she worried, and not necessarily about her son's pending performance.

She knew that Sheriff Robert Torrez, Captain Eddie Mitchell, the two Toms, and photographer Linda Real had spent most of the day out at the airstrip, combing the area where the three bodies had been found.

Working with them were Lieutenant Mark Adams of the New Mexico State Police and two of his officers, along with Agent Barker Rutledge of the Border Patrol. An area roughly the size of a football field had been meticulously gridded and would be searched and combed foot by foot. Estelle was skeptical that the search would uncover anything—she was convinced that the three victims had arrived by plane, taken a few dozen steps, and been murdered. The killer had then left as unobtrusively as he had arrived—long gone from the country, certainly from the county.

At the same time, the bike race organizers were putting the finishing touches on their first-year project, and no doubt County Manager Leona Spears was in the thick of it. EMTs would follow the cyclists in chase vehicles, and in those sections where a truck or car couldn't go, organizers had arranged for motorcycle or four-wheeler coverage. There was no way to make a bicycle race entirely safe—that was both the nature of the beast and its attraction for riders. There was a price for carelessness or inattention. But the organizers had a myriad of volunteers to watch the route during the race. If there was a section *not* covered foot by foot, it would be out on the flat sections of Country Road 14, out on the prairie where the biggest safety threat was an occasional wandering prairie dog or slithering rattlesnake.

And so, with phone near at hand and *nana* Irma Sedillos, the younger sister of Gayle Sedillos Torrez, the sheriff's wife, on hand in case Estelle had to be called away, the undersheriff spent a rare Saturday at home.

Well aware that he would be performing in front of a small crowd of family and friends, Francisco worked his practice sessions as diligently as his effervescent personality would allow.

The afternoon was broken by a single phone call. Dr. Alan Perrone announced that preliminary toxicology tests showed that the older male victim had a residual blood alcohol level high enough to measure—in Perrone's words, the victim would have been "comfortably sauced" when he stepped off the plane.

"Odd to travel that way," Estelle remarked.

"Maybe he hated flying," Perrone said. "Or a case of the nerves. Or maybe he's an alcoholic. Or, or, or…We'll know more after the full autopsy."

Knowing that one victim was a drinker got them nowhere, and Estelle shoved the whole affair toward the back of her mind, letting it stew. She had left word with dispatch that she would be unavailable for any calls that evening, unless the world itself came crashing down. The phone stayed mercifully silent, and at 6:30 p.m., they drove to the school as a family, a rare treat.

The acoustics of the Little Theater were as elegant as the gymnasium that the "theater" had once been. A decade before, when the original Posadas High School gym had been declared insufficiently grand for athletic events, the district had built a new facility, leaving the old, open-girdered hulk to be divvied up between the special education and the home economics departments. Somewhere in the planning, the modest theater had been included in the old gymnasium's renovation.

The metal folding chairs were arranged in a dozen crescent rows, each row including fifteen seats, far more than the modest recital required. A section had been reserved for the sixteen student musicians at front and center.

Estelle snuggled up as close to her husband as she could, her shoulder nestled into his. Sitting on Dr. Guzman's right, Bill Gastner, former Posadas County sheriff and *padrino* to the two Guzman boys, was engrossed in quiet conversation with Leona

Spears. The large woman had worn one of her most flamboyant muumuus for the occasion.

Estelle tried to relax, but a collection of butterflies danced in her stomach. From where she sat, a few seats to the left of center and five rows back, Estelle could see Francisco's dark little head bowed in deep conversation with a fifteen-year-old girl whose piano lessons at Mrs. Gracie's were scheduled immediately after his. Both children ignored the small audience around them. Estelle also recognized Melody Mears, Sergeant Tom Mears' daughter. Melody was half-kneeling on her chair toward the end of the row, surveying the audience. She caught Estelle's eye and waved, her smile brilliant. Melody's parents, Tom and Pat Mears, sat to Estelle's right and two rows closer to the front.

She could imagine Sheriff Bob Torrez's growl of impatience at having two of his officers wasting time watching children play music while a multiple homicide remained unsolved.

Although she understood the purpose of having the children sit separated from their families—encouraging dependence on their own hard work, their own music to comfort their preperformance fidgets—Estelle found herself wishing that her son was sitting beside her now. On the short drive to school, Francisco had been his usual loud, excited self. But nervous? It was hard to tell. He had talked about his music, and about Melody's—and she found it odd now that her son had chosen to sit several seats away from Miss Mears.

Normally, she would have taken an interest in the audience—scanning the faces, watching the whispered conversations as part of an occupational habit. Now, she watched her son—what she could see of the top of his head, that is—and wondered just how much the seven-year-old understood about what the various adults seated behind him expected of him. Did he know how excited they were?

Onstage, Francisco's piano teacher, Edith Gracie, conferred with the other instructor with whom she had coordinated the evening's recital—the high school band director. He shrugged helplessly at something the elderly woman said, and Mrs. Gracie took him by the elbow. The conversation continued at the bass end of the grand piano's keyboard.

"Maybe they're missing a chord," Francis said in a conspiratorial whisper. His arms were locked around their younger son, Carlos, and the little boy's eyes were huge and watchful.

Estelle grimaced. "When I was a senior here," she said, "a couple of my classmates sprayed foam insulation in the piano before an assembly. That stuff you can buy in aerosol cans? That same piano, I'm sure. That's how long it's been around."

Francis laughed and with Carlos' hands in his mimed playing a piano. "Thunk, thunk, thunk. Maybe that's what we need for this gig. Some insulation." He nodded at the program. "At least no one is torturing a violin tonight."

The confab onstage ended with Mrs. Gracie giving a quick, appreciative nod at something her colleague said, and then she walked to the edge of the stage, facing the audience of forty-five people. Estelle glanced at the single-sheet program as the audience hushed. Her son was listed toward the end, followed by Melody Mears and two other more advanced students.

"Good evening," Mrs. Gracie said solemnly. Her voice was deep and rich, and she smiled affectionately at the row of student musicians for a moment before looking up at the audience. "We have a treat for you tonight, as I'm sure you'll agree. Mr. Parsons and I are so proud of these young people. Now, some of our musicians are seasoned veterans. Jaycee Sandoval and I were discussing this very thing earlier today, and tonight marks her twentieth recital since she started playing piano when she was five years old. Can you imagine that?" She beamed at the older student sitting toward the end of the row whose name appeared last on the program.

"It would also be appropriate to announce at this time that Jaycee has earned the prestigious Marks Scholarship for musical studies at the University of New Mexico." Mrs. Gracie waited until the applause had stopped.

"We expect grand things from all of these young musicians. Four of them have not played before an audience prior to tonight, and isn't that wonderful?" She held out her own program toward the musicians, letting them bask in the moment. "We'll begin tonight with Toby Escoba, a student of Mr. Parsons. Toby is fourteen, he's an old hand at performance, and you may recall his beautiful trumpet rendition of Mozart's 'Laudate Dominum' at the Christmas concert last winter. As your program notes, he'll be playing Wahlberg's 'All That Jazz,' with Mr. Parsons accompanying on the piano." She turned and patted the Baldwin's broad flank and then waggled a finger at Parsons, who had settled on the piano bench. "We certainly hope this old thing doesn't fall to pieces."

A student with shoulders suited for a linebacker vaulted onto the stage, ignoring the two steps. His trumpet looked fragile in his beefy hands. He took a moment to smooth out his music on the rack, blew silently through the trumpet's mouthpiece, and fluttered the valves. Mr. Parsons, a large, well-padded man, sat quietly at the piano bench, waiting. Finally, Toby took a deep breath, shook his right hand as if the fingers had gone asleep, and then nodded at his accompanist. A dozen bars of the dissonant music left Estelle wondering how it was possible to distinguish correct notes from strays. The Baldwin held together, the trumpet blasted and screamed, and Toby Escoba beamed when the audience burst into applause twice before he finished.

Through it all, Estelle's son Francisco remained remarkably quiet, occasionally bouncing half out of his chair, or turning to the girl on his left for another whispered conference.

From Toby's romping beginning, the recital continued demurely with a simple piano solo played by a beginning student so tiny that her feet swung twelve inches from the stage floor. She played solemnly, brows beetled with concentration, her stiff little fingers robotic. As the concert progressed from student to student, Estelle found herself referring back to the printed program, as the names marched toward her son's.

When Pitney Clarke was introduced, the tall girl seated beside Francisco rose, and to Estelle's surprise, so did her son. They made an interesting pair—seven-year-old Francisco darkly handsome in black slacks and shoes and his favorite plum-colored pullover, Pitney tall and graceful in a black skirt and long-sleeved white blouse, frilly around the throat.

Pitney carried a portfolio of music, and she took her time arranging it on the piano. She whispered instructions to Francisco, who apparently had been nominated to be her page turner. He nodded quickly, even impatiently, as if he'd attended to this chore a thousand times. Serenity and ferocity appeared to be Pitney's favorite emotions as she tackled the long and complex Schubert piece, with many passages sounding as if they required at least a dozen fingers.

The young musician managed Schubert's intricacies well enough, but to Estelle's untrained ear, it sounded as if the composer had written one page nicely, then copied it a dozen times, with each copy held at a slightly different angle for variety.

The communication between the two children at the piano was easy and natural. As each set of pages drew to a close, Estelle saw Francisco lean a little so that his shoulder touched Pitney's side, and at the right moment, Pitney would offer just a hint of a nod. Francisco would reach forward, perilously close to the keys and the young lady's lap, and snatch the page. At one point, Estelle sensed that her husband was looking at her. She glanced over at him and saw his raised eyebrow. She wound her hand around her husband's, including Carlos in the process. There were plenty of secrets in Francisco's little head—apparently Pitney Clarke was one of them.

The Schubert concerto worked toward its conclusion, and after he turned the last page for Pitney, Francisco sat back on the piano bench, frowning darkly, concentrating on the keyboard. Estelle realized that she was holding her breath. Sure enough, the little boy's hands reached out, fingers soundlessly caressing the bass keys. Pitney's fingers floated downward through the concerto's final resolution, but it was Francisco who played the final, complex chord so infinitely pianissimo, so seamless with the girl's own playing, that it blended perfectly.

And then he was a joyful seven-year-old again, snatching his hands off the keys and bouncing off the piano bench as if springloaded. Pitney, far more demure at fifteen, stood and acknowledged the audience, then turned and held out her hand to Francisco. The two of them left the stage.

"That's an interesting expression on your face, *querida*," Estelle's husband whispered.

Chapter Seven

Estelle took a deep breath, listening to the applause.

"Who's Pitney Clarke, do you know?" her husband asked, tapping the program.

"Her lesson with Mrs. Gracie is right after Francisco's. Her mom works for New Mexico Cellular."

"Ah," Francis said. "Interesting rapport between those two kids."

"Apparently so."

If she had a problem deciding how to introduce Francisco, Mrs. Gracie had solved it neatly. Mike Parsons, the band director, stepped onstage. Applause greeted him and he nodded curtly, all business.

"Do you like what you're hearing?" he asked, his foghorn voice reaching effortlessly to the farthest corners of the theater. The audience applauded politely. "So who's next?" Glancing at the program as if he might have forgotten, he continued, "Francisco Guzman is seven years old, and is already one of Mrs. Gracie's stars…as well as being a veteran page turner." He frowned with mock severity at Francisco, who was already half standing. "Please welcome a remarkable talent playing a composition by another rare one…Mozart's Sonata in F."

"Relax, *querida*," her husband whispered. "My hand's about to fall off."

Estelle flexed her fingers, realizing that she'd been crushing every hand she could reach into a clammy ball. She tousled

Carlos' silky black hair, and he leaned back against his father, perfectly confident and at ease, ready to listen to the stories his older brother was about to tell.

Now all by himself on the stage, Francisco was diminutive against the black expanse of the piano. He slipped onto the bench and regarded the keyboard as if someone had switched the blacks and whites while his back was turned. With his left hand, he reached out as far as he could, spanning the bass keys. He straightened, then did the same, reaching to his right. Estelle could see that in a year or two, her son might be able to reach the pedals without straining and pointing his toes. The little boy looked out at the audience and grinned impishly.

He had not carried any music onstage, and the piano's black music rack was empty. His left hand curled under his chin in a gesture that Estelle recognized as the little boy's way of holding on to some inner, personal delight. Finally, both hands drifted down to the keyboard, and the first chord, a full, rich F, burst forth. He held it longer than he ever had in practice, longer than the composer indicated it should be, but it was Francisco's story now, not Mozart's.

The piece that reminded Estelle of squirrels arguing over nuts continued without hesitation until the presto movement, the opening measures of which had always reduced the little boy to hopeless giggles. Carlos emitted a tiny squeak and instantly clapped a hand over his mouth, but this time his older brother was undeterred. He pushed the piece faster and faster, then let it gradually relax, as if the squirrels, now sated with acorns, were too fat to move. The story ended with the same F chord that started it, played so softly that the sound disappeared in the big room before Francisco removed his hands from the keys. Only when he turned a bashful smile toward them did the modest audience erupt in applause.

Bill Gastner leaned forward, reached across Francis and Carlos, and patted the back of Estelle's hand. "You can relax now," he whispered. "The kid did good."

After a brief stop for a chat with Melody Mears, Mike Parsons lumbered back onstage as the applause continued.

"Well," Parsons said, pausing as Francisco took his seat. "Remember you heard it here first." He beamed at the audience and rubbed his hands. "Melody, are you ready?" The girl nodded, and Parsons silently clapped his hands once. "I call Melody Mears 'Miss Sunshine,' because she lights up every room she enters. And so does her music. She's been playing piano for six years, and the piece she's going to play for you tonight is one of the all-time classical hits." He beckoned toward Melody, who bounced out of her seat.

"Pachelbel's Canon in D," Parsons announced, and left the stage. He met Melody on the stairs, and she reached out a hand and whispered something to him.

"Sure," he said to the girl, then turned to the audience. "Can we have our talented page turner back for an encore?"

Estelle watched with amusement as Francisco shot out of his seat and practically skipped to the stage. The Canon was another multipage opus, and Melody's copy was tattered from handling. She smoothed it carefully on the rack, taking her time. Francisco squirmed on the bench beside her, then took a deep breath as his partner prepared to play.

The piece struck Estelle as repetitious but elegant, a haunting tune that once poured into the ears was hard to erase. Even though it was entirely possible that he had never seen the music before this moment, Francisco did a flawless job turning the battered pages.

Finally, as the applause swelled, Francis leaned close. "Company," he said. A hand on her shoulder startled Estelle at the same time that she heard the unmistakable clank of hardware and creak of leather. She turned to look up into the face of Deputy Tom Pasquale, who then knelt in the aisle beside her.

"We're going to need you," the deputy whispered as quietly as he could, and pointed discreetly toward the rear door.

Francis laughed ruefully. "Too good to last," he said. "I'll make sure the kid makes it home through the crush of his adoring fans."

"Ay," Estelle sighed. Her eyes searched Pasquale's face. "This can't wait?" she asked, knowing the question was a waste of time. Her pager and phone were turned off, and instructions had been left with the dispatcher—and she had felt no quake of the world ending.

"No, ma'am. It sure can't." Pasquale straightened up, and she slipped out of her seat with an apologetic smile at her husband and *padrino*. Gastner, retired after twenty years with the Sheriff's Department and knowing the drill, shrugged philosophically. Two rows ahead of them, Sergeant Tom Mears turned and looked at her, and Pasquale crooked his finger at him as well.

"A minute," Estelle said, and she crossed quickly to the front row, kneeling by her son. Francisco hugged her fiercely, and she wasn't sure if the heart she could feel banging away was her own, or her son's.

Onstage, Mrs. Gracie waited politely.

"I'm proud of you, *mi corazón,*" Estelle whispered in her son's ear. She gave him another hug and then rose. As the door closed behind them, Estelle could hear the elderly woman's voice introducing Jaycee Sandoval, the final star of the show. The undersheriff wondered if Jaycee would need help turning pages, too.

Chapter Eight

"One of ours?" Estelle asked incredulously, and Pasquale nodded. "The sheriff thinks so."

The evening away from work hadn't lasted long. Both she and Sergeant Mears had driven with their families to the recital, leaving patrol vehicles at home. For the altogether too fast ride back to her house, Estelle's mind churned. She had a dozen questions, but they all could wait. Pasquale dropped her at the curb, and she raced into the house, changed clothes, and was heading toward the front door when her mother hobbled out of her bedroom.

"And so?" Teresa Reyes said.

Estelle hugged the tiny, birdlike frame gently. "I have to go, *Mamá*."

"Always, you have to go. Am I going to hear how the concert went?"

"Beautifully, *Mamá*. I wish you could have gone."

"There will be others," the old woman said. She had never offered an explanation why she had *not* wanted to attend the concert, although the hard metal chairs in a cool gymnasium would be torture enough. "You be careful."

"Everyone will be home in a few minutes," Estelle said.

"Then maybe I'll stay up." She reached up with parchment fingers and touched Estelle's cheek. "You be careful," she said again.

A few minutes later, as Estelle neared the airport gate, she saw Bob Torrez's county Expedition parked in front of the last hangar in the row of five buildings, nosed in with an older model BMW sedan and airport manager Jim Bergin's Dodge pickup. Pasquale evidently hadn't returned to the airport.

The main hangar door was closed, but the regular "people door" off to one side stood ajar. As Estelle pulled her car to a stop, Jim Bergin stuck his head out of the hangar door and lifted a hand in greeting. He waited in the doorway as Estelle approached.

"Thirty-two years in the business, and this is a first for me," Bergin said, a surprising admission for someone who cherished his "seen it all, done it all" image. He stepped to one side to let her pass, and behind him Estelle could see what appeared to be a perfectly unremarkable airplane sitting inside an unremarkable steel hangar. She hesitated in the doorway, letting her eyes adjust to the dim light.

"Somebody's been havin' some fun at Jerry Turner's expense," Bergin said.

Estelle glanced at him, wondering how much the sheriff had told the airport manager.

The uncertain light inside the hangar came from two fluorescent shop lights suspended from the corrugated steel ceiling high overhead. Four old bulbs, one of them flickering and humming, turned the large hangar into a shadowy cavern. Estelle saw Torrez standing in front of the blue and white Cessna's left wing. He held up a hand in greeting and then walked over toward her, looking over his shoulder at the airplane as if it might try to slip away while his back was turned. In the shadows behind the plane she saw another figure moving, but couldn't make out who it was.

"Pretty bizarre," he said. "Turner thinks someone's been using his airplane without his permission."

"I *know* someone's been using it," Jerry Turner called from the other side of the plane. He held a large, boxy flashlight, and was examining the rear of the fuselage around the horizontal stabilizer, glaring at this and that. He didn't actually touch the aircraft, and Estelle got the impression that the businessman might be angry with the airplane, rather than the alleged tres-passer. The comment and response made it clear that Jerry Turner knew nothing of the multiple homicide out at the gas company's airstrip.

"Using it," Estelle said. "You mean as in flying somewhere and then bringing it back?" She frowned, knowing that her question sounded dumb, since there the Cessna sat. She glanced around the hangar, seeing nothing but sheet metal panels on steel girders, with a steel ceiling forming a black night sky over-head. The hangar was plenty large for the one airplane and, in a back corner, what might be either an old car or a boat had been covered with a tarp. A stack of used tires was stored along a side wall beside a well-worn set of cabinets that might once have graced someone's kitchen. The concrete floor of the hangar was reasonably free of debris.

Turner walked around the back of the plane, shaking his head. A large man with a vast belly and unusually narrow shoulders, he looked like a giant pear dressed in a business suit. He stopped, hands on his hips, and his wide, doughy face wrinkled in vexa-tion. "I don't believe this. I really don't." He nodded at the hangar doors. "You want those open so you can see something?" The twin sodium vapor lights outside might have helped some, but Estelle shook her head.

"Wait on those for a minute," she suggested. "Since I don't understand yet what I'm supposed to see." She saw the look of impatience flash across the man's face. "Let's step outside and you can tell me what happened here, Mr. Turner." Until she had heard the full story, she was loath to have an audience tromp around the inside of the hangar, planting size 12's over any evi-dence that might remain. Enough of that had happened already.

The big man turned his back on the plane and followed the sheriff and Estelle outside.

"Look," Turner said, holding out both hands in exasperation, "Bobby here called me and said that he wanted to check out my plane. I don't know why, and he sure as hell didn't *say* why. So I come out and open up, and you're probably going to think

I'm nuts, but sure as I'm standing here, *someone* has used that airplane." The outburst subsided for a moment. "And yes…by that I mean they used it. There's damn near eleven hours on the Hobbs that aren't mine—I can sure as hell tell you that. Now I need to know what the *hell* is going on."

"How did you happen to notice all this?" Estelle asked.

"All you got to do is look," Turner snapped. "I don't go drivin' her around in the dirt."

"In the dirt?"

"Jesus H. Christ," Turner barked. "Yes, the goddamned dirt. You want to see?"

"In a minute."

Bob Torrez had said nothing, but stood bemused, hands in his back pockets, regarding the interesting surface of the tarmac. "Excuse me, will you? Give us just a minute." She left Turner fuming and with a hand on Torrez's elbow led him a few yards away, toward the corner of the hangar. A light breeze from the west whispered around the building.

"You think this is it?" she asked, keeping her voice low.

"Could be," Torrez said. "Measurements fit. Our tire cast is for shit, but this one's got rubber that's consistent. That's the best we're going to get. Wheel base is right on the money. Lemme show you something." At the same time, another set of headlights pulled onto the airport apron, and when it passed under the first sodium vapor light by the fuel pumps, Estelle saw that it was Tom Mears.

"Let's wait for him," Torrez said. He motioned for Mears to park beside his own vehicle. "Truck smells like perfume," he added. "You didn't bring her majesty along?"

"She's at the concert," Estelle replied. "How did you stumble on this?"

Torrez flicked his flashlight beam toward the corner of the hangar. "I'll show you." When Mears joined them, he nodded at Turner, who had retreated to his BMW, where he leaned on the front fender, arms crossed over his chest, in conversation with Jim Bergin. "Stick with him," the sheriff said to Mears. "There's some things we don't know yet."

He motioned with the flashlight. "Jimbo? Come on back with us. Step kinda careful."

Saltbrush, koshia, ragweed, and a host of other opportunistic weeds surrounded the hangar, a crackly dry barrier just beginning to green up after the rare May precipitation. Estelle followed the sheriff closely, stepping in his footprints. He led them around the building to a point about a third of the way along the back wall, stepping carefully and avoiding open patches of ground that might yield shoe prints. He stopped like a proud guide about to expound on the next attraction on the tour. "Check this out," he said. Before she pressed forward, Estelle played the light carefully under the base of the creosote bush that grew tight against the hangar's back wall. Seeing no short-tempered reptiles coiled in the shadows, she pushed the bush to one side and stepped closer.

Torrez waited until she had regained her balance and then pointed at the wall. A football-sized rock had been rolled against the bottom of the corrugated siding in an attempt to hold in place one of the steel panels whose bottom and a portion of the side seam had been pried loose. Elsewhere, rusted pop-rivets secured the siding where it wasn't spot-welded to the hangar's steel skeleton. Running diagonally downward from above the loose seam was a subtle disruption in the sheet metal's surface, the sort of mark left by gently folding the metal back without creasing it.

"Move the rock and you got a six-foot-high section that can fold back out of the way," Torrez said. "I would bet far enough to slip through."

"I'll be goddamned," Bergin muttered. He reached out a hand, but Estelle caught him gently by the forearm. He jerked back as if stung. "Somebody sure as hell has been busy," he said.

Without touching either rock or hangar, Estelle examined the sheet metal closely for a moment. The evidence of a fold in the metal extended all the way down to the foundation. And once folded, the steel panel would never close back against the stud properly. At midpoint, it gaped more than an inch. When folded back, the panel formed a clever entry, but one for a pint-sized intruder. Someone as burly as Jerry Turner would have created a far larger doorway than this, where the rough edges of the metal would grab and tear at fabric or skin.

She pivoted and surveyed the jumble of scrub behind the hangar, looking out toward the roadway. Twenty yards of open space separated the row of hangars from the dilapidated chain-link boundary fence. Unless the intruder stood up and waved his arms, he would blend with the shadows and scrubby vegetation, impossible to see. At night, a simple crouch would make him invisible.

During their patrols, sheriff's deputies routinely swung into the airport. Sometimes it was for a quick cup of coffee with Jim Bergin, sometimes just to check for vagrants or unlocked hangars. If the security gate was open—as it always was if airport manager Jim Bergin was working or if one of the aircraft owners was on the premises—the officers would drive onto the tarmac. If the gate was closed, deputies turned around in the parking lot, using the vehicle's spotlight to inspect each of the buildings and the gate.

Despite the fence, with its three loose strands of barbed wire atop six feet of chain-link, the airport was not a secure area. Each aircraft owner had a key to the main gate, as did the county manager's office and the sheriff's department.

The gate was left open as often as not. Estelle had found it so a dozen times herself. In addition, the security fence did not extend the length of the taxiway, but marked only the perimeter of the outer parking lot. If the facility was locked, anyone wanting access had only to trot west a hundred feet and slip through the four-foot-high barbed-wire property fence.

Estelle turned back and looked at Bergin. "This isn't something that Mr. Turner had told you about before?"

Bergin scoffed. "Hell, no. If this was flappin' in the wind, he'd likely say something. But who's going to notice?"

"This isn't a setup for a one-time thing, though," Torrez said. "Someone made themselves a door. Pretty clever."

Estelle examined the undisturbed rivets beside the suspect panel, comparing them with the bright-rimmed holes left when the metal was pried loose. "Planning ahead, it looks like," she said. "Interesting, interesting." She stepped back and looked at the rock-strewn gravel that passed for prairie soil. "The only way we're going to find tracks that amount to anything is to pour some plaster and hope they come back and step in it tonight."

Bergin chuckled. "Now that's a thought. I wondered how you guys did that."

"How'd you happen to notice this?" she asked Torrez, and the sheriff just shrugged.

"Drivin' in. Spotlight picks it up."

"I wouldn't have noticed it in a thousand years," Bergin said.

"And you say Turner wouldn't have seen it, either, at least under normal circumstances. How often does he use this airplane?"

Bergin's left eyebrow drifted up. "Not nearly enough. But that's true of most hobby flyers."

"Once a week? Once a month?"

Bergin hesitated. His fingers drifted toward the cigarette pack in his shirt pocket, but he thought better of it. "Maybe once a month or so. And I'll tell you one thing—that ain't enough flyin' to stay current or safe, either one, Estelle. That's flyin' on luck." He shrugged. "Lots of pilots do that. For most of 'em, a plane's like a boat, or an RV. When the novelty wears off, the thing just sits."

"Turner's plane just sits?"

"Most of the time, yep. Like I said, he's flyin' on luck. That's what I call it. As long as nothing goes wrong, as long as he don't fly into some sort of problem, then it's okay. That's a nice airplane Jerry has there, that 206. Older model, but still real strong. A real workhorse."

"Maybe on both sides of the border," Estelle added. "What's he actually use it for?"

Bergin grinned. "Drinkin' coffee? That's another one of his hobbies I think. He flies over to Cruces with a friend and has a

cup. Or to Socorro. Or Grants. Wherever there's a coffeepot."
He shrugged. "There's good Mexican coffee to be had south of
the border, but that would surprise me, Jerry doin' something
like that."

"I was under the impression that coffee was always part of
your operation right here at home, Jim."

"Well, it is. But it always tastes better after a good flight,
Estelle. Old Jerry just likes to cruise, is all. He don't need a 206
to do that…but that's the plane he likes, and he can afford it."
He shrugged. "He should fly it a little more often, is all."

"So most of the time the airplane just sits inside the hangar
gathering dust?"

"Sits, anyway. He keeps 'er clean and waxed up, fair enough.
But he don't fly 'er enough. That's no way to treat a lady." Bergin
grinned.

"Somebody's using her now," Estelle said, turning back to the
bent wall section. "I want to take a few pictures of this, and then
can I ask your help to fold this back? I want to see how it works."

"You bet."

"I called Mark," Torrez said. "He's bringin' Sebastian over."
Sebastian, a State Police dog who had earned his stripes dozens
of times, lived in semiretirement with the State Police lieutenant.

"Good move," Estelle said. "We need his nose." More vehicles
turned into the airport driveway. Linda Real's small red Honda
sedan was followed by a county pickup truck, County Manager
Leona Spears' preferred wheels.

"Something else," Torrez added. "Tell her about the fuel,
Jim."

"Well," Bergin said. "She's just about full, Estelle. Maybe a
gallon or two down. Both wing tanks. You don't fly eleven hours
and end up with full tanks."

She studied Bergin for a moment, digesting the possibilities.
"So the pilot refueled somewhere."

"Yep."

"You sell gas right here."

"Not to this airplane. Not recently. You can check my fuel logs if you want."

"Then he stopped in someplace like Deming? Lordsburg?"

"Not and arrive back here with full tanks. That bird burns somewhere between eight and twelve gallons an hour, Estelle. She's only down maybe one or two in each wing."

"Could he have fueled it himself? Right here in the hangar? Estelle asked.

Bergin looked skeptical. "Could, I suppose. I ain't sold avgas to someone with five-gallon cans." He held up a hand, halted by another thought that burst into his mind. "Something else we should check," he said, but before he could explain, two State Police cruisers braked hard and turned into the airport.

"Here's Sebastian," Torrez said. "Let's do it."

Chapter Nine

"Can you give us about ten minutes?" Estelle asked the State Police lieutenant, and Mark Adams grinned.

"You can have all night as far as I'm concerned. We're not going anywhere." He bent down and looked through the windshield of the patrol car at his backseat passenger. Sebastian sat on the wreckage of the backseat, tail thumping his blanket expectantly. Estelle was eager to learn what the dog's awesome nose would discover, but once that process started, other evidence could be destroyed forever.

She turned to Jerry Turner. "Show me the grass," she said, and followed him back into the hangar.

"Bobby called me sayin' that someone might have been in the hangar, so we came down. Now, in a preflight check, we always look at the tires pretty carefully. And it's obvious when you do that. See right there?" He aimed his flashlight, and Estelle knelt beside the right main wheel skirt. "I saw that tuft of grass stuck where it shouldn't be stuck. I saw that, then I saw some other marks on the skirts...like I don't know what. Then I looked at the prop tips." He lowered his voice as if the information might be confidential, and squatted down beside Estelle. The wheel skirt's fiberglass was cracked in various places, including around one of the bracket bolts. Several bits of grass had been caught there.

"Show me the prop," Estelle said, and pushed herself upright. Turner warmed up to his role as tour guide.

"Rev it up, and the tips of that prop are traveling just short of supersonic, you know. They suck in just about everything." His eyebrows raised as he extended one hand to within an inch of the rounded propeller tip without actually touching the metal. He traced the smooth edge. "Real vulnerable part of the airplane. What I'm looking for is nicks, of course. Nicks from stones and crap off the macadam. You get a big enough nick, and it causes vibration, and *that* can ruin your whole day, lemme tell ya. Anyway, there's residue on the prop tips that shouldn't be there. She's been in the grass. Dust and grass. I'd bet the farm on it."

"That's not just from gathering dust sitting here?" Estelle asked.

"Hell no, it ain't that. Lookit." He held the light so that the beam shot down the prop blade. "Look at the tip, now, right there on the black paint. I clean that prop every time I fly, and I clean it when I put the bird away. There's dirt and crap all over it."

Estelle saw the reddish film, maybe enough to prove Turner's point, maybe just his overactive imagination.

"You don't operate out of any locations that might—" she asked, but Turner interrupted her with an emphatic shake of the head.

"Never. Never. I don't land on dirt roads, I don't taxi anywhere but on the macadam or concrete. The last time I went up in this airplane, I flew over to Cruces International with Jimbo to pick up the new rotating beacon for the airport here, and the International sure as hell don't have grass growing up through the cracks of the runway."

"That's a fact," Bergin said, his head jerking up as if he'd been dozing.

Estelle regarded the taciturn Bergin for a moment. "What do you think?" Estelle asked him, understanding his need for prompting.

Bergin shrugged. "The airplane has been operated off the dirt," he said. "Dirt, grass, whatever. No doubt in my mind. You don't get grass in your wheel skirts by sitting on concrete floors in a locked steel hangar."

"You were saying something about the gasoline," Estelle said. "Explain that to me."

Bergin stood on his tiptoes, pointing at the wing. "Filler caps are on top of each wing."

"You want the ladder?" Turner asked. "I got me that old aluminum one over in the corner."

"I don't think so," Estelle said.

"This is what I was thinkin' outside," Bergin said. "If whoever used this airplane was dumpin' automotive gas in the tanks, say from jerry cans, then he could park it here and fill it."

"They better not be putting auto gas in my airplane," Turner said. "You want to drain some?"

"That's what I was gettin' at," Bergin said.

"Can I?" Turner said to Estelle. "I got to open the left door to do that. Sampler's in the pouch behind the pilot's seat."

"The plane is locked?"

"Nah," Turner said. "I don't lock it. The *hangar's* locked." He opened the door gingerly and retrieved the plastic fuel sampler. Thrusting the pin into one of the vents under the left wing, he squirted a jet of fuel into the sampler. "There you go," he said, and handed it to Bergin.

The airport manager sniffed it carefully and looked dubious. "I don't know." He held it up, holding a flashlight off to one side. "Auto gas is red, avgas is blue. Maybe this is a mix. Who the hell can tell in this light?"

"But it *could* be," Estelle prompted.

"It could be." He walked to the engine cowling and stooped down, drawing another sample. "If she was running on avgas when she was parked, and then the wing tanks were filled with auto gas, we might be able to tell—maybe." He shot a skeptical glance at Estelle. "If our lab was good enough." He eyed the engine fuel sample, then flipped it out on the concrete floor.

"These are ladder marks?" Estelle asked, playing her flashlight on the floor where scuff marks were obvious.

"Most likely," Turner said. "But I clean off the top of that wing, and I check the filler caps every time I fly. Them could all be mine."

"Huh." She stood back and regarded the airplane. "Eleven hours, you say?"

"Damn close."

"Is maintenance on the aircraft done here, Mr. Turner?"

"You bet. Jimbo here does it all for me."

"Then chances are good that I'll want to see your logs, and the maintenance records. We want to nail down exactly when *you* last flew, when Jim last worked on the aircraft…simple things like that to give us a window of opportunity."

"Okay. We can do that. All that's in the airplane. And after all this, I'm going to have Jimbo go over this old crate with a finetoothed comb after you're through with her. Make sure someone hasn't monkeyed with anything. Hell of a note."

"The hangar door is always locked?" Estelle asked.

"Yep. I go in the side door there, which is dead-bolted. We can only access the main door from inside. It's got that big slide bolt."

"Go ahead and open that."

She watched as Turner pushed the massive door to one side. It rolled easily on well-greased wheels. She beckoned to Bob Torrez, who broke off his conversation with the State Police lieutenant.

"Bobby, I don't think we're going to find much on the floor, but it's worth a try. We could use those portable lights." She held up both hands, framing the airplane. "If we set them up off to the left there, we can get a good angle. If there are any interesting shoe prints on the floor, they might show up better."

"God, I hate to put you to all this trouble," Turner said. "It's not like we found a corpse or anything inside the plane, after all."

"No trouble, sir." She smiled at him. "And you never know what we'll find. I'm going on the assumption that you're correct about someone using your plane. There's no reason why you would be wrong about something like that. If someone used it, that means they had a way to gain access without breaking down the door. They took it, flew somewhere, landed, and then returned, and tucked the plane back in its hangar here, with no one the wiser."

"Remember those three teenagers who stole a plane down in Houston, was it?" Turner said. "Someplace like that, several years ago. One of them was a student pilot, and he took his friends up for a nighttime joyride around the city."

"They were all drunker'n skunks," Bergin added. "Tower had to talk 'em down. That sure as hell isn't what's going on here, though."

"And that was in a little puddle jumper," Turner said. "A trainer. Someone with just a few hours could fly one well enough to get her off the ground and back again, with a little luck. But it's a different story with this one." He nodded at his aircraft.

"This is a..." Estelle prompted.

"Turbo 206," he said proudly. "There's a lot of horses under that cowl, and she's a complex, heavy airplane. It's not something a kid is going to take on a joyride."

"And worth some money, I imagine."

"Sure. This is probably the most popular model to steal, especially along the border here," Turner said. "Good freight hauler." He paused with evident pride. "We got us right at eighty grand parked here."

"And you don't keep it locked?"

"Nope. Somebody gets in this hangar, I don't want 'em ruining the aircraft door to get in. You know how much that would cost to fix?"

"There is that," Estelle said. She pushed the door open and looked inside. The ignition key was in place, a small evergreen air freshener and a second key hanging from the ring.

"Do you normally leave your key in the airplane, sir?"

"You know, I do...." Turner hesitated. "Stupid, huh?"

"Yep," Sheriff Torrez said, and his one-word utterance jerked Turner around as if he had forgotten that Bob Torrez was standing nearby.

"But see, I look at it this way," he said. "The hangar's locked. Always locked. I make sure of that. It's a steel building with a dead bolt on the access door, there, and steel lock bolts on the main door. I figure that if someone is going to go to the trouble of breaking in to steal my airplane, then what the hell. They're going to take her whether there's a key in the ignition or not. Airplane's just about the easiest thing next to a power lawn mower to hot-wire."

"Uh huh," Estelle said, keeping her tone neutral.

"And what the hell. Jim, your Citabria?" he called to Bergin, who stood just outside the open hangar door. "That doesn't even *have* an ignition key, does it? Just a couple of switches."

"True." Bergin sounded noncommittal.

"What's the second key on the ring for, sir?"

"Well, now I'm going to sound even stupider," Turner said. "That's an extra door key."

"You mean for the hangar?"

"Yes. Well, hell. That way I know where it is."

"I see," Estelle said, managing to keep the amusement out of her voice. People routinely did dumb things, but that never seemed to lessen the umbrage when their habits caught up with them.

"Well, now…" Turner started to say, then bit it off.

Estelle added the dangling keys to the list of photographs that she wanted Linda Real to inventory.

"What's all that tell you?" Turner asked. "Are you able to do anything with that grass sample?"

"I don't know, sir," Estelle said. "Grass is sort of a ubiquitous thing, you know. And the red dust on the propeller? I wish we had a magic computer where we could feed a sample into a program and it would instantly locate where in the world it came from—but that's still Hollywood sci-fi."

"The grass caught in the wheel skirt could tell you something, couldn't it?" Turner persisted.

"I suppose it could, if it turned out that it was a rare, endangered species that grows only on a small peninsula in the Yucatán."

"What you're saying is that we may never figure this out," Turner said.

"Been known to happen," Torrez said. "Just for fun," he continued to Estelle, "let's go over the inside with black light when you're all done lookin' for hairs and fibers and all that shit."

"What's that do?" Turner asked.

"Shows some interesting things," Torrez said, and let it go at that.

"Body fluids show up," Estelle added for Turner's benefit.

The possibilities of that weren't lost on the aircraft owner. "Well, yuck," he said with a grimace. He'd grimace even more if he knew about the family of corpses currently reposing in the basement morgue at Posadas General, she thought.

"Let me ask you something, sir," Estelle said. "How long could this airplane have been missing without you noticing?" When he didn't answer immediately, she added, "From the last time you closed and locked the door to right now."

"Well, like I said—I guess when Jim and I flew down to Cruces. That was last month sometime."

"Early in the month," Bergin said. "Today's the ninth of May. That's a month."

"I guess so," Turner said. "About a month."

"*Ay,*" Estelle whispered to herself. "That's quite a window of opportunity. All these nice flat surfaces can gather a lot of dust in a month."

"Could. But what's on that prop isn't something that sifted down from the ceiling in here," Turner said doggedly.

"Eleven hours of flight time in a month." She leaned inside again, examining the instrument panel. "Which one of these is the Hobbs?"

· Turner reached across the seat and tapped a small, black-ringed clock. "Right there. Hobbs meter gives true time, and the tach records engine hours."

"They're not the same thing, then?"

"Ah, no," Turner said indulgently. "They're not the same."

"You have a record of what the Hobbs read when you flew last time?"

"Sure. The logs are in the pocket behind the seat. Lemme come around."

Estelle pulled back and let Turner rummage. He flipped open a black book and leafed through the pages. "When we came back from Cruces, and that was on April fourteenth, the Hobbs read 2134.6 hours. And now, it reads…" He paused as he squinted at the dial. "It looks like 2145.9. That's—" and he looked upward as he did the math in his head "—a little more than eleven hours."

"How far could you fly in that time?" Torrez asked. "Or half that time. You gotta come back."

"To keep it simple," Bergin explained, "a hundred and forty miles an hour gets you seven hundred miles in five hours. But that's not counting fuel stops or anything like that."

"Seven hundred."

"That's right. Hell of a ways from here to Los Angeles, or Dallas, or Denver. Or a hell of a ways into Mexico."

"And back," Estelle added.

"You have any ideas?" Turner said, looking first at Estelle and then at Torrez.

"A couple or three," Torrez said. "It wasn't just pleasure flyin'."

"We could be looking at five trips of two hours each, more or less. Or three trips, or whatever," Bergin said.

"Yep." Torrez nodded. "Interesting that they went to the trouble of bringin' the airplane back when they were done."

"Pretty darn thoughtful," Bergin said.

"Oh, yeah," Torrez grunted. He turned to Estelle. "You ready to have Linda go over it? Then we can let the dog out."

Turner looked even more uncomfortable. "You think somebody used my plane to run drugs, or what?"

"We'll find out," Torrez said.

Chapter Ten

Sebastian stood beside the airplane, his leash hanging relaxed from the State Police officer's hand, tongue lolling and eyes looking expectantly from human to human. Neither luck nor his phenomenally precise nose had located any trace of the fragrant little red ball with which he had been so meticulously trained.

Estelle knew that it often came as a surprise to drug dealers that the dogs didn't know hashish from hot dogs, or blood from grape juice. Find the source of the smell for which they had been trained, whether it was the real thing or the essence smeared on a rubber ball, and win a treat. It was as simple as that.

The trick was keeping distractions to a minimum. As soon as he had been released from the backseat of the State Police car, Sebastian had caught sight of Bob Torrez. The dog did a little dance, uttering a girlish yelp of greeting.

"He loves you, Bobby." Lieutenant Adams laughed. Aloof with other human beings except his handler, Sebastian went to pieces with Bob Torrez—no one, including the sheriff himself, knew why.

Socializing turned to work in short order. Keeping Sebastian on short leash, Lieutenant Adams led him into the hangar. For the next ten minutes, he guided the dog's efforts, covering the perimeter, the exterior of the plane, and finally the inside.

Tail wagging furiously, Sebastian leaped through the large door of the aft baggage compartment, eager to please. No matter how thoroughly he thrust his nuzzle into dark corners, even wedging his wet nose into the seat pockets, he found nothing.

After several attempts, Adams led the dog out of the hangar, where he collected a single pat on the head from Sheriff Torrez.

"Nothing," Adams said. "Absolutely nothing. If this aircraft has been hauling freight, it wasn't coke or grass or any of that shit." He looked approvingly at Turner, as if somehow the cell phone salesman's reputation had been at stake.

Fifteen minutes later, they had another answer—another negative one. The black light wand produced nothing. The interior of the airplane hadn't been splashed with bodily fluids—certainly not blood, anyway.

A perceptive businessman, Jerry Turner watched the circus with nervous interest. At one point, he sauntered with exaggerated calm over to where Leona Spears waited by her county truck. Leona had stayed well back from the crime scene, but her natural curiosity—especially since the airport was county property—kept her from leaving.

"What do you think?" Torrez asked.

"I want to know where the gasoline came from," Estelle said.

"That shouldn't be too hard. How many places in town sell gas? Six?"

"About that. And I would think that they'd remember someone filling multiple cans."

"And it don't have to be gas stations," Jim Bergin offered. "Any rancher that has a storage tank. Probably another half a dozen outfits in town have tanks."

"It still ain't that many," Torrez said. "Let me get someone started on that."

"Eddie's still out at the airstrip?"

"Far as I know. Him and Jackie. I'm going to leave her out there, get the rest combin' the area for gas sales."

Estelle shook her head slowly. "*Ay,*" she whispered. "If this is the plane…"

"Then it's somebody local," Torrez finished the thought.

"Or somebody who *knows* the community as well as a local." She reached out a hand to Bergin, taking him by the left shoulder. "How many pilots do you know in Posadas who fly well enough to do something like this?"

"Oh, shit," Bergin said. "You mean steal an airplane and bring it back? Just about anybody with a pilot's license, Estelle. Now, if they're flyin' at *night*, that's different. And if they're dodgin' border security, that's something else again. I don't know anybody who'd be crazy enough to do that."

"Well, taking the plane is the least of it." She drew him several steps farther away from Jerry Turner's hearing. "Jim, we think that this plane was used to fly in from somewhere— maybe Mexico, maybe not—with at least four people." She released Bergin's shoulder and held up four fingers, then bent one down. "One was the pilot. The other three were murdered. Shot to death."

Bergin looked at her in silence.

"The sheriff found the bodies out at the west end of the gas company's airstrip, off County Road Fourteen."

"Jesus," Bergin murmured.

"We don't know who they are, but we think they may be from Mexico, maybe somewhere else south of the border."

"You're tellin' me that somebody took this airplane, flew down south, picked up passengers, brought 'em back into the country, then killed 'em?"

"Yes."

"Then *returned* the airplane. Just parked it back in the hangar and walked away."

"That's the possibility we're looking at, Jim."

"Well, I wondered why all the fuss. I don't guess you'd have the whole department out lookin' for a stolen car—or airplane. Least of all a *borrowed* one. Unless there was something else goin' on."

"There is. Three homicide victims. Maybe a family. We don't know."

Bergin held up a hand. "I don't need to know no more," he said. "Does Turner know any of this?"

"No. He's going to *need* to know, though. I want to borrow the plane. With you flying it."

Bergin cocked his head incredulously. "Now what? What are we talkin' about here?"

"I'm going to repeat my original question: how many pilots do you know of around here who fly well enough to pull this off? For the sake of argument, let's say, fly deep into Mexico, pick up passengers, fly back, and land at the airstrip—all, I'm going to guess, at night. Daytime is too risky. He lands, shoots the three, then piles back into the plane, and returns to Posadas. Again, at night. If you're not here, he's going to be able to slip in without anyone noticing."

"Sure he is. And I'm not here all the time, either."

"Just so."

"Who could do that? Well, I could. Jerry, there. He *could*. He wouldn't, but he *could*. There's maybe half a dozen at most."

"In Posadas."

"Here in town. Now, you include Deming and a few other towns, there's more. But if what you're sayin' happened the way you think it did, that's…well, I don't know." Bergin groped for words. "That's something kind of different."

"Yes, it is. Very, very different. That's why I want the ride."

"That's not one of your better ideas, Madame Undersheriff," he said.

She regarded Jerry Turner's Cessna 206 critically, trying to push commonsense agreement with the airport manager out of her mind. "There's nothing that says this *isn't* the plane that landed out on the gas company's strip, Jim," she said. "The wheelbase measurement is consistent."

"Hell, that could change," Bergin said. "Loaded heavy, your tire track is going to be one thing, empty and it's going to be somethin' else. I don't see how you can measure that close."

"May we can't—but it's close enough to suggest a match."

"Look," Bergin said, and his fingers groped for a cigarette. It was half out of the pack before he remembered that he was standing near an aircraft hangar, in close proximity to a full load of volatile fuel. He thrust it back and patted his pocket closed. "I don't think anybody ought to be flying this airplane until we have a chance to really go over it, nose to tail. If she's got auto fuel mixed in with avgas…and I realize that ain't no big thing. But just the same…"

"Whoever used it didn't have any qualms," Estelle said. "Would he necessarily know the difference?"

Bergin laughed dryly. "Yes, he'd know. And we ain't him. Havin' a few of those qualms keeps us alive. Not to mention that it's the middle of the goddamn night, with a short unlighted airstrip that has a fence at either end. Besides, what's the difference? Maybe this is the plane…maybe it is. So what? What's flyin' it out there in the dark going to tell you?"

"I don't know what it's going to tell me," Estelle said. "It's just helpful. What I know is that it's a link we need to explore—the sooner the better."

"Helpful," Bergin repeated. "Seems like it could at least wait till light."

She nodded, not knowing how to explain what she felt. "It could. But they landed at night. I'd bet on it." In her mind's eye, she could see the Cessna sinking downward, with the apprehensive eyes of the passengers glued to the windows, staring out into the inky blackness of the desert. The landing lights would cut a swath, making the desert seem all the more ominous. The plane had touched down solidly, no bounces, no swerving—a perfectly executed landing followed by a long, straight rollout. And then the drift to the right, slowing more, swinging hard left perhaps with a burst of power—and then the first sign of a miscalculation, so out of place with the rest of the command performance.

"We can't jump to easy answers," Estelle said. "We're so far out of the loop it's pathetic, Jim. We don't even know for sure where the three victims are from—most likely someplace south of the border, but we're not sure. We haven't found any paperwork, no personal belongings. The plane could have flown five hours south, and that would have put it pretty deep in Mexico, but where the passengers were actually picked up might just be a staging area." She shrugged. "If I can put myself in the same situation, it might tell me something about the pilot. About the way he thinks."

"You think the pilot is the killer?"

"I don't know. He would almost certainly be involved some-how. He would have to know. And if the pilot did the shooting himself, that means the plane had to be parked for a few minutes untended while he got out to do his business. Right now we have no way to tell if that's what happened. If the victims had any personal belongings, those stayed in the plane—we didn't find anything scattered in the desert. I'm hoping you can help me with that."

"Huh," Bergin grunted. "And parked is parked, Estelle. When he stopped to let out passengers, he was parked. Whether for thirty seconds or five minutes don't matter much." He looked at the floor thoughtfully. "This airplane don't have any seeps. No oil puddle from bein' parked. So you can't tell from that." He heaved a sigh. "Tell you what. You want to fly out that way, let's take my plane."

"There's no point in that."

Bergin almost smiled. "I was afraid you'd say that." He fumbled with his cigarettes again and laughed. "I don't know why I let you talk me into these things." He sighed. "Okay, tell you what. If Turner says it's okay, fine. You got to give me a couple hours to check this bird over real good. Maybe even drain out the gas, if that's in question. I don't want any surprises."

"Done. I'll talk with Jerry."

The big man turned a shade more pale as Estelle recited a short version of events to him. As she described the victims and how they were found, she saw his shoulders slump and his weight sag onto the fender of the BMW.

"Why would someone *do* something like that?" he asked finally. He looked quickly first at Bob Torrez and then at Estelle.

"I hope to heaven you folks don't think *I* had something to do with all this."

"Someone used your airplane, sir. That's what we think. If we can have your cooperation, we'd appreciate it. We'll fill it up when we're finished."

"With avgas," Turner said, trying to smile.

"You bet."

"I don't want to go, if that's all right. For one thing, I'd have to put the seats back in."

"That's fine, sir. We won't be gone long."

She checked her watch. "Midnight straight up?" she asked Bergin.

"That'll work. It's crazy, but it'll work."

Chapter Eleven

Sheriff Torrez agreed to meet airport manager Jim Bergin and Estelle out at the gas company's airstrip. "Somebody's got to be there when you two crash through that barbed-wire fence," he said. With the sheriff coordinating the search of local gas stations and fuel dumps, Estelle took a moment to prepare a brief statement for the media. Word of the triple homicide would certainly leak out, and the city papers and television stations would be calling, if they hadn't already.

Each police agency would have its own spin on events, and she couldn't count on the Border Patrol or the State Police or the INS to suggest that reporters call the Posadas County Sheriff's Department for information. Some of them would anyway, and she didn't want Gayle Torrez, who would be taking over from dispatcher Brent Sutherland at six the next morning, to be blindsided.

Without doubt, Frank Dayan, publisher of the *Posadas Register*, would be calling, searching for some angle to put his small weekly newspaper ahead of the metro media.

The cyclo-cross bike race, in its first year and just hours away, didn't offer much news value—certainly not enough for metro news teams to travel to Posadas, wherever that was, to shoot footage of a crowd of spandex-clad people pedaling laboriously up Cat Mesa. But throw in a multiple homicide on the same turf, and the attraction would escalate.

The media interest would be sparked until everyone made the easy assumption that the three dead people were just another unhappy statistic—Mexicans whose drug deal in the desert had gone wrong, or migrants who had been ill-prepared for a long trek in the wilderness. That would lead to more sidebar stories in the Sunday papers about the growing problem of the border drug trade, or of illegals running afoul of border vigilante groups, or the push to finish the transcontinental border fence, or to a dozen other takes on the "border problem."

At ten minutes after eleven on that Saturday night, Estelle pulled into the driveway of her home on South 12th Street, parking beside her husband's SUV. The front porch light was on, and a single light glowed through the living room curtain. Her mother was a fitful sleeper, and often chose her rocking chair in the living room, in company with her friendly books, rather than tossing and turning in bed.

Estelle let herself in and stopped abruptly. Her mother wasn't in her chair, but Estelle could see her older son's tousled little head peeking out from behind the music rack of the piano. Their eyes met for just a fraction of a second, and then he ducked down, hunching his shoulders.

"You're up late, *hijo,*" she said as she crossed the living room. The dark circles under his eyes hinted that he hadn't just popped out of bed. She dropped her jacket on the sofa, then crossed to the piano. "May I?" she asked, and slipped onto the bench beside him. She circled his thin, bony shoulders in a hug. His hair smelled vaguely musty, reminding her of an old man's. Her right hand stroked his forehead, pushing the flop of curly black hair out of his eyes. He didn't look up at her, but she felt him lean against her.

"You got called out," Francisco whispered.

"Yes. A bad time, *querido.* But I heard you play. I'm so proud of you."

He nodded and fell silent, looking down at his hands. His fingers rested on the piano keys as they might on an unresponsive tabletop. After a minute, his right index finger reached out tentatively and touched the face of the black C-sharp key just above middle C. His fingers were long and strong, and she saw that his muscles had already taken on definition resulting from hours of unrelenting exercise.

Estelle waited, sensing that the little boy was wrestling with something far beyond his seven-year-old capabilities to articulate. Perhaps, after the intense excitement of the recital, his first time in front of an audience other than family, the adrenaline rush hadn't subsided yet.

"Are you going out again?" he asked.

"I have to, for a little bit."

"Right away?"

"Yes."

"Are we going up on the mesa to watch Tommy race tomorrow?"

"I hope so." She felt his shoulders rise with a little sigh of resignation. "You know I can't promise, *mi corazón*. But Daddy will take you up if he can. Or *Nana* Irma. Or *Padrino*."

His index finger tickled the front of the C-sharp again. "Did you hear Melody play?"

"Yes, I did." She didn't release her hug. "And I thought it was nice that she asked you to turn pages for her. Have you ever played that piece?"

"No. But it's easy. And it's boring."

"Maybe she doesn't think so."

"Pitney is mad at me," he said after a minute. "She wouldn't talk to me after the recital."

"Why ever not?" But already part of the scenario was obvious to her. Her seven-year-old son, adorable in so many ways, had wandered into the unpredictable turf between two older females.

"'Cause I turned pages for Melody."

"Why would that make her mad at you?"

"'Cause. She said I should play Pachelbel," and he pronounced it *patchy-bell*, "to show Melody how it should go."

"You mean instead of your own piece?"

"Yes. But I don't like that old stairway song."

"Stairway song?"

He sighed. "You know. Up and down. Da, da, da, da, da, da, da, da," and he continued, the fingers of his right hand once more over the keys, marching down and then back up, soundlessly touching each one, following the opening motif of Pachelbel's Canon.

"Pitney wanted you to play Melody's piece, instead of your own? Instead of the Mozart?"

He nodded. "But that's mean, isn't it, *Mamá?*"

"More than mean," Estelle said. "Why would Pitney want you to do that?" She could imagine perfectly well why, but wanted to hear her son's version.

"'Cause. She doesn't like Melody, *Mamá.*"

"I see," she said. "But *you* like Melody, don't you?"

He nodded.

Oh my, Estelle thought. *He's seven, and the women are fighting over him already.*

"You know that what Pitney asked you to do was wrong, don't you?"

"Yes. But she wouldn't talk to me when Melody finished playing."

"Maybe that's not important, *mi corazón.* When people ask you to do things, you must always think about it. You must think about what they ask of you. And you know, Melody has always been kind to you, Francisco. I've seen her at school, and she always asks about you. She's so proud of you. She doesn't try to make you do things that you shouldn't."

Her son drew his hands off the keyboard, curling them under his chin in that characteristic gesture of delight.

"She's a clown," he said, but his tone welled with kindness rather than insult. "She played well, don't you think?"

"She played beautifully. You all did. Does Daddy know you're still up?"

"No. I don't think so."

"You should go to bed. Tomorrow's a big day."

He nodded and rubbed his eyes. "I've been working on a story," he said.

A *musical* story, she knew, and wondered what images he was seeing in his head. If they had returned home from the concert by 8:30, Francisco had been at the keyboard for several hours. "You've been here since you came home from the recital?"

"I didn't make any noise," he said, and a note of childlike conspiracy entered his tone. "Just like this." With left hand curled under his chin, his right hand spidering over the keys, and after a moment his left hand joined the music, the touches on the keyboard as soft as a kitten's tread, so soft that the piano's mechanisms never moved under the strings.

"Start over," Estelle said. She reached across and with thumb and index finger twisted an imaginary knob on her son's left temple. "Turn up the volume so I can hear."

"*Abuela* is still asleep," he said.

"I bet not," Estelle said. "She can hear ants crossing the sidewalk. And anyway, she'd like to hear, too."

He took a breath, and once more the right hand started, this time touching three notes in succession, lingering on the last. "That's her name," he said, and played the three notes again. "Me-lo-dy."

"I hear that it is. Should I hear the rest, or will you save it for her?"

That thought obviously hadn't occurred to Francisco. His fingers hesitated, and he looked around at his mother for the first time. "Should I do that?"

"It's up to you, *mi corazón.*"

"I want you to hear it."

"All right."

Estelle found herself wishing that she could somehow tune in to the pictures that paraded through her son's mind as he played, but that remained his private world. The music was simple, the two hands talking to each other as he'd learned to do by playing the Grump, *el Gruñón,* as he called J.S. Bach. But the music went beyond that, and Estelle wondered if her son heard the difference between his soundless hours of practicing and what now swelled from the huge piano, lyrical and rich.

The music finally wound down, ending with the same three notes, played so softly that they barely escaped the piano—a whisper of affection that Estelle understood so clearly that it made her heart ache.

She realized that her husband was now standing in his bathrobe in the hallway, leaning against the wall. She grinned at him and he winked back.

"He's figured it out?" he asked.

"Oh *sí*," she said, and hugged Francisco fiercely.

"I want to play that for her," the little boy said.

"That's what you should do," she said. "Can we record it?"

Francisco instantly shook his head. "It's just for her."

"What if *she* wants to record it, so she can hear it whenever she wants?"

Francisco's eyebrows almost met in the center of his nose, and then he brightened with a wide smile. "Then she's got to learn to play it," he said. "I'll teach her."

"Would you like someone else telling you what you must play, *hijo?* Wouldn't it be nice to play the piece for her, and then give her a copy so that she could hear it again whenever *she* wants?"

"Yes," Francisco said, the thought that Melody Mears might *not* want his composition never crossing his young mind. "But I don't know how to write it down."

"Before long, you will, *hijo*. You will. But for now, a CD would work just fine. Then, if she wants to play it, she'll have something to listen to."

"I'll play it for her on Tuesday, at my lesson," Francisco said, the matter settled in his mind. Estelle watched him carefully close the black hinged cover over the keyboard, and made a mental note that it might be productive to change Francisco's music lesson day to another day of the week, a little bit more removed from the creative Pitney's teenaged conspiracies.

"Bed now," Estelle said, and kissed him on the forehead.

"Okay," the little boy said. He made it across the living room, then leaned heavily against his father's left leg. That comfortable contact flipped the switch on his overtaxed system. Francis knelt down to gather up the little boy, whose eyes were already shut. Her husband glanced back at Estelle as he headed down the hall with his cargo. "You, too," he added.

Estelle watched them go, wondering how much she should burden her husband with her plans. The clock ticked to 11:40, and she rose from the piano bench. In a moment, Francis reappeared, shutting the boys' bedroom door carefully. "Out like a light."

"*Querido,* I need to go back out again."

"You're kidding."

"No."

"Progress? Do you know who the three are? Were?"

"Not a clue. But we're following up on some other ideas."

"None of which can wait until morning."

She snuggled against him. "Actually, no. There's some aerial surveillance that Jim Bergin has agreed to fly for us. That has to be done at night."

He looked askance at her. "You're going along, I gather."

"Yes."

"Do I want to know more?"

"Just that I think this is very important, and that we'll be very careful."

"Oh, I trust Jim," Francis said. "If he says it's safe, it's safe."

Well, he didn't say it was safe, Estelle thought. "I told him I'd meet him at the airport at midnight," she said instead. Francis walked her out to the car and held the door for her. "Irma is spending the night," he said. "If I get a call, we're covered."

She took a deep breath and put her hand over his. "No calls, please."

"Not until tomorrow, when we have more cliff divers." He laughed.

Chapter Twelve

Jerry Turner's plane waited on the tarmac beside the fuel pump island. The aircraft looked a good deal smaller out of its hangar. Bergin had fussed over the Cessna, including taking the time to drain any suspect fuel from the wing tanks and refill them with fresh avgas.

Bergin stood under the left wing, one hand resting on the strut. "All set?"

"As ready as I'll ever be," she replied, and clambered inside.

"All the way across to the right seat," Bergin said.

"Odd that there's no door on the passenger side," Estelle said, feeling claustrophobic immediately. As she strapped herself into the cramped confines of the Cessna, she felt a surge of adrenaline. Had the killer strapped himself into this same seat, in command of the situation? Or had he curled up in the back with the others, smelling their sweat, their excitement, eventually their fear?

She turned and looked back through the empty cabin, trying to picture how the three people had squeezed some comfort out of the cramped quarters, with nothing but the flat aluminum floor to sit on. Only the two front seats remained—Turner had taken out the other four when he and Jim Bergin had flown the new beacon back to Posadas.

And not a scrap of luggage—not even a plastic bag filled with underwear and socks to use as a pillow.

Her position suggested one small answer, even as Bergin climbed into the left seat. If the killer had ridden up front, as she was doing right now, he would have had two choices when the aircraft stopped—squeeze into the back between the two front seats or wait for the pilot to exit the plane, allowing the killer to follow.

The other choice was simple enough: the killer had piloted the airplane. Perhaps the father had ridden in the right seat up front, leaving only the woman and her son to make do in back.

"You thought about the route you want to take?" Bergin asked. He held a small flashlight and scanned a printed checklist clipped to an aluminum thigh-board.

"I don't think it matters," Estelle said. "We're betting that the victims came into the country from the south—nothing else makes sense to me. Whether they flew across to the east, over by María, or through Regál…we have no way of knowing. What *doesn't* make sense is thinking that they came in right over the top of the mountains." Looking through the freshly polished windshield, she could not see the San Cristóbals, but she knew they loomed ahead to the southwest, a long dark lump of rock waiting to reach out and grab aluminum.

Bergin held both hands out to form the shape of a football. He lifted his right. "Regál's at one end of the mountains." He lifted his left hand. "María's at the other. You want to try west?"

"That'll work."

He nodded and returned to his preflight chores. As an afterthought, he said, "And the mountains don't matter, Estelle. Not with this airplane. She's got the power to handle anything, even loaded on top. If they wanted to come straight in over the mountains and then drop down, well…that's easy enough. A lot of folks don't understand mountains. As long as you don't fly *into* one, it don't matter a whole hell of a lot how high they are, or how rugged. To an airplane that can easily top sixteen, eighteen thousand feet, a ten-thousand-foot mountain doesn't amount to a thing."

He finished the first portion of the list, scanned the dashboard again, and then started the engine, coaxing it gently to life. The big six-cylinder shook the entire airframe until it settled into quiet idle. Bergin relaxed the brakes and let the plane move away from the fuel island. As they rolled down the taxiway, he continued his checklist, glancing ahead now and then to make sure some night beast wasn't standing in the middle of the taxiway. As they neared the turnaround donut at the east end, he turned and glanced at Estelle. His voice through the headset was relaxed.

"You want me to use the runway lights? We turn 'em on with the mike," and he held up the handset. "But I don't think someone comin' in with a stolen plane would do that. He *sure* as hell didn't have lights at the gas company's strip."

"Whatever you think is best," she said.

He laughed, the crackle of the radio making his voice sound metallic and artificial. "What I think is best is to be home and curled around a nice glass of bourbon."

"Afterward," Estelle said.

"Yeah, sure." He completed the run-up, the plane shaking against its brakes, watching the rpm's carefully as he checked each magneto and cycled the propeller three times. Finally satisfied that the engine would behave itself, he toggled the mike button on the control yoke. "Posadas Unicom, Cessna niner two Hotel is taking two seven. Lights inoperative." The words shot out into the electronic airways, and Bergin waited for a moment, the Cessna parked perpendicular to the active runway. "He wouldn't have done that, either," he said after a minute. "You all set?"

"Sure."

"Then let's boogie," Bergin said. He fed in power and the Cessna trundled out onto the asphalt runway. Estelle rested her feet lightly on the pedals, feeling them work. The landing lights in the Cessna's left wing picked up the white centerlines, and the thrust pushed Estelle back in her seat as Bergin firewalled the throttle. In a thousand feet or less, the vibration of wheels against pavement ceased and Estelle felt an odd surge of disorientation as the landing light halo on the asphalt disappeared.

They thundered up into the night, and as they turned south, she saw the spread of village lights off to the left.

"It makes a good landmark," Bergin said. He reached forward with his right hand and popped a circuit breaker, dousing the plane's dash lights, plunging them into complete darkness. His left hand held the yoke back, keeping the Cessna in a steep, spiral climb. "You want to be scanning for moving lights, things that aren't stars," he said. "Red light on the right, green on the left. There's not a lot of traffic out here, but there's some—and it ain't all legal."

After a minute, the nose sank as Bergin pulled back on the power and spun the trim wheel. Receding behind them, the mat of lights that was the village spread thin and frayed around the edges, and Estelle strained to see the dark outline of the mountains to the south. "How high are we?"

"About fifteen hundred feet." He rested a hand on the dash cowl, pointing off to the right, over toward the Torrance Ranch to the northwest. Headlights inched across the desert, then abruptly disappeared. "See that vehicle? A turn, a tree, go behind a barn—it don't take much to hide lights," he said. "Not when you have a picture this big. It'll take your eyes a while to get used to it. Just relax and drink it all in."

A set of lights appeared far out to the southwest, just a pin-prick through the trees.

"That's comin' over Regál Pass," Bergin said.

"And it's unlikely that he could see us," Estelle said.

"Especially if I turned out the nav strobes," Bergin said. He looked over at Estelle. "But I ain't about to do that. They don't bother us none. But chances are good your flyboy had his off. Flyin' dark."

She leaned forward, staring into what first looked like an endless void. But as her eyes adjusted, she could make out the smooth shadow that marked the mountains against the sky. Here and there, a single faint light marked a ranch or vehicle. "You have to know where you are," she said. "Are we on someone's radar now?"

"We might be. Get a little higher, and we might show up on the screen at Cruces. Other than that, someone would have to be *lookin'*. And contrary to popular belief, they aren't always. One thing's for sure—whoever did this knew the country." He relaxed back, eyes still scanning the heavens. "There's three ways to fly at night. One is to know the country. Or you can trust your instruments—and this plane's equipment isn't adequate for IFR. Or you can be damn fool lucky."

"Can you fly west to about Encinal? That would put us past the mountain. Then turn around and come back to the strip."

"We can do that." Bergin pointed again. "If you look northwest, way out, you can see that faint wash of light? That's Lordsburg. And stare right through the spinner, you'll catch the glint of the state highway heading down to the pass at Regál. We got just enough moon that it picks up on the shine of the asphalt."

"That's how he found the gas company's airstrip, then."

"Helps. But he had to know it was there, Estelle. He had to. For one thing, no matter what direction you approach the runway, you got the village lights in your eyes. It ain't much, but it's enough to kill a lot of your night vision and be a distraction."

A surge of air bumped the airplane upward, and then just as smoothly let it back down, like riding a small boat over a large smooth wave. Bergin paralleled the San Cristóbals, staying as far south of State Highway 56 as he could and still keep an obvious margin of safety between the plane and the sawtoothed mountain ridge. Estelle picked out the single small light of the Broken Spur Saloon, and knew that just a mile or so farther down the highway, County Road 14 came in from the north.

"If he flew around the west end of the mountain, he's got a pretty good valley there. He could stay low, out of anybody's radar," Bergin said.

"How low?" Estelle asked.

Bergin's electronic chuckle crackled in her headphones. "Two feet? Ten feet? You got one set of power transmission lines that runs east-west down there, and that's it. It's marked on the nav chart. Other than that, the tallest thing is a runty juniper. And those dirt roads show up pretty well at night, too. Good land- marks. See," and he shifted a little in his seat, fingers resting feather-light on the control yoke. "Most folks think it's a hair-raising, dangerous thing to fly low. But I gotta tell you—low ain't what kills you. It's *hittin'* things that ruins your day. Trees, barns, stock tanks, trains…even power poles. The truth is, you can leave a nice trail down a dirt road, flyin' so low that your tires suck dust. Don't hurt, as long as you don't catch a post, or a tree, or a power pole. You got to pay attention. No trick to it." He adjusted his position in the seat. "Crop dusters do it on a daily basis. When they kill themselves, it's almost always from hitting something they should have avoided. Like the ground." His chuckle sounded like static in the headphones.

"In fact," he added, "you get down low enough, and you have a good cushion of compressed air between the wings and the ground. That's called ground effect, and you can make it work for you."

"So he could avoid being spotted on the radar."

Bergin grunted in disdain. "'Course he could. That's one of the great myths, that radar sees all. Radar is good—if it's turned on, and if someone is *looking*. But it can't see through mountains, and it can't bend around corners and peek down valleys."

In a moment, Estelle saw a faint twinkle to the southwest, the lights of three or four ranch houses that marked Encinal, a tiny settlement near the far west end of the San Cristóbals, well out of Posadas County. Farther to the northwest, the spread of Lordsburg's lights had grown, and she could see the necklace of traffic on the interstate.

"For what it's worth, my guess is that they came around the mountains," Bergin said. He pointed toward Encinal. "Come up the valley there, and you're out of sight. You got just the one power line to remember, and a road to follow." He turned in a quick, sharp bank southward toward the mountain, flying directly toward Regál Pass until Estelle felt the slight sag of air flowing over the peak. Bergin turned then, and cut the power, letting the Cessna sink in a graceful turn back around to the north, away from the mountain.

"I'm going to take us down to about five hundred feet," he said. "That's low enough to give you the impression."

"How high do you think he was?"

"A lot lower than that. *He* was. Not us."

Twisting in her seat, Estelle searched the darkness off to the northeast until she once again found the two sodium vapor lights in the parking lot of the Broken Spur Saloon. A faint mark that might have been the gas company's runway stood out only because it was perfectly straight and defined in a dark world of smooth, dark shapes. A couple of miles north, two faint lights marked what would be Herb Torrance's ranch.

She held up her cell phone. "Can I use this in here?"

Bergin nodded. "You won't hear diddly, but knock yourself out. They'll hear you okay." She slipped off the headset, blocked her opposite ear, and held her cell phone tight to her head after dialing. Torrez's response was difficult to hear on any phone, but this was all but impossible. She spoke loudly and slowly, hoping he could hear her.

"Bobby, we're southwest of your position, and we'll be heading in." He said something she couldn't understand, and she added, "Not a single flashlight," although she knew that the sheriff didn't need the reminder. "No headlights."

"Got it," he said, and this time she could hear him clearly.

They banked sharply, turning back toward the northeast. Bergin backed off the throttle again, and the sensation of the ton of aluminum sinking out of the sky was unsettling. "He would have wanted to land headed toward the west," he said. "The other way, the village lights on the horizon are in his eyes. That'd be tricky as hell. I don't feel like bein' tricky. And most of the time, winds would have been in his favor, coming out of the west."

After a moment, the flaps spooled down and the plane humped as if someone had pushed it in the belly. "You see the runway?" he asked. Estelle stretched up, trying to see over the high dash. "Right there."

If she imagined hard enough, she could see the ghost of moon- and starlight on asphalt, and what she thought might be the white roof of a vehicle pulled off into the grass.

"When we line up on the runway, Posadas will be behind us," Bergin said.

They were so low that as they banked north on the base leg to the runway, Estelle could count four vehicles in the saloon's parking lot.

"They would have heard it," she said to herself, but Bergin's voice popped in her earpiece.

"Not necessarily," he said. The engine was idling, the prop windmilling as they settled. "We ain't stealth, but it don't make much noise when it's not pullin' power. And if the wind's right..." In a few seconds, he added, "That's pretty good," and the Cessna banked left again, lining on its final approach. The strip looked ridiculously tiny through the windscreen, still indistinct and ghostly. Her stomach rose as the flaps hung low, two aluminum barn doors rattling gently in the airstream.

The approach seemed terribly steep, and Estelle glanced across at Bergin. His left hand held the yoke firmly, his right resting almost nonchalantly on the throttle. "It's all visual," he said, as if sensing his passenger's unease, and Estelle tensed, wishing he'd narrate some other time. "If you turn on the instrument lights, you lose your night vision."

He reached out and flipped a switch, and the shaft of the landing light lanced ahead from the left wing. The air was so smooth that it felt as if they hung suspended and motionless while the dirt county road approached at dizzying speed, rushing up to meet them. Only at the last moment did the rusted wire of the fence catch the light, and then they were over it and settling onto the pavement. The tires kicked dust and Bergin pulled the throttle to the stops, holding the front wheel off the tarmac as long as he could, using the big, flat wings and flaps for drag.

"Lots of room," he said with satisfaction. The landing lights picked up asphalt and, along the edge, prairie vegetation, but nothing else.

"Can you swing around right at the end of the runway?"

"Going to have to." Bergin laughed. "This boat don't have reverse." He swung wide to the right as the end of the strip approached, and Estelle could see the yellow crime scene ribbon. "You say when," he said. "You want me to drop a wheel off, too?" He had been amused earlier at Estelle's description of the maneuver.

"Yes." She slipped off the headphones again and keyed the cell phone. "Bobby? Have someone mark the tire marks for us." Bergin slowed the Cessna to a slow walk, and they saw Eddie Mitchell appear out of the darkness, pointing with both hands toward the cast print.

"We need to miss that, Jim," she said. "Maybe you can swing around this side of it a bit."

"Prop wash is going to blow sand," he said. "Will that hurt anything?"

"I don't think so."

As they started their turn, Bergin shrugged. "He didn't have any reason to drop off a wheel," he said. "Runway is plenty wide, and this old bird will turn on a dime and hand you lots of change. With differential brakes, you can just pivot around one of the mains."

That was evidently the case, since Bergin had to relax his turn considerably to run off the pavement on the opposite side of the runway.

"Maybe something distracted him," he said. "You want me to stop?"

"Yes," she said, and the plane jerked a little, the right wheel off in the sandy gravel beside the macadam. "He let them out while he was parked off the strip." Her hand groped for a good handle as Bergin pulled the throttle back, the engine idling with a deep-throated burble. She paused, remembering that she had no passenger door. If the killer had been riding in the right front seat, he would have had to slip into the back—a contortionist's maneuver if there ever was one—or wait for the pilot to deplane. If the killer was the pilot, he would have to leave the airplane untended while he got out and did his business.

She twisted in her seat and tried to look out the back. The Cessna's small, sloping rear windows provided little visibility. Anyone deplaning would have done so into the darkness, with nothing other than their personal flashlights—if they had them. None had been found. There were no parked cars, with head-lights to guide the arrivals. In all likelihood, she realized, the three victims had been herded like sheep, around the rear of the airplane, out beyond the end of the runway.

The prop ticked to a stop as the engine died, and Bergin set the plane's parking brake.

"My side," he reminded Estelle. "Take your time." He slid out and Estelle followed, impressed with how awkward the whole process was.

Had the pilot not been involved, he might have remained with the Cessna, the engine running, unable to see what was happening behind his airplane. Estelle stood just aft of the wing. How many in the plane, then? Three victims, one pilot. A minimum of four. Maybe five. Perhaps even six.

Estelle turned at the sound of boots crunching on gravel. Sheriff Torrez appeared out of the darkness.

"Well?" he asked.

She moved away from the plane, toward the tail. "Why here, Bobby?" She reached out and rested a hand on the Cessna's horizontal stabilizer. "We need to find out the answer to that."

Chapter Thirteen

"He had to know this area intimately, Bobby," she said. "And he's top-notch. That much is obvious. It was no accident that he chose the airstrip."

"We knew that." Torrez regarded the Cessna skeptically. Bergin had switched off the engine and then remained with the plane, waiting patiently. "And so? What did you find out?"

"Awkward," Estelle replied. "The airplane is awkward. The pilot has a door on the left side of the plane, but the passenger in the right front seat doesn't. You have to climb across."

"Okay. But you can fly from either seat, can't you?"

"Yes. There are dual controls."

"So there you go." Torrez shook his head. Without giving Estelle time to respond, he added, "If someone was standing out in the parking lot of the saloon, they would have heard him come in. They sure as hell would have heard him leave if he took off to the east. I was thinkin' that maybe Herb Torrance might have heard something. I sent Abeyta over to check that out. He was going to swing by the saloon, too."

"We don't know if the pilot was the killer," Estelle said. "That's the trouble. And *heard* isn't the same thing as *noticed.*"

"He coulda been the pilot. Or not. Kinda don't like it either way." The sheriff shifted his weight with a sigh. "If he was flyin' the plane, then we know where he went. We know where the plane ended up."

"If he was a passenger, he might have been dropped off any-where," Estelle amended.

"For true. And I guess there's a possibility the pilot didn't know what was goin' on. Visibility out the back of that plane can't be too good." He nodded at the Cessna.

"It isn't. And it's noisy. There's every possibility that the pilot might not have heard the shots."

"If the killer didn't get back on that airplane out here, we got us a different problem," Torrez said. "Where'd he walk to? Assumin' there was just one of 'em."

"The county road is just a half-mile away," Estelle replied. "But I don't think that's what happened."

"I don't guess so," the sheriff agreed. "Anybody with this situation under control the way he had to have it ain't going to leave himself on foot out in the middle of nowhere. Somebody was waitin' here for him, or he got back on the plane." He turned a full circle, hands on hips. "Ted Weaver was out, by the way. He's not too happy about all this."

"I imagine not," Estelle said. Weaver, a gas company executive, would join Jerry Turner as someone uncomfortable with being an innocent bystander.

"One way it coulda worked," Torrez said, and paused. "If the pilot saw what was goin' on and spooked, he might have bolted. Took off and left the shooters behind."

Off to the north, following the circuitous route of County Road 14, headlights glinted briefly through the scrub. As if reading her thoughts, Torrez added, "Abeyta's on his way up to the Torrance Ranch—that's the closest dwelling—then on over to the saloon to talk with Vic Sanchez. But all this happened two, maybe three days ago. That's what Perrone's givin' us for the time of death. The killer's long gone."

"Maybe he is," Estelle said. "Back to Mexico?"

"Most likely. That's what the Border Patrol thinks. Rutledge sees this as payback of some kind. Drug deal, maybe. Something like that. He ain't impressed."

"I suppose he isn't." Estelle had worked with Barker Rutledge on several occasions, never by choice. In this instance, Rutledge had arrived earlier at the crime scene in company with two other federal agents, and stayed less than an hour. Estelle had not had the opportunity to talk with him, but she was reasonably sure that at some point, Rutledge would have sucked in his considerable belly and announced, "Well, that's three more we don't have to worry about."

"No word yet from Naranjo?" Eddie Mitchell asked. He had been standing quietly in the dark, well away from the airplane, watching and listening.

"Not yet. He'll work on it. I'll call him back in a bit," Estelle said. "I sent the morgue shots to him. He'll do what he can."

"Which ain't much," Torrez said.

"You never know," Mitchell said, not so quick to write off the Mexican efforts.

"These three weren't laborers," Torrez said. "At least they didn't spend much time workin' with their hands."

At the far end of the runway, a pair of headlights materialized and then flicked out, the vehicle driving down the center of the runway guided only by its parking lights.

In a moment, Jackie Taber's older-model white Bronco idled to a stop.

"Collins thinks that he's found where the gasoline came from," Jackie said. "The lock's been cut on the tank behind the school's auto shop."

Estelle's heart skipped a beat. "Recently, he thinks?"

"I asked Collins that. He says it's hard to tell. He's trying to find the shop teacher now."

Torrez patted the door panel and stepped away from Jackie's truck.

"Meet you there," he said. "You flyin' back with Jim?"

She nodded. "I'll be back as quickly as I can." She walked to the plane and Bergin held the door for her. She settled back against the hard seat and closed her eyes.

"Long day, eh?" Bergin said. He slammed the door and snapped his seat belt. "Won't take long goin' home. You learn anything useful?"

"Yes." She reached across and touched his right wrist. "And thanks, Jim. I appreciate it."

"Not a problem." He scanned the checklist briefly and then the Cessna shuddered into life. The taillights of Jackie's Bronco were fading down the runway, and Bergin gunned the Cessna out of the gravel and back onto the asphalt. Spinning it against the left wheel brake, he turned the plane around and taxied the remaining yards to the end of the pavement. They turned around once again just shy of the yellow crime scene tape.

"Short strip like this, it's a good thing to use every advantage," he said, and fed in the power. The takeoff roll was short enough that they were a couple hundred feet in the air by the time they flashed over the county road. To the right, Estelle could look down to the saloon, less than half a mile south.

She knew how quiet the prairie could be. An odd noise stood out, begging to be noticed. Without much effort, she could imagine a couple of patrons sitting at the Broken Spur's bar, sipping the brew. When they heard the plane, one might smile and turn to the other. "'Nother load dropped off," he might say. And that would be that.

Bergin banked left, and they headed directly toward Posadas Municipal Airport. He let the Cessna climb to five hundred feet, and then trimmed it forward to a fast cruise. It seemed like seconds before he keyed the radio.

"Posadas traffic, niner two Hotel is five southwest, inbound for right base, niner zero." He clicked the mike button twice, and ahead of them, the runway lights illuminated as if by magic, two long strips to guide them in. "Makes it easy," Bergin said. "We already proved we can land in the dark."

In a moment, they were down and taxiing quickly toward the hangar. Jerry Turner's BMW was still parked off to one side.

"Nervous parent," Bergin said. "His baby's become a criminal." As he shut down the engine, he looked across at Estelle. "Any questions?"

"Several million," she replied. "Thanks so much."

"You're welcome. Any time." He opened the door and slid out. "'Course, I don't really mean that. Keep me posted, will you?"

"Certainly."

"I was thinkin' of spending a few nights out here, till you get this thing wrapped up."

"Not a bad idea," Estelle said. "But if someone stops by to steal an airplane again, just let them take it. We're not dealing with an amateur here."

He laughed. "I ain't no hero. Anyway, they're going to have to work harder at it. I'll get that sheet metal siding welded in place, and we'll change the lock on the dead bolt. That'll slow 'em down some."

Chapter Fourteen

The state highway back to Posadas was a reminder that all was not normal this quiet night. Estelle passed two State Police units, running five miles apart, both officers cruising well below the speed limit, no doubt looking in every arroyo and behind every abandoned ranch building. They wouldn't find anything, she knew. No doubt, they knew it, too.

Closer to town, she saw an SUV pulled into the shadows by an abandoned gas station. She slowed, and the vehicle's lights winked at her. As she passed, she could see the broad stripe down the vehicle's flank that was part of the Border Patrol's insignia.

"Everybody is looking," she said aloud to herself. "And no one knows who to look for." Most of the coverage was token, she realized. The shootings, now two, three, maybe four days cold, were long in the killer's rearview mirror. But the old saw was true—every additional hour only benefited the killer. For want of anything specific to do or someone specific to chase, officers looked in the shadows for things that shouldn't be there.

As soon as she had heard where the deputy had discovered gasoline thefts, a new theory had crept into her mind, an uncomfortable one that fitted her instincts. The more she thought about it, the more her apprehension built.

Her telephone chirped as she drove past Pershing Park, and she groped it out of her pocket.

"Hey," Bob Torrez's voice announced. "I'm at the school. Where you at?"

Fast and direct as the flight might have been, her brief conversation with Jerry Turner at the airport had consumed several minutes. The cell phone salesman had promised not to let his delinquent aircraft leave its hangar without notifying the Sheriff's Department first.

"Just about into the village. Give me a minute."

"Okay. I got Archer over here. Grider is on the way," the sheriff said, not bothering to elaborate where "over here" was. "Some other stuff, too," he added cryptically.

By then Estelle was turning left on Piñon Street with the high school in view on the other side of the athletic field ahead, its security lights making it look like a row of five various-sized boxes attached end to end. "We're over behind the vo-tech wing," Torrez said. She could make out the gathering of vehicles as she turned onto Olympic and skirted the athletic field. There were just enough outside lights around the school to make an intruder's job easier, pools of bright light alternating with inky darkness.

She eased in behind the sheriff's Expedition, and before she had shut off the engine, Deputy Dennis Collins trotted out of the shadows cast by the nearest building.

"We're over behind the auto mechanics wing," he announced as she got out of the car. "The back gate is open."

"Is that the way they gained entry?"

"We think it is. The lock is cut."

The chain-link fence started at the corner of the redbrick building, extending outward a dozen yards to enclose an eclectic assortment of junk. Until the chop of budget cuts ten years before, the building had housed the wood and metal shops, auto mechanics, and vocational agriculture, and the area behind the building had been the natural overflow area. The vo-ag program had been the first victim of the budget woes, but the boneyard behind the building still housed a fair collection of portable steel stock panels, two partially disassembled tractors, and one dual-axle stock trailer.

Collins led her around the fence to a rolling gate. He paused, pointing with his flashlight. "They cut this chain. Real tricky."

He held the light close. "See that?" Two links of the chain, almost behind the side post and well away from the padlock, were tied together with a short piece of insulated black electrical wire. "They didn't touch the lock. If you don't look close, it looks okay. It's hidden behind the post."

"This is what you noticed first?"

Collins nodded. "My brother did this once," he said. "Back in Akron, though," he added hastily.

"Ah," Estelle said. "Clever. Make sure Linda shoots this." She looked through the fence toward the dark corner of the building where the other officers were gathered. "How do we get in?"

"When I saw this, I called Matt Grider," Collins said. "'Cause I knew exactly what was happening. The guy can slip through here whenever he wants. No one the wiser." He flashed the light toward the building. "The gas storage tank is over there beside that metal shed. I called Matt, and he opened the side door of the building for me so I could get in. Sure enough," he said with considerable satisfaction. "The lock on the tank is cut."

Estelle turned and looked at the street behind them. The gravel lane provided obvious opportunities—out of the way, out of sight.

"Let's see the rest," she said.

The rest was simple enough. The storage tank, a 250-gallon drum on short pipe legs, included a hand pump—the sort of arrangement that was standard on farms and ranches, or any-where that the long arm of OSHA didn't reach. Matt Grider, an angular, morose young man with a shaved head that accentu-ated his speed-brake ears, was talking to Sheriff Torrez as Estelle approached from the back door of the school's shop.

"Kinda interesting," Torrez said. He pointed his flashlight first at the padlock on the pump. "The hasp is cut. Just swing the lock off, and we're in business." He swung the light to the door of the storage shed. "Matt says there's a couple of jerry cans in there. We ain't touched the door yet. Don't take a rocket scientist to figure out what we'll find."

"Linda?" Estelle asked.

"She'll be along. Take a couple of shots, though. We need to get in there," Torrez said, and Estelle nodded. She rapped the side of the gas storage tank with a knuckle.

"Mr. Grider, thanks for coming out," she said. "Do you use this often?"

"No, ma'am," Grider replied. "We used to. When we work on a vehicle, once in a while we need gas."

"When was it filled last?" Torrez asked.

Grider fell silent, mouth pursed in thought. "Sometime last spring, I guess."

"Not exactly fresh, then," the sheriff said. "Not too bright dumpin' it in an airplane."

"You guys want to tell me what all this is about?" Grider asked uneasily.

"Someone's stealin' gas," Torrez said, and let it go at that. "How much did you have in this? Do you remember?"

"Honestly, I don't. Maybe half. Maybe three quarters. Like I said, we don't use it much. I could look up the paperwork." He looked first at the sheriff and then at Estelle, perhaps wondering why the theft of a few gallons of gasoline would attract such attention. "What happened?"

"Good question," Torrez said. He turned to Estelle, ignoring Grider. "Gravel parking lot," he said. "No tracks for shit." He took her by the elbow and together they walked toward the gate. "This don't fit," he said when they were out of earshot of Grider and Collins. "We're barkin' up the wrong tree. This is the work of some kid. Some punk who wants gas for his four-wheeler. At three-fifty a gallon, even old gas is worth takin'."

"I think that's who we're dealing with, Bobby."

The sheriff stopped short, waiting.

Her stomach tightened its knots now that she had voiced the notion. "Look at the pieces. Number one, he climbs the airport fence, or slips through somehow, and does it with full cans of fuel. Even if he pulls a pickup truck up beside the fence where it's only four feet of barbed wire, hops in the back, and then goes over, that takes strength and agility."

The sheriff remained silent, his signal for her to continue.

"That's one. Number two, he goes through the *back* of the building, slipping through a small piece of bent siding. That takes strength and agility, too. And he's no giant. Maybe he only did that once, because after he was inside, he had the keys. Then he takes the plane and, more important, *returns* it—that takes some guts and some planning, too, and that flair for risk that appeals to kids. He flies a route to who knows where, at night—and then returns, again at night, making a risky landing on a small strip with a plane carrying a heavy load." She paused. "It just seems to me that the odds are *so* stacked that most adults would hesitate. This pilot doesn't. Have you ever met a teenager who didn't think he was immortal?"

Torrez grunted. "They all do."

"What's a professional drug runner do?"

"Meaning what?" the sheriff said.

"Meaning this: They take an airplane, or actually *buy* one. Load it full. If there's any sign of trouble, the plane is abandoned. Not a look back. They cut their losses and run to fly another day. But think about it. What's *this* guy doing? He's being cute, Bobby. So clever that he's leaving kid prints all over everything."

"Kids don't shoot whole families."

"That's the joker in this. Forget the murders for a minute and concentrate on Jerry Turner's stolen airplane. It's a kid. I just feel it. It has all the earmarks. *Especially* now. Who would be most likely to steal the gasoline from this particular storage tank? Someone who knows it's there, for one thing. Maybe someone who can figure out that there might be jerry cans in the shed."

"Yup. That's teachers or kids." He turned and gazed across the dark compound to where Collins now talked with Linda Real, with Grider standing by the door, hands thrust in his pockets.

"Cutting the chain and then retying it with a piece of wire? Putting the tank lock back so that it looks okay at a passing glance? It all fits. That's a kid's mentality, being clever so he isn't caught. Collins said his brother did the same stunt years ago."

Torrez traced idle circles on the gravel with his flashlight beam as he mulled over what Estelle had said. "If we got us a kid flying Turner's plane, then the pilot ain't the killer. That's the work of a professional."

"I think so."

"And it ain't going to be hard to figure out who did the flying, either," the sheriff said. "There ain't a teenager alive who has that kind of skill and experience who wouldn't talk about it to his buddies." He nodded toward Grider. "Good place to start."

Chapter Fifteen

Matt Grider's classroom was well on its way to being a poster museum. From the yellowing lithograph of a Ford 9N tractor being driven across an idyllic pasture by a checkered-shirted farmer, to current flyers for synthetic motor oils, nearly every square inch of wall space was covered. Little Carlos would love it all, Estelle thought. The desks were in a hodgepodge, not rows of organized groups. Grider made his way toward the front of the room and then stopped, uncertain.

"I need to talk to Dr. Archer first," he said, and glanced at the wall clock. "I don't think I can call him now," he added. Estelle knew that Glen Archer was used to being called at all hours, even at 2:10 on a Sunday morning.

"We already did," Torrez said. "Relax a little." That was easily said. Matt Grider fidgeted, looking miserable.

"How many students are enrolled in auto mechanics, Mr. Grider?" Estelle asked.

"Is Dr. Archer coming over?" he repeated.

"I'm not asking about any specific student, sir," Estelle said. "And yes, the superintendent is on the way."

"Look," Grider said, and he turned to leaf through a grade book that lay on his desk without turning it toward them. "I need to know what this is about."

"Somebody's takin' gas from your tank," Torrez said.

"But that's not all," Grider said quickly. "I don't think that's why we're having a convention in the middle of the night, is it? And whatever it was, what makes you think that it was one of our students that did—whatever it was?" He looked expectantly from Estelle to Torrez.

"It's a logical place to start," Estelle said. "Students and school staff would be the first ones to know about the fuel storage tank out back."

"Or anyone who graduated from here in the last fifteen years," Grider added. "I don't know what you're after, but it isn't the theft of five or ten gallons of gasoline."

Estelle didn't respond to that, but watched Grider's face as he skimmed down a class list where his thumb had opened the grade book, seemingly at random.

A swath of headlights danced through the window as another vehicle pulled into the parking loop out front. "That's Dr. Archer," Grider said with some relief. He closed the grade book.

"What else do you teach, sir?" Estelle asked. "You must not have more than a dozen students in auto mechanics now, do you?"

"I have nine," he replied. "And I teach three sections of consumer math and one section of welding."

"That would keep you busy."

"Sure. And one class of study skills—that's just like a study hall sort of thing."

"You teach all of them here? In this room?" She turned in place, scanning the small classroom. In the back of the room, a double door led out to the shop area.

"Auto and welding. The others are over in one-twelve, behind the gym."

They heard the outside door rattle open and then close, and in a moment Glen Archer appeared in the classroom doorway. Even in the middle of the night, he managed to look natty, dressed in a light tan jacket over a salmon-colored polo shirt with spotless blue jeans and golf shoes.

"Good evening, all," he said, not a cheery greeting, but not frosty, either.

"Thanks for coming down, sir," Estelle said.

"You're entirely welcome," Archer said. His gaze swept the room quickly. "I think, anyway," he added quickly. He flashed a smile at Estelle. "I was having trouble sleeping, so here we are."

"Sir," Estelle said, and then hesitated. She was loath to explain the details of what happened—once the information was out, it would spread like wildfire through the tendrils of the gossip vine. Still, enough time had already passed that the killer enjoyed a significant head start. Sheriff Bob Torrez remained silent. "Sir, we think that someone is taking gasoline from the storage tank out back."

She saw Archer's right eyebrow rise, as if to say, *You got me up in the middle of the night for this?*

"We think that there's a chance that they're stealing gasoline from here and using it to fuel a stolen aircraft."

Archer's broad, ruddy face went blank. "Say that again. You lost me."

Estelle repeated what she had said word for word.

"That's what I thought you said."

"Yes, sir."

"I know both of you, and know that neither one of you is given to thinking up jokes like this in the middle of the night... or any other time, for that matter. But stealing an airplane?"

"Yes, sir."

"From out here? Jim's airport?"

"Exactly."

"Well...that's a new one. Whose plane was it?"

"Jerry Turner's."

"Oh, my gosh. And how do we know all this?"

"We don't, sir," Estelle said. "Not for sure, anyway. We're making some assumptions about what happened."

"I see." Archer turned sideways and sat in one of the awkward chair–desk combinations. He pulled a small notebook from his pocket, along with a gold ballpoint pen. "Stealing an airplane. Huh." His pen hovered but he didn't mark the paper. "Well, Estelle," he said, and nodded at Torrez. "And Robert. Again, I know you both well enough to know this isn't some wild goose chase. If you're here, it's serious, whatever it is. So that's that. What do you need from us?"

"We have reason to believe that the person who used the airplane is possibly a student," Estelle said, then amended that. "I think so."

Archer regarded her skeptically. "Really."

"Yes, sir."

"And the gasoline? What's up with that?"

"Whoever used the airplane wanted to do it without being noticed, sir. It was flown at night, probably south into Mexico. After returning, the aircraft was refueled and replaced in its hangar, no doubt in hopes that the owner would never notice."

"But evidently he did."

"In part, yes. When we posed the possibility of someone gaining entrance to his hangar, he made an examination. He saw some irregularities."

"So they didn't just steal the airplane, then," Archer said. "Someone used it without permission. Sort of borrowed it, as it were."

"Yes."

"They're running drugs, you think? Isn't that what everybody does with an airplane these days?"

"No. We don't think that's what happened."

"What, then?"

"We think that the airplane was used to bring at least three people into the country."

"Wow." Archer whistled. "We have enough troubles with the folks who try to *walk* across the desert. This group is going first class. What did they do, drop 'em off here in Posadas, or what? Fly 'em to the city someplace?"

"That would have been better, sir. We found the bodies out at the gas company's airstrip down by Regál Pass."

"You're kidding." For a long moment, Archer stared at Estelle, speechless. "Three, you say? Murdered, or died of exposure?"

"Shot."

He looked down at his pad, even though he hadn't written a word. "You're saying that someone *stole* an airplane from right here...What, Jerry left the keys in it, or what?"

"That's right, sir."

"Not the smartest thing he ever did. So they stole the airplane, flew it down into Mexico somewhere, picked up three people, brought them back to a remote airstrip, and killed them there?"

"That's essentially it."

"Whatever for? Drug deal gone sour?"

"We don't know, Dr. Archer."

"Wowser." He looked at Grider, who shrugged helplessly. "You know any of these people? The ones who were killed?"

"No."

"Now, for some reason, you think that one of our kiddos is in on this? Am I hearing that right? I can't believe that."

"Involved somehow, yes. If not as the pilot, then at least as an accomplice."

"Why a child, for heaven's sakes?"

"Not a *child*, sir. I would guess a teenager. Someone old enough to drive a car. Someone with some experience."

"My lord. This world is going nuts. What do we do, then? What do you need from us? You've got prints and things like that?"

"We're still processing what we have," Estelle said, avoiding adding, *What* little *we have*. She hesitated again, looking at Grider. "One thing that kids have trouble with is keeping their mouths shut," she said.

Archer laughed ruefully. "Adults, too."

"Here's what I'm thinking, sir. I can't imagine some teenager who has these kinds of aviation skills being so close-mouthed about it...never letting something slip. Never saying anything."

"But say again...You're *sure* that a youngster is involved? I just can't believe this. You really are?"

"No. But at this point, that's what I *think*."

"Ah...woman's intuition," Grider said, managing to make it sound vaguely condescending. "How do you know it's some kid from Posadas?"

"We don't, for sure. But it doesn't make sense to me that someone from Deming would drive over here to steal your gasoline—and then drive to the airport and know the place well enough to steal the right airplane, and then return it? I don't think so."

"What do you want from us?" Archer asked again.

"I'd like you to look through that," Estelle said, indicating the grade book. "I want you to think about your students. Do any of them fly, or come from families who do? Do any of them *talk* about flying a lot? Do any of them spend time out back with the smokers?"

"Nobody smokes out there," Grider said quickly.

"Well, then they're emptying their ashtrays out by the fence," Estelle said, and sensing Grider's animosity, changed tacks. "Or is there anyone who you know who is intimately familiar with Mexico? That's another angle. Someone who knows the country really well."

"Huh," Archer said. He beckoned at Grider, and the teacher handed him the grade book. "I've been in this district for a long, long time," he said.

"I know you have, sir." In fact, no one was as completely familiar with the demographics of his student body as Glen Archer—a teacher of mathematics and history for years, then high school principal for a decade, he had finally taken the new position when the superintendent's and principal's job were combined. Estelle watched the older man thumb through the grade book, and reflected that, between former sheriff Bill Gastner and Glen Archer, there were not many unknown faces in Posadas County.

He scanned each class in turn, running a finger down the names. Finally he flipped the book closed almost too quickly and handed it to Grider. "No bells ring for me," he said. "How about you?" Grider shook his head.

The superintendent pushed himself up and out of the awkward desk. "Let's take a walk," he said to the officers. "Matt, thanks for coming down. Are we finished here?"

"I think so, sir. If you'll lock things up, we'll probably come back when it's light for more photos."

"Buy a better lock this time," Archer said with a grin, but Grider didn't share the humor.

"They cut the chain, not the lock."

"Ah. We probably need to rethink having that tank," Archer said, and beckoned at Estelle and Torrez. "If you have a few minutes?"

Out in the hall, Deputy Collins was talking with Linda Real, who had just arrived.

"Tomorrow," Estelle said to them, "let's rethink this with some light on the subject. I took a couple shots of the cut chain. Make sure things are secure, and then let's wrap it up."

Archer led Estelle and Torrez out of the annex, through a short breezeway, and into the main building of the high school. He fumbled with the keyed light switch for a moment, and then nodded down the hall. "This way." As he walked, he reached out and touched Estelle on the elbow. "I saw when you left the recital last night," he said. "Great timing, eh?"

"It never fails," she replied.

"That's quite a boy you have there."

"Thank you, sir. He's a challenge."

Archer laughed, the sound echoing in the empty building. "Aren't they all." They rounded a corner, and fifty feet of hallway extended in front of them, ending in the main foyer behind the double-glass entry doors. He stopped, surveying a display of artwork that hung on the north wall. "Some really fine things," he said. "Starts with primary students, and goes right through the high school seniors down at the other end." He strolled slowly, examining the work as if for the first time. "We have two shows a year, as I'm sure you're aware."

He had nearly reached the end of the display, a collection of sophisticated artwork that leaned heavily on fantasy, video game violence, or Middle Earth. Beside one piece, the principal stopped and turned to look expectantly at Estelle and the sheriff. "Impressive, isn't it?"

The watercolor was large, perhaps eighteen inches wide and thirty inches tall. In the lower left of center was a rambling adobe home, neat and tidy but entirely ordinary with chile *ristras* hanging from the *vigas* on either side of the doorway. Two figures were in the front yard, waving wildly. Pulling up steeply to avoid the family and the home was a bright yellow biplane, a crop duster, the mist from its sprayers still wisping off the nozzles.

"Caramba," Estelle said. "This is amazing."

"Yes, it is," Archer said. "You know, when I first saw it, my reaction was a bit negative. For one thing, I've seen the picture before, only in different form. There's a picture that I've seen several times in some of those aviation junk-mail catalogs—the crop duster pulling up sharply to miss the barn? This is the same perspective. He's changed the barn into a house, changed the Stearman, I think it is in the original, into a Grumman Ag Cat. But technically, he's really got the touch, doesn't he?"

"Hector Ocate," Estelle read from the label, and her stomach felt as if it were full of lead.

Chapter Sixteen

"I didn't say this back in the classroom, but I need to now, before we go any further with this." Glen Archer spoke with his eyes locked on the painting. "I guess nothing surprises me anymore in this crazy world, but what you're telling me…I don't know what to think." He fell silent for a moment, still lost in the painting.

"I want to be sure that Mr. Grider has nothing to do with any of this," Archer said. "I sensed some hostility in his attitude toward you folks, and that's unacceptable. We're here to cooperate."

"He's just protective," Estelle said. She glanced at Bob Torrez, who had played the role of silent stone-face to perfection. That in itself had been enough to make Grider nervous.

"Well, maybe," the superintendent said. "I'd like to think that."

"We appreciate your concern, sir. But a lot of folks don't care to have us snooping into their lives," Estelle said. "That doesn't mean they have anything to hide."

"I would hope not," the superintendent said. "But I want to be sure. Mr. Grider does a good job with a difficult program, but we don't always see eye to eye on things—especially money matters. We just don't have any extra funding, and Mr. Grider takes any cut or refusal personally, I think. You may remember some of his letters to the editor in the *Register*." He made a face of impatience. "But that's his right, and that's not why you're here, is it? This youngster," and he touched the matting of the picture, "is an incredible talent. He's an exchange student, as you may already know. Just a wonderful boy. He's in Mr. Grider's welding class—I know that for sure. I would hope that he isn't into something. I can't even imagine something like you describe. Do you really think that a *youngster* took that airplane? And murder? That just doesn't…You really think he did?"

"I think so," Estelle said. "I'm not one hundred percent sure. But I think so. We need to remember that a teenager isn't just a kid anymore."

"Oh, I know, I know," Archer said. "They'll do anything an adult will."

"Or more," Torrez interjected.

"Or more," she agreed. "I know this young man a little bit. I spoke with the senior American history class last month. He was in it." She could picture Hector Ocate, sitting about halfway back in the room, quietly listening to both her presentation and the questions and answers that followed. After the presentation, she had talked with a handful of students for another fifteen minutes, and Hector had finally worked up his confidence to ask her several questions about her own experiences as a child growing up in northern Mexico.

If first impressions counted for anything, Hector would be far, far down her list of suspects in the theft of an airplane—and certainly the murders that followed. Of average height, a bit chubby, he had seemed innocent, bright, and eager, and obviously had been adopted already by a considerable circle of friends.

"He's living with Pam and Gordon Urioste and the two kids," Archer said. "Martin and Lorietta. But still—a boy is interested in airplanes. How is that enough of a connection to put him in…" He groped for words. "To put him in the epicenter of something like this?"

Estelle nodded. "It doesn't, necessarily."

"Someone gets themselves run over by a drunk driver, you look for drunks," Torrez said.

Archer waited, expecting more explanation, but the sheriff apparently didn't feel his analogy needed clarification.

If one were to judge by Hector's host family, the boy's involvement seemed all the more unlikely. Gordon Urioste worked as a maintenance man and custodian for the Baptist church, and his wife, Pam, had been with Posadas Insurance Agency for as long as Estelle could remember.

The undersheriff moved closer to the painting and examined the details. "Remarkable," she said. "No matter how he did it, it's remarkable."

"In this particular case, I know that it's entirely original—I mean, other than the obvious borrowing of the basic idea. On several occasions, I've strolled through his art class. He's been working on this and a couple others right in class—he doesn't paint at home. He told me he has too many other things to do."

"I bet," Torrez said laconically. "Where's the kid from?"

"Near Acapulco, I think. Or at least that general area. He told me once, but the name of the actual town? It's about twenty syllables long, and I couldn't even come close—assuming I could remember it in the first place."

"Cuajinicuilapa? I think that's what he told me."

"I just don't know, Estelle."

"We'll talk with him. But being able to paint a realistic airplane doesn't mean he knows how to fly them," Estelle said.

"Nope," Torrez said. "But he's a kid, and kids talk. Could be he has an idea who went on our little jaunt. And he's from Mexico."

"Acapulco is more than a thousand miles south, as the Cessna flies," Estelle said. "We're dealing with eleven hours unaccounted for. Those hours would get you one way to Acapulco, maybe a little more."

"You think Turner keeps accurate track?" Torrez asked. "He don't seem the type to care much one way or another."

"True enough. But Jim Bergin keeps meticulous records, and he's the one who services Turner's airplane."

"Well, *Jerry* certainly wouldn't do a thing like that," Archer said. "Heavens, at least I hope not. I have lunch with him every Tuesday in Rotary."

Estelle thought about the refueling process, of someone lifting the awkward cans up onto the wings of the Cessna. "No... Mr. Turner wouldn't. Has Hector been in school every day the past couple of weeks?"

"Good heavens, I couldn't tell you that. We'd have to check in the office."

"Can we do that now?"

Archer glanced at his watch and smiled bleakly. "What the heck," he said. "This is going to be one of those nights anyway."

"Already is," Torrez said. "We might as well check this through, but it's way too easy."

"Too easy?" Estelle asked.

The sheriff jerked his chin toward the painting. "You think a kid flew the plane? Well, maybe. Now we got a kid with art talent who likes airplanes. About half of them do. Now we hear that he's from Mexico. Ain't that convenient. Just way too easy, is all I'm sayin'."

"Well, I surely hope so," Archer said fervently. He fumbled a large set of keys from his pocket. "Let's see what the computer tells us about Master Hector's attendance. Do you have any idea of the time frame we're looking at?"

"No," Estelle said. "Just the past few days. Probably not yesterday, maybe not the day before."

"Good heavens," Archer muttered, and shrugged with resignation. "Let's check."

They followed Archer down the hall to the office complex, and he waved them to chairs by the secretary's desk. "Sit, sit. This is going to take a minute while we boot up."

"Sorry to put you through this," Estelle said.

"No problem," Archer said. "You're doing what you do, Estelle. I have to admit that the timing of all this brings back memories of your previous boss. As I recall, Bill Gastner used to work right through the night about half the time." He glanced at Estelle. "Have you run any of this past him, by the way? He knows everybody there is to know—and their parents, and grandparents, back to the dawn of time." He glanced up and grinned. "Not quite, maybe, but you know what I mean."

"Yes, sir. But we haven't had the chance. We've been on a dead run since we were called out of the recital."

"Ah," Archer said. "And that was a delightful performance, I must say. Most impressive. Most impressive. And here we are. Almost." He hunched over the keyboard, staring into the bright screen as he scrolled down through the data. The cursor stopped and the superintendent highlighted a line. "The only time Hector was absent this week was for three morning classes on Wednesday. The code says that the absence was excused."

"What for, do you know?"

"The code is for family medical. That's all it tells me. Claudia could fill us in, I'm sure." Archer didn't offer to ring the principal's office secretary in the predawn hours of a treasured weekend.

"Thanks, sir. This has been a help."

"You're going to talk with Hector about this? I'm sure that he had nothing to do with stealing an airplane. Let alone—"

Estelle nodded. "We'll just have to see, sir."

"I guess we really never know, do we? I should just say I *hope* he had nothing to do with it. If there's anything else I can do, you just let me know, all right?"

Estelle and Bob Torrez left the school through the front door, walking back along the sidewalk toward the vocational wing. "I'll check back with Collins and Grider and wind up this end," the sheriff said. He nodded toward the compact car that was parked behind Estelle's. "Anything specific you want from Linda that you don't already have?"

"Just her perspective," Estelle said. No one needed to explain to Linda Real how to photograph a crime scene—her talent seemed innate.

"Are you going to roust the kid?" Torrez asked.

"I'll give the family an hour or two."

"Why?"

Estelle hesitated. "Because, that's all. We don't have a single thing that actually links Hector Ocate with this. Just an interest in airplanes…just a painting. And some evidence that gasoline was taken from behind his school. That doesn't mean that *he* took it. That's just circumstance. A couple of hours gives Tom Mears a chance to process the two gas cans in the shed for prints. He was going to go over the plane once more, and see if there wasn't something there—a print on the throttle, or on the flap handle…something."

"Naranjo? You still holdin' your breath on him?"

"If we're lucky, he might have something for us. Odds are long."

"Yeah, well," Torrez said. He took a deep breath. "It's gonna be tight. We got to be able to spring a few people free for the race, too. Unless we just want to cancel it."

"We can't do that, Bobby." She groaned. "*Ay. El tiempo pasa inexorablemente,* as my mother is fond of saying. I hadn't even given the race a thought." She looked at her watch again. "The first rider is off at nine o'clock this morning. That's in six hours."

"You better tell Pasquale there ain't no point in trying to squeeze into his spandex. We're gonna need him."

"We'll find a way to cover, Bobby. I don't want to pull him out of the race at this late hour. He's trained for months, he helped organize it, and he deserves the time."

"He also ain't had no sleep," Torrez said. "We'll probably find him lyin' under some piñon up on the mesa, blowin' z's."

"Well, he might need that, too. I'm going back to the office for a few minutes to make sure that our coverage schedule for the race still works. I need to stop by the house when the kids are getting up. Then I'll swing over and talk with Hector."

"Good enough. We'll finish up here."

By the time Estelle reached the Public Safety Building, the dawn of Sunday was only an hour off. She could see streaks near the eastern horizon, wide bands of thin clouds. By race time at nine o'clock, the clouds would burn off and race competitors would face the rigors of Cat Mesa in sunshine so hot that the stunted piñons and junipers would perfume the thin air, rich and sweet.

As her hand touched the door handle, Estelle's phone chirped as if her touch had triggered the mechanism.

"Hey," Sheriff Torrez said. "Abeyta just called me. He's got a time."

"A time for…" Estelle opened the door and stepped inside. Looking down the narrow hall past the offices, she could see that dispatcher Brent Sutherland was also on the telephone. Deputy Tony Abeyta wasn't scheduled to be working at this hour, but he'd been caught up like everyone else.

"One of the kitchen help saw the airplane."

"Really." It took a few seconds for her to catch up with Torrez's habitual shorthand.

"Yep. Corrie Velasquez? She stepped out back to toss some leftovers to the coyotes. Or some shit like that. Anyway, she claims that she saw the plane. It attracted her attention because it was just sort of whistling in, no lights, engine idling."

"Huh." Estelle pictured Corrie standing by the back door of the Broken Spur. She would be facing north, toward the arroyo behind the saloon. The aircraft would have passed within a quarter mile of where Corrie stood if it was landing from east to west, low on final approach to the gas company's runway. "Does she remember when?"

"She thinks Tuesday night. She knows it was after midnight, but the saloon closes at one, so it wasn't much later than that. Two at the most."

"That would make it Wednesday morning, then." The growing pall of fatigue lifted a bit, and Estelle walked into her office, closing the door behind her. *And Hector was absent from school Wednesday morning,* she thought. "How does Corrie remember that it was Tuesday, and not some other night?"

"I don't know. Maybe Abeyta asked her that, but he didn't tell me. He's inbound, if you want to talk to him. He was lookin' for a couple hours' sleep before he pulls race duty."

"Some sleep sounds good."

"You still going to talk with the kid?"

"Yes," she said. "He's not going anywhere."

"We best hope not," Torrez grunted. "If he gets wind that we're snoopin' around, the border ain't very far away."

Chapter Seventeen

An hour's wolf nap wasn't enough, especially with the rest of the household enjoying the quiet of early Sunday morning slumbering. It would have been too easy to roll over, snuggle up against her husband, and doze off again. She sat on the edge of the bed for a moment, trying to focus. She had folded into bed at three fifteen. In a blink, the clock had leaped to 4:30 a.m.

"What's the deal this morning?" Francis asked, his voice muffled by the pillow.

Estelle rubbed her face and double-checked the time. "I need to talk with a kid who might have taken the plane," she said. "There's a chance. Slim, but a chance. I need to follow up on it."

"You be careful. You're tired."

"I know. I'll try to be back in time for the race. If it looks like I can't make it, I'll call." She turned and patted his hip. "Can you take the boys up on the mesa if I'm not back?"

"Chances are," he replied. A finger appeared from under the pillow and wagged at her. "Don't you be sending more work our way."

"I'll try my best, *querido*." After a long shower, she dressed quickly and forced down a small microwaved breakfast burrito and a cup of tea. By five thirty, she was parking in front of a nondescript double-wide mobile home on the southwestern outskirts of Posadas. She paused by her car, noticing two things. First, she could see the end of the vocational wing of the high school, no more than a quarter of a mile distant, across a scrubby field and a single arroyo. Second, her arrival had not gone unnoticed.

Two pit bulls watched her with interest. They were tethered with their light chains running up to a wire clothesline, allowing them to course back and forth in front of the home, in an area lighted by an irritatingly bright streetlight. Both dogs could reach the path to the front door with ease.

By the time she had gotten out of the car and walked around the front fender, both dogs were wagging so hard it appeared their backbones were in jeopardy, their voices sounding like two frantic children. If they thought that a stranger approaching their house in the wee hours of the morning was unusual or cause for alarm, they didn't show it.

"My long lost pals," Estelle said aloud. As she approached, one of the dogs, a butterscotch female splotched liberally with white, stood on her hind legs, balancing against the pull of the leash. The other, a brindle female, took the low road and flopped on her back, presenting a white belly that had nursed its share of puppies.

"They're harmless," a man's voice said, and Estelle glanced up to see Gordon Urioste standing at the front door of the double-wide. "As long as you don't mind the slobber."

"Good morning, sir," Estelle said.

"Get down, Squeak," Urioste said sharply, and the dancing female dropped to all fours instantly, stubby tail still flailing. "How are you this morning, Ms. Guzman?" he added. "You're out bright and early."

"I'm okay," she said, pushing past the two wet, snuffling muzzles that blotched her previously spotless tan pantsuit. The two dogs couldn't reach the front step, and both of them sat down at the full stretch of their chains, butts wiggling. Urioste stepped the rest of the way past the storm door and closed it behind him. A short, burly man, his heavy-featured face was one of wary good humor.

"What can I do for you? You want a cup of coffee? The wife's got it going."

"No thanks, sir." She turned, surveying the neighborhood, a hodgepodge of older trailers and double-wides situated on irregular two-acre lots. The neighborhood had started its sprawl during the last heydays of the copper mine on Cat Mesa, and now struggled with vacant lots left when the trailers pulled out, leaving behind the stubs of plumbing pipes and chopped-off electrical wiring. Fences were choked with tumbleweeds, and the dirt streets were dismal. The two dwellings on either side of Urioste's were vacant—on one side, a single trailer whose carport was sagging over a vast pile of trash, and on the other, a ten-year-old double-wide bordered by a rickety cedar fence, the place recently abandoned when the elderly owner had died.

"Going to be a beautiful day, I think," Urioste offered, a polite way of asking, *What do you want at five thirty in the morning?*

"I'd like to talk with Hector, if he's around," Estelle asked.

"Hector?"

"Yes." Estelle smiled cordially. "He and I chatted some when I did a career day presentation at the high school."

"Oh." Gordon Urioste nodded. "Oh, really? That's right, I guess I remember. He talked about that." An even shorter, wider form appeared in the doorway behind him.

"Good morning, Pam," Estelle said. A loose housecoat, her short hair unruly, Pam Urioste's early-weekend-morning uniform was a far cry from her polished, carefully groomed image that greeted clients at the insurance office.

"Hi," the woman replied. "I've got coffee on..." And her voice trailed off expectantly.

Each of the three knew that police officers didn't routinely show up on the doorstep at five thirty on a Sunday morning for idle chitchat about high school career days. Estelle knew the Uriostes well enough to greet them by name—that was all. Gordon glanced across toward the vacant double-wide, and Estelle saw something in his expression that might have been resignation or irritation.

"Look," he said, "is this about the truck?"

The truck. She was tempted to ask, *What truck?* But Urioste had opened a door, perhaps unwittingly, and she didn't want it slammed shut. Instead she said, "Mr. Urioste, I really do need to speak with Hector. I know it's early, but I have a lot on my plate today, with the bike race and all the rest. If he's here, then it will only take a minute."

"Well, sure he's here," Pam said, and she began to sound more like the efficient administrative assistant that she was. She started to turn away, but her husband held up a hand.

"Now wait a minute," he said, trying to sound reasonable. "We need to know what this is all about. I mean, after all, we're Hector's guardians while he's in this country."

"I realize that, sir." Estelle watched his face, and after a minute, he acquiesced.

"Okay. You want to shag him out here, honey?" Gordon smiled a little. "That might be a trick. He's been dog-tired these past couple of weeks. Final exams, you know. He takes 'em serious."

"I'm sure he does."

They waited silently, and Urioste studiously avoided looking at Estelle. More than once, he glanced next door, and it wasn't difficult for Estelle to guess what the attraction was.

In a moment, Pam Urioste reappeared, and she looked first at her husband. "He's not here," she said.

"What do you mean, he's not here?" Urioste said, but it didn't sound convincing.

"What else could I mean?" Pam snapped. "He's not in the house." And sure enough, Gordon Urioste's eyes flicked to the right, toward the abandoned double-wide trailer next door.

"So," Estelle said, "tell me about the truck, sir."

"What's this?" Pam asked. "What truck?"

"Look, I *told* him that he shouldn't use it again…well, not too much, anyway. You know," Urioste said, "after the old man passed away over there—" and he waved a hand toward his neighbor's "—things have just sat there, you know. That old Chevy—I guess the bank will end up taking it. I was going to see about maybe putting a bid on it."

Estelle turned and surveyed the double-wide. "There's usually a truck parked there?" She racked her memory, trying to form a picture.

"The old man—you knew him?" Urioste asked.

"Reynaldo Estrada," Estelle said. "I'm sure just about everybody knew Reynaldo." One of the community's perennial bachelors, Estrada had been a talented stonemason when not wrapped around a bottle, and before advanced years turned his knuckles to arthritic crystal.

The old man had died long before young Hector had arrived on the scene, but an abandoned Chevrolet pickup posed an attractive nuisance. A teenager with a finely honed sense of trespass might find it tempting to investigate. "Hector has the keys to his truck?"

"Well, they were in it," Urioste said. "The old man, he used to tuck the keys under the floor mat so he wouldn't lose 'em. He told me that himself once, just in case I needed to borrow it for wood or something like that."

Estelle took a deep breath. "When was Hector here last?" Urioste started to waffle, and Estelle cut him off. "Look, sir, this is important. When—exactly—did you see Hector last?"

"I went to bed at about eleven," Pam offered. "Hector was reading in his room then."

Her husband nodded. "Yeah, I guess that's about right."

"Did you hear him go out, sir?"

He started to shake his head, then thought better of it. "He got up early."

"What time?"

"Five, maybe."

"Did he take the truck?"

Gordon hesitated.

"Sir?"

"I heard it start up," he said finally. He nodded toward the dwelling next door. "And it's not there now, so—"

"Do you know where he planned to go?"

"He and his girlfriend were going to hike in a ways on the mesa to find a good spot to watch the race. That's what he told me yesterday."

"Who's the girlfriend?"

"I'm not sure who he's seeing now. Last week, it was Penny Mendoza." He laughed weakly. "I'm not sure about who it might be this week. He's something of a lady killer, you know."

Not just ladies, Estelle thought. "But you think that's where he planned to go today?" she asked. "Up on the mesa?"

"I think so. Yes." He seemed relieved that the story had finally come out.

"We can hope that's where he's going," Estelle said. "If he comes back before I have a chance to talk with him, make sure you let me know, all right?" She handed them one of her cards. "It's very, *very* important."

"We should keep him here, then? When he comes back?"

Estelle had already turned to tackle slobber alley again. She paused, fending off the first flailing tongue. "Yes," she said. "That would be a *very* good idea. I'll be in touch." When she backed the county car out of the driveway, Pam and Gordon Urioste were still standing in the doorway of their double-wide, wondering what had just happened to their lives.

Accelerating hard out the dirt road, Estelle palmed the phone and touched the auto-dial for dispatch.

"Brent," she said quickly, cutting off Sutherland's slow-paced greeting, "what's Taber's twenty?"

"Just a sec, ma'am." Estelle's county car reached the pavement of Bustos Avenue, and with a howl headed eastbound on the quiet street. Flashing past the center of Posadas, she then turned north on County 43.

"Estelle, Jackie's west, out toward Regál Pass."

"Good. Look, find out what license plate old Reynaldo Estrada had on his Chevy pickup. Alert Jackie and ask her to keep a watch for that truck, possibly driven by a Mexican national teenager." Estelle glanced at the dash clock. The border crossing at Regál would open in just a few minutes. "Have her check with Customs."

"I'm on it."

"I'm headed to the airport."

"Ten-four."

She pushed the car even harder after turning westward on the state highway that headed out toward Posadas Municipal Airport. If Hector Ocate was bumping the old pickup up Cat Mesa with his girlfriend riding beside him, looking for the perfect vantage point to watch the race, Estelle would breathe a deep sigh of relief.

But she also knew that, if Hector had been the pilot of Jerry Turner's airplane, he could have had opportunity to hear about the investigation—about the officers snooping around the airport, or about the discovery of the three bodies. Anyone driving past Posadas Municipal Airport on the state highway would have seen activity. Anyone driving south on State 56 toward Regál would have seen the gathering of lights at the gas company's airstrip. Anyone at the saloon would have heard Jim Bergin's landing and takeoff.

Estelle hadn't been listening, but it was likely that at least one of the area radio stations had carried some item, however sketchy, about the tragic events.

Had he glanced out the window of his bedroom, likely in the back of the house where bedrooms always were, he might even have seen the gathering of vehicles at Matt Grider's room. It wouldn't be rocket science to put all the numbers together. Knowing that something might be amiss, Hector Ocate would know that safety lay just minutes south of the border.

Chapter Eighteen

She hadn't stayed at the airport after the flight to make sure that Jim Bergin and Jerry Turner had locked everything up. She could only hope. Jim had said that he planned to stay at the airport, but he might not have meant that very night. And Turner? Hopefully, he had taken the Cessna's keys with him this time—but for an enterprising repeat burglar, that didn't pose much of a problem. Several places in town could duplicate keys for a buck. How handy it would be to have a spare ignition *and* a spare door key.

Although there was inadequate personnel to have a deputy sitting at the airport full-time, the airport was under close patrol. Several times each shift, deputies cruised by, checking locks, checking for illegal access. That didn't prevent much. With the prairie whisper-quiet, a patrol vehicle could be heard a mile away—certainly easily enough when its tires crunched the gravel of the airport's driveway. Anyone could step into the shadows and wait until the cop was gone.

And Estelle grimaced to herself as she realized that they had all made a fundamental mistake, thinking from the beginning that the killer was long gone after the three homicides.

She found herself wondering how long it would take to push the big doors open, jump into the Cessna, crank it up, and flee. Less than a minute without checklists and careful run-ups?

The county car rocketed down a state highway thankfully devoid of traffic at that early hour. Three miles east of the airport, she overtook a diesel pickup, and caught a glimpse of a startled Jim Bergin as she blew past at nearly twice his speed.

"Three-ten, PSO."

She picked up the radio mike. "Go ahead."

"Three-ten, be advised the license number you requested is one-eight-three, Tom Kilo Lincoln. It should appear on a blue 1978 Chevrolet half-ton. Registration expired eleven of oh-six."

She acknowledged.

"Three-oh-four copies," Jackie Taber's quiet voice said. "Negative contact at the border crossing."

A quarter mile east of the airport, a large RV with a pudgy SUV in tow was parked at the scenic area pull-out, a spot that afforded a view of the sweeping prairie and the San Cristóbal Mountains beyond. So massive was the vehicle that Estelle almost didn't see the second vehicle parked so that the RV was between it and the highway.

She stood on the brakes, swung wide, and executed a U-turn with tires squealing, then pulled into the west access for the parking area. The RV carried Wisconsin plates, as did the vehicle in tow. Estelle regarded the pickup as she reached for the mike.

"PCS, three-ten."

"Go ahead, three-ten."

"I'll be out of the car with one-eight-three Tom Kilo Lincoln at mile marker one-oh-six on State Seventy-eight. I don't see an occupant."

"Three-oh-four will expedite up that way," Taber said.

"Negative. Cover the border crossing until I see what's what, Jackie."

"Three-oh-eight's ETA is about ten," another voice said, almost inaudibly soft. Bob Torrez hadn't been able to sleep, either.

Estelle stepped out of the county car and circled the truck. It was empty, with no keys dangling from the ignition.

"You with the cops?"

She turned at the voice, and saw an enormously fat man standing beside the door of the RV, the huge inner tube of belly hanging out beneath his white T-shirt. He supported himself on two aluminum crutches.

"Sheriff's Department," Estelle replied. "Was this vehicle here when you stopped?"

"Sure was."

"How long ago?"

"Oh." He grinned, looking at his watch. "I guess we've been here about thirty seconds, the wife and me. Gonna have us some breakfast."

"Did you see anyone around this pickup?"

"No, ma'am. Who are we looking for?"

"We're just checking," Estelle said.

"Fair enough. And by the way, I think we're lost. Is this the highway down to the border crossing?"

"No, sir." She pointed east as she strode back toward her own vehicle. "Go east to the caution light, turn right. Head south through Posadas and catch State Fifty-six. That'll take you to Regál and the crossing. You folks have a good day."

Before the man had a chance to reply, she was back in the car and accelerating out of the rest area, beating Jim Bergin's truck by a hundred yards. As soon as she turned into the airport access road, she could see that the hangar door had been run out, the door rail framework extending well beyond the corner of the building.

The car slithered to a stop in the loose gravel, and Estelle dashed to the gate, stabbed in the key to the county lock, and snapped it open. The long, heavy chain-link gate rolled easily. As she slammed the gate open, Bergin's truck pulled in behind her county car. She held up a hand to stop, and then ducked back in her car. As she drove in around the office building, she heard the powerful engine.

Accelerating around the gas pumps island as hard as the police cruiser would go, she looked down the row of hangars and saw the Cessna outside, its back already turning to her. It trundled along smartly, headed for the west end of the runway.

The plane did not have rearview mirrors, and if the pilot concentrated on watching over the cowling, he might never see her. She kept the accelerator flat to the floor, and by the time she reached the end of the last hangar, closing in behind the taxiing airplane, the Crown Victoria was rocketing along at close to a hundred.

Just a few feet behind the plane's stabilizer, she braked hard and swerved left, shooting obliquely across the smooth median between taxiway and runway. Not touching the brakes until she had careened back onto the asphalt of the runway, she managed to slow enough to take the turnaround donut at the end of the runway, racing toward the Cessna head-on.

She saw the astonishment on Hector Ocate's face. He had three choices: charge his airplane head-on into Estelle's patrol car, try to swerve past her to the runway, or spike the brakes and turn around. The heavy airplane was no ballerina on the ground, and Estelle saw that she could run the nose of her patrol car into the prop if necessary.

He chose the third course, and Estelle saw the Cessna 206 dip its nose as he braked. He telegraphed his intentions with a swing first to the right, taking all the asphalt possible, then started to swing left. Estelle punched the gas and cut him off.

For a moment, the big snout of the Cessna, its three-bladed prop a menacing blue, approached within a yard of the Crown Victoria's driver's door. Hector braked so hard that Estelle saw the front gear collapse the oleo strut to its stops. Without a handy reverse, Hector was trapped. If he rammed the car—if he so much as kissed it—the propeller would be destroyed.

He stood on the left brake and the engine roared in one last desperate effort to lurch around and clear the car, but Estelle pulled the sedan forward and to the left, cutting the plane's maneuvering distance to a hairsbreadth. She released her seat belt at the same time, ready to dive to safety when the prop started chopping the Ford.

She rammed the gear selector into park and clawed across the clutter between the seats, digging her knee painfully into the corner of the computer. Diving out the passenger-side door headfirst, she pushed away from the car and came to her feet with the stubby .45 automatic in hand.

Hector Ocate was caught, and knew it. He slumped back in the seat as Estelle rounded the front of the patrol car and ducked under the left wing, advancing as far as the strut. Without being told, the boy reached forward to the dash, and in a few seconds, the engine ran rough and then died.

Jim Bergin's truck slowed to a stop twenty yards away on the taxiway, but he stayed inside.

"Step out of the airplane," she commanded. The door popped, and she moved to her left, putting the strut and door between her and the boy. "Put both hands where I can see them." He did so, hesitantly, one foot showing below the door. Estelle held the gun in both hands, watching the boy over the sights. "Step out of the airplane with your hands on top of your head, Hector."

The second foot appeared, and the youth slid down from the cockpit. He closed the door gently with both hands, and then turned to face Estelle. He laced his fingers on top of his head, and stepped to one side to avoid the wing strut.

"Stop there," she ordered. Hector was dressed in blue jeans and a colorful short-sleeved shirt, and he looked smaller than she remembered. His knees quaked and he almost staggered before regaining his balance. "Face down on the ground," Estelle ordered, and when he hesitated, she commanded in Spanish, *"¡Al suelo, boca abajo!"* Instantly, he sank to his knees, one hand reaching out toward the Cessna's wing strut for balance. *"¡Al suelo!"* she repeated, and he sagged forward on his stomach on the cold concrete. *"¡Extiende los brazos!"* When he was down and spread-eagled, and she could see both hands and both feet, Estelle moved toward him, shifting the gun to one hand.

"I speak English," Hector shouted, his voice now shaking.

"I know you do," Estelle replied. *"No te muevas."* Not only would he speak English, but he would be familiar with police tactics in his home state. There were only two alternatives to obeying police commands—a savage beating or a bullet. She had seen his fear in his quaking knees.

Slipping the cuffs out of her belt, she advanced on him from behind. *"Pone una mano detrás de la espalda,"* she ordered, and seeing the speed at which he complied, wondered if he had considerable practice. In deft movements, she snapped the cuffs on his wrist. *"La otra,"* she said, and secured both hands.

"Up now," she said, and applied some force while he scrambled awkwardly to his feet. She let him lean against the aircraft's fuselage behind the wing.

"Mr. Ocate," she said, her tone softening from the standard felony-stop commands. "Shopping for an airplane?"

He ducked his head and she saw his eyes flick toward the sound of an opening car door. Jim Bergin had stepped out of his vehicle, but he stayed well back.

"I..." Hector started to say, then fell silent. She waited for a full minute before he added, "I was deciding." He started to shift his weight forward, but Estelle reached out and with three fingers against the center of his chest pushed him back against the airplane, keeping him off-balance.

"Deciding what, *joven?*" Estelle glanced at her watch. The boy had had plenty of time to make good his flight. Something had made him hesitate. Had he been sitting in the hangared plane with the door open, he could have heard her car hurtling toward the airport, hitting the gravel so fast she had almost slid into the fence. He had hit the ignition just about the time she had been fumbling with the lock on the gate.

The teenager took a long shuddering breath and closed his eyes for a moment.

"Three-oh-eight is thirty out," Bob Torrez's voice crackled from Estelle's handheld radio. Estelle pulled the radio off her belt.

"Three-ten copies. We're at the end of the taxiway. One juvenile in custody."

"Ten-four." Torrez sounded almost disappointed. Even as he spoke, they could hear his county vehicle approach on the state highway, then slow and turn onto the gravel access road.

As if the arrival of reinforcements was what he had been waiting for, Hector Ocate looked plaintively at Estelle. "I had decided that I could fly home," he said. He turned and nodded toward the cockpit of the Cessna. "He must have insurance, no? I thought to fly to the airport at Culiacán. Do you know of that place?"

"And then?"

"I could leave the airplane there. Perhaps it could be recovered. It is easy. I fly right down the highway." He looked out the door toward the San Cristóbal Mountains to the southwest. "Just there. That's all. No one would care."

"And then?" Estelle repeated.

"Just home," Hector said.

"Where's that?"

"A small village…some distance south of Acapulco."

Hector stood a little straighter, and his voice took on an urgency that hadn't been there before. "You must help me," he said, and Estelle looked at him in surprise. "Please."

"Help you?"

"That is what I decided. That you must help me."

"Ah. It didn't look that way, *joven*. Flying away in someone's airplane isn't asking for help."

"I know now," he said, nodding vigorously. "If I go home, he will find me again. And there, no one will help me." The white Expedition roared down the taxiway, and for a moment it appeared as if Sheriff Robert Torrez was planning to rear-end Jim Bergin's pickup. He swerved around it at the last minute, took to the grass, and stopped a dozen feet in front of Estelle's sedan.

Estelle reached out again, hand on the boy's chest. She saw Ocate's eyes flick first to Bergin, then to the sheriff, and then back again. "It is possible that you can help me," he said with finality. "And you must. That is the only way. That is why I didn't take this airplane just now."

"You didn't take it because you would have crashed into my car, Hector. Don't take us for fools. Who are you running from?" Estelle asked, and once more she saw Hector Ocate's eyes flick back down the taxiway, past the airport manager and the sheriff, to the open hangar door as if he expected someone else to appear.

"Please," the teenager pleaded.

"We won't let anyone hurt you," she said. "Will you talk with me?"

"Not here, please," Hector said. The boy's eyes were those of an injured rabbit watching the coyote circle ever closer. Sheriff Torrez approached without a word, grabbed the boy by the collar, and spun him around, pushing him hard against the airplane's fuselage.

"Spread," Torrez said, kicking his feet apart and back. The pat-down was anything but gentle or perfunctory. The boy looked back toward her, and she felt a stab of sympathy. To plead with police for protection had to be counter to all of Hector Ocate's instincts, coming from a "guilty until proven innocent" culture where fairness was more often a function of the ability to pay the right people. Torrez's rough handling was more familiar, and perhaps expected.

"Keys," Torrez said, holding up a set of keys that included three—perhaps to the old man's pickup and house. He pulled the boy's wallet out of his back pocket and thumbed it open. "Well now," he said, and held it so Estelle could see the hefty wad of bills. Satisfied that there was nothing else, he spun the boy around. Hector shrank back against the plane. Torrez was a head taller, fifty pounds heavier, and ferociously calm. He held out the keys and wallet to Estelle. "You want to keep track of these?" He then thrust his hands in his pockets, regarded the shaking boy dispassionately. "How many times have you used this airplane?" he asked, his skepticism heavy.

"I caused no damage to it," Hector said.

"Oh, and that clears everything up," Torrez muttered.

"Please," Hector said again, and he looked past Torrez to Estelle. "I have this." He twisted, digging one of his thumbs behind his belt and pulling at the leather.

The belt looked expensive, with basket-weave tooling and a silver buckle. What was tucked inside the belt was far more valuable, no doubt.

"Yeah, I saw that," Torrez said.

"Tell us what happened to your passengers," Estelle said.

"Please, you must help me." It sounded as if the boy was beginning to panic, odd behavior for a kid with steely nerves who could pilot a stranger's overloaded aircraft across desert and mountains at night, landing on a narrow, unlighted strip of macadam.

"Help you?" Estelle asked. "Help you how?"

"Please—I will tell you what I know."

"Let's get him out of here," Torrez said impatiently, and he turned to the airport manager, who waited quietly beside his truck. "Jim, will you make this thing secure?"

"You bet," Bergin replied. "He leave the key in it?"

"Yes. Can you find a way to button up that hangar so this doesn't happen again?"

"Bigger lock is about all I can do," Bergin said.

"Well, we'll find somebody to sit the place until we know what's what," Torrez said. He reached out and took Hector by the elbow. "Let's go," he said, and the boy looked to Estelle beseechingly. It seemed clear to her that the youth wasn't going to talk to the brusque sheriff—if Torrez gave him the chance in the first place. But the sheriff was right. There was something to be said for keeping Hector Ocate off-balance and apprehensive.

Chapter Nineteen

Three morgue photos were fanned out on the table in front of Hector Ocate. He tried not to look at those incriminating, grotesque faces. Instead, he concentrated on his hands clenched in his lap.

"Tell me who did this," Estelle said. "You know what happened."

The teenager didn't respond. Despite his momentary eagerness out at the airport, now that he was sequestered inside the county building, Hector had retreated to some distant place. The boy knew he was in trouble, that was obvious. But it was equally obvious to Estelle that he was having difficulty weighing his options.

"Right now, you have two choices," Captain Eddie Mitchell said, understanding the boy's dilemma. Mitchell sat on the edge of the conference table, his fingers busy pinching a corduroy pattern in the rim of his foam coffee cup. He wore his best neutral expression, perhaps encouraged by being awakened after so little sleep. "You can spend a hell of a lot of time in a prison here, or you can spend the rest of your life in a prison in Mexico." He turned his head to regard the boy. "I'm sure there are some folks who'd like to talk to you down home, *¿verdad?*" The Spanish grated, the one word using up about half of Mitchell's fluency. "That's just about the extent of your choices."

"Tell me their names." Estelle pushed one of the photographs toward Hector. The high-contrast black-and-white photo, a head and torso shot, showed the corpse who had been found closest to the runway. Cactus thorns studded the man's right cheek. The 9mm slug had not exited after its path from back to front through the man's skull, but it had lodged in the globe of the left eyeball after bursting through the thin orbital bone, leaving the left side of the man's face pulpy and grotesque. The other eye was open, death coming before surprise.

"You don't know who this is?"

"They called him Guillermo. I heard her say that." He touched the edge of the photo of the heavy-set woman without picking it up. "This one talked so much—"

"Her name?" Sheriff Torrez snapped.

"I…I don't know."

"So now we're supposed to believe you've never seen these people before," Torrez said. "Who did the shooting? You know that?"

"I picked these ones up outside of Culiacán," Hector said. "They are from El Salvador. That is what I heard. I was told to meet them…at Culiacán."

"Told by who?"

"The man who promised to pay for the flight. That is where he got on the airplane as well," the boy amended.

"He is not one of these?"

"No."

"His name?" Estelle asked.

Hector hesitated. "Manuel, I think. No…*Manolo.*" The boy took a deep breath. "I knew when I saw him that…that…*no sé,*" he finished lamely.

"You knew him, you mean? Before all this happened?"

"No," Hector blurted. "But he had a…I don't know the word. *Actitud.*"

"A way about him? An attitude?"

"Yes. *Exactamente.* The command."

"Is he the man who hired you in the first place?"

"Yes. I think so."

"You *think* so?"

"I cannot be sure, *agente.* But I believe he is the one who contacted me originally."

"While you were living with the Uriostes?"

"Yes."

Estelle sat for a moment, regarding the boy. "I don't under-stand, Hector. A group of Salvadorans somehow make arrangements to rendezvous with a flight north out of Culiacán, across the border at night into the United States. The assassin—whatever he is, *who*ever he is—contacts a kid who is a student in the United States to steal an airplane and do the flying? That doesn't make any sense."

"But is true."

"I don't think so," Estelle said. "How did he contact you, then?"

"Through the e-mail, *agente.*"

"Don't be ridiculous," Mitchell said. "How would he know your e-mail address unless you had sent it to him? What, you met him on an assassins' chat room, or what?"

Hector frowned deeply, his lips pressed into a white line.

"You may be a hell of a pilot, fella, but you're a piss-poor liar," Mitchell observed.

"All your communication was by e-mail?" Estelle asked.

"Yes."

"His address?"

"I have it, yes."

"I suppose you do," Estelle said. "What *is* it?" She slid a small pad of paper across to him, along with a pencil.

"E-mail," Mitchell scoffed as Hector jotted down the electronic address. "All that tells us is that he's on this planet…probably. And half the world has e-mail with that same search engine."

"It's something," Estelle said. She turned the paper and looked at the address. "Neat. All numerical." She handed it to Mitchell, who in turn passed it to the sheriff. "When did he first contact you?"

"In March. *Yo creo que sí.* It was early in March."

"Two months ago?" Estelle asked incredulously. "How would he know *your* e-mail address?"

"I…I don't know." His eyes flicked toward Torrez, as if he feared the silent sheriff was going to reach out and smack him.

"So out of the blue, somehow," Estelle said, "*cuando menos se lo esperaba*, here comes an e-mail asking that you do this, and you jump at the chance."

"No…yes."

The undersheriff sighed loudly. "*Caramba*, Hector." She tapped the table with the eraser end of the pencil. "We'll come back to this. Tell me what he asked you to do."

"Only that I should pick up these people at Culiacán, and that he would ride with us north across the border, because he had unfinished business in the north."

"Business with whom?"

"He did not say."

"When he first contacted you, how did you know you could find an airplane to use?"

"Is easy," Hector said.

"I see. *Is easy.* You chose a time, figured out how to take the plane without being noticed, and flew south."

"Exact."

"To Culiacán."

"Yes. Direct there."

"The four people were waiting?"

"Yes."

"Then what?"

"When we were in the air, Manolo told me that he needed to deal with people in Albuquerque."

"Deal how?" Estelle asked.

"I don't know. But…" He stopped again. "He did not want me to fly him to Albuquerque. To be exposed at the International Airport, perhaps. I don't know."

"Tell us what he looked like," Mitchell said.

"Not too tall, perhaps," Hector said. "As tall as me, I think. Heavy." He held his fists clenched, flexing his muscles. "He is like the bull. Strong. And quick."

"Features? What does he look like?" Mitchell repeated patiently.

Hector frowned. "Nothing to notice. A small scar is at the corner of his right eye." He flicked a finger to his own face. "Here, like so. Just a little one. Black hair. Brown eyes, I think."

"What was he wearing?"

The boy grimaced. "I did not…do not…remember. A black jacket, I think. And blue jeans." He circled his left wrist with his right hand. "A large gold watch."

"Did the three passengers appear to know him?"

"I don't think so."

"And he paid you?"

"Some. And promised more when we were safely in the United States."

"Between Culiacán and Posadas, you didn't see any relationship between this Manolo and the other three? Did they talk?"

"No. Manolo sat in the front seat. The others in the back."

"What did you think?"

Hector shrugged hopelessly. "I thought that…I don't know."

"Why did you choose to land on that little strip by Regál? That could not be where the three wanted to go originally."

"No. I was to take them to Socorro. It is easy to fly low up the valley of the river, and that is where this Guillermo and the talking woman had a relative. That is what they said. They were most excited."

"So what happened? Why the change of plans?"

"We had been in the air for only a few minutes, and Manolo ordered me to go to Posadas—not the airport, but this one."

"He used your map?"

Hector shook his head. "He already knew the way. I agreed. How could I not? I could see that he had a pistol."

"Ah. Now he has a weapon. He threatened you?"

"No. But in the airplane, the pistol was obvious, so." Hector leaned back and jabbed his hand in his waistband, on the left side.

"Did he say anything to the other passengers? About landing near Posadas? About the change of plans? About *not* going to Socorro?"

"No. He did not speak to the others. He sat in the front, with me. I believe they thought he was with me, somehow."

Torrez leaned back, expression skeptical. "They—Guillermo or any of the others—didn't talk like he was the one who arranged their flight?" he asked.

"No."

"But that was *your* understanding…that he had made the arrangements."

"I…I think so. But maybe not." The boy looked at each of the officers in turn, as if trying to judge who was his ally.

"So you landed here, and everyone bailed out," Torrez said.

"Not right away. I land, and we are…taxi? Is that what you say? We taxi down the pavement, and this man demands that they give him the money. Each. He took them all."

"Them all what?" Mitchell asked.

"The…the *cinturones? Con dinero.*"

"Money belts," Estelle prompted. "They were each wearing a money belt?"

"Yes. Each the three of them. He used the pistol to threaten these people. I think that he kills them if they do not agree. I think at that time, they think about robbery, and that they were going to be abandoned there, in the desert."

"They gave up the money without a struggle?"

Hector shrugged. "He had the pistol, *señora*. They did not want to give him the belts. But they had to."

"What kind of weapon? Do you know?" Mitchell asked.

"Yes. A large pistol with a…" and he made a round shape with one hand, screwing it onto the invisible pistol in the other.

"*Silenciador?*" Estelle offered. "A silencer. A suppressor?"

"Yes."

"That would convince a lot of people," Torrez said.

"Guillermo said they would give the money, if they were not to be hurt. Manolo took all the belts, and ordered the people out of the plane. He gave one of the belts to me."

"Tom, would you get the effects?" Estelle said, and Sergeant Mears disappeared for a moment, returning with a brown manila envelope. He dumped it out on the conference table: ninety-seven cents in change, a wallet, a small pocketknife, sunglasses, and a heavy leather belt.

Hector reached across the table and touched the belt's tooled leather. "There is money, I think."

"You know damn well *there is money*," Torrez snapped. "Try four thousand five hundred in hundred-dollar bills. That's what I counted." He lifted the inside fold and spread the belt, revealing the tightly folded bills. "Five grand and ninety-seven cents, counting the change and the money that's in the wallet. Not bad pay for a night out on the town."

"He said that if I had to take him home, sometime, that he would give me another."

"If," Estelle repeated. "He didn't tell you where he was going?"

"No. Only north."

"How did this Manolo know that the people had money?" Mitchell asked.

"I think that is why he came here," Hector said. "I don't know so much, but I think the men he works for…I think they would know."

"And how do you know that?" Estelle said softly. "The *men he works for*. Did he actually tell you that he worked for someone?"

"Well, that is what I think. This kind of money—"

"This is Salvadoran money coming north?" Estelle asked. "Is that what you think?"

"I am not so sure. But I think so. That is what I guess." He gulped as if his throat were full of cotton. "I did not ask. He had the pistol. And he seemed like a man to use it. That is all I know."

"I bet," Torrez said. "What do your parents do?" The change of subject was jarring, and Hector coughed violently until his eyes teared. Mitchell left the room and returned promptly with a can of soda. The boy sipped eagerly, and they waited until he had regained his composure. "Your parents?" Torrez repeated.

"He…" And Hector stopped abruptly. Estelle could see that it wasn't any lack of facility with English that made him so hesitant. Eventually, he said, "My father flies the charter out

of Acapulco. Sometimes it is the tourists, sometimes…others."
Quickly, he added, "He does nothing against the law. Nothing."

"You learned to fly from your father?" Estelle asked.

"Yes. I learned to fly with the big Grumman. He used to…
what is the word…to spray?"

"He was a crop duster?"

"Yes. He doesn't do that now. I have flown since I was ten.
I am licensed now."

"Whether you have a license or not is the least of your problems, *joven,*" Estelle said.

"I am licensed." His eyes strayed to the wallet, and the watchful Mitchell leaned forward, took the wallet, and examined the
contents.

"This?" he asked, holding up an official certificate. Hector
nodded. Mitchell handed it to Estelle, who read both sides.

"Is this accurate?" she asked.

"Yes."

"It says your date of birth is April of 1989. That makes you
eighteen, doesn't it?"

Estelle turned to one of the chairs, pulled it forward, and sat
down beside Hector Ocate. "It's hard to believe anything you say,
señor." She emphasized the salutation, and its obvious contrast
with *joven,* the generic greeting for a teenager.

"You landed, got out of the plane, and popped those three. Is
that what happened?" Torrez asked. "There ain't no goddamned
fifth passenger."

"That is *not* what happened," Hector said, a trace of panic
creeping into his voice. Despite the circumstances, it was still
hard to look at the young man's round face, his expressive brown
eyes, and think him a killer.

"What did?" As he asked the question, Eddie Mitchell leafed
through the remainder of the wallet's contents, finally tossing
the scant documents back on the table.

"I landed the plane as you say," Hector pleaded. "That is all.
Manolo ordered everyone out, and he followed."

"You had to get out of the airplane as well," Estelle said. "There's no passenger side door on the right side of the cockpit. For Manolo to exit the plane, you had to get out first—to get out of his way."

"Yes. That is so. Then I climbed back in."

"And waited."

"And waited, yes."

"You knew what he was going to do?"

"Yes." The single word was nearly inaudible.

"You saw what happened, then?"

"No, I did not," Hector said quickly. "I was inside the airplane. What happened was...was behind me. I could not see."

"But you knew," Estelle said, and Hector nodded.

"Who are these folks?" Mitchell asked. He held up a photograph that had been framed in one of the wallet's plastic inner pockets. The photo had been folded, a crease running through the picture between the boy in the middle and the man on his right. "This is you in the middle." He held out the photo to Hector.

"Yes," the boy said. He took a deep breath.

"The others?"

"That is my father, just so." He touched the photo, indicating the man standing to his right, isolated by the crease where the photo had been folded. "Rudolfo Villanueva. But he is not my *father*. He is *padrastro*. I do not remember the word in English."

"Stepfather," Estelle prompted.

"Yes, I think so."

"And this?" Mitchell tapped the photo. The third figure, a heavy-set man with black curly hair, stood with one arm draped around Hector's shoulders. The man, perhaps fifty years old, wore only a pair of bright yellow shorts—and a lot of muscle. His left foot rested on a cooler, and his calf muscle looked like a football. Estelle examined the photo. The family resemblance was striking.

Once again, Hector hesitated. "He is...a friend of my father."

"His name?"

"I...I do not know."

"Shit, you don't remember," Mitchell snapped. "You two are standing there like old buddies."

"Really. He is just a man we met that day. We were fishing, and when we posed on the boat, my mother, she took the photo."

Estelle fingered the crease.

"He's a lyin' little shit," Torrez said affably.

"He is just a friend. *Mira*," he added. "My father knows nothing of this. Please…"

"You're lying, Hector," Estelle said abruptly.

"No," he said.

She held up the photo again so Hector could see it. "This is the man who flew north with you, isn't it?"

"I…I…he was just there that day. We were fishing," he said lamely.

"He's the one, isn't he?" When Hector refused to answer, she grimaced with impatience and turned to Eddie Mitchell. "We need to bring the Uriostes in. Both of them. I don't believe that all this went down without them knowing something. While you're doing that, I'll see if I can reach *el capitán* Naranjo. He may have contacts that will be useful. We're going to need to talk with this alleged *padrastro*." She picked up the photo. "And we have this. This other face." She leaned close, examining the photo. The man wore a heavy watch, perhaps a Rolex. All three men were relaxed in the photo, not a moment among strangers.

"I…" Hector said, and put his head in his hands.

"I'll do it," Sheriff Torrez said. "You want 'em both? Mom and Pop?"

"Yes."

"No, please," Hector said from behind his hands. "They know nothing of this. And…"

"And what?"

"Please…"

Estelle nodded at Torrez. "Go ahead. Give me a minute with him." When the door had closed, she leaned closer to Hector. "So tell me, *señor*. You waited for this Manolo to finish his business?" When the boy looked up at her, confused, she added, "You waited in the airplane, and after a little while, Manolo returned to the airplane? You got out so he could climb back inside?"

"He entered through the big door. The cargo door in the back."

Estelle pictured the tight confines of Jerry Turner's Cessna. "There's no easy way from there to the front seats," she said, and looked at the photo again. "And he's a big man, Hector."

"No, no. He remained in the back."

"And the two of you flew where?"

"Here," Hector said. "We flew to the airport. I parked in front of the hangar, and got out to open the doors. When I returned to the airplane, he was gone."

"Sure thing," Mitchell scoffed.

"He was gone," Hector insisted. "I do not know where."

"You just locked up and went home?"

"Yes."

"What time was it by then?"

"Perhaps two or three in the morning."

"Your host family—the Uriostes—they knew nothing of any of this?"

"Nothing."

"What time did you leave the house that night?" Estelle asked, as if "that night" was a time in the distant past and not just days before.

"Eight in the evening," Hector said promptly. "Maybe a little earlier. The Señor Bergin had a meeting. I know that. The…I don't know what it is called, but the businessmen of the town all meet."

"The Chamber of Commerce?" Estelle prompted.

"Yes. That is it."

Tuesday evening's dinner meeting of the Chamber had been an important one, by all accounts—and well-publicized. "How did you know that?"

"He told me," Hector said.

"Ah." Estelle looked across at the others. "Jim Bergin told you?"

"Yes."

"You've talked to him?"

"Yes. Several times. He came to school once, and I have visited the airport."

Estelle turned to Mitchell. "See if you can reach Jim, will you?"

"You got it," Mitchell said, but he paused before turning to the door. "What did you tell the Uriostes when you left the house?" he asked Hector.

The boy ducked his head, as if loath to reveal the subterfuge. "I go to study with one of my friends," he said. "He lives just a short distance."

"But instead, you went next door and took the old man's truck," Estelle said. "You park in the rest stop along the highway, just east of the airport." She relaxed back in the chair, regarding Hector Ocate. His story included some grains of truth, no doubt. Her flight with Jim Bergin, over rough country at night, had surprised her. What to the uninitiated might seem suicidal or at best foolhardy was hardly that; they had managed the flight with comfort and ease.

"What time did you return home?"

"It was nearly four in the morning," Hector said.

"Your host family doesn't mind that you're gone all night?"

"They are sure that I'm with the Grahams."

"Your study partner."

"Yes."

Captain Mitchell reappeared at the door, cell phone in hand. "Jim's on his way in." He beckoned to Estelle, who joined him outside the conference room.

"What do you think?" he asked.

"Bizarre, is what I think," Estelle said.

"He's a real piece of work," Mitchell said. "Woulda been nice to run an NAA on his hands. But it's been too long now."

"I don't think he fired the gun, Eddie."

"I don't either, but it was a thought. At the same time, I'm not sure I buy all this *Manolo* shit, either. But it's a fact—we've got *somebody* who is as cold-blooded as they come. Like some shootin' gallery. *Pop, pop, pop.* And in the dark, even with a laser sight, it ain't easy. It ain't something that a kid does. And that's what bothers me. Here's a kid who's a hot-dog pilot. All right, I can buy that. Motorcycle, four-wheeler, airplane, it doesn't make any difference. Kids are immortal and know it."

"The flying is one thing," Estelle said.

"That's where I'm going," Mitchell agreed. "He knows what went down out there in the desert, and he still flies back, calm as shit, makes a perfect landing, puts the plane away, remembers to fuel it…Shit." He shook his head. "Don't jibe. That's cold."

"The money troubles me," Estelle said. "Three money belts, and maybe five thousand in each. That's petty cash, Eddie. You don't run those kinds of risks for fifteen thousand dollars. Not in this day and age."

"Well, now, I don't know. We have people walking across the desert every day and every night without a peso between 'em."

"This is different. Someone from El Salvador makes complicated, risky arrangements to flee north, carrying enough money for the trip without being weighted down? I have to wonder… Where's the rest?"

"Transferred to some bank stateside," Mitchell said. "Or a million other places. Caymans, Switzerland, wherever money is going these days." He nodded as the possibilities opened. "Odds are good it isn't their money," he said. "That's an obvious motive." He frowned. "But why not just pop 'em in Mexico, when he caught up with 'em? What's the point of takin' the risk?"

"That's the part that doesn't make sense to me," Estelle said.

Mitchell grinned. "Just that part, eh? That puts you way out ahead of me." He looked across the small lobby toward the clock. "We're going to keep after this little shit until he gives us some answers," he said. "The Uriostes will be here in a minute. They have some explaining to do. Are you going to talk with Naranjo?"

"Yes. If the Judiciales can help in some way, he'll be the best contact that we have. If this is all out of El Salvador or some such, there's not much they can do." She held up the picture of the boy and his two guardians. "Maybe this will help as well. I'll e-mail it to Naranjo's office right now so he can have a look. That and the name of the boy's stepfather might ring a bell with someone." She shook her head slowly. "Hector makes things up as easily as breathing." She tapped the photo. "Who knows. This guy in the bathing suit might be an innocent shrimp fisherman, just minding his own business."

"Maybe."

"But I'll bet a lot that he isn't. He looks more like Hector than his stepfather does."

"If there is a Manolo who needs a return flight, he might be coming back this way. Be nice to be at the plane to meet him."

Chapter Twenty

Estelle Reyes-Guzman's pulse clicked up several notches at what she heard. Jim Bergin was contrite that he hadn't remembered his conversations with Hector Ocate from days earlier. Perhaps in the dim light of dawn, in the excitement of the moment as he watched the speeding patrol car chasing the airplane, and then later standing well back from the scene as the boy was placed under arrest, he simply hadn't recognized Hector.

Estelle ushered him into the privacy of her office, and she could smell the sweet tang of aviation fuel and motor oil on his clothes. "His name is Hector Ocate, Jim."

"Yep. When Eddie got me on the phone, he told me. I feel kind of stupid."

"Apparently he knew that you had a Chamber of Commerce meeting this past Tuesday night," she said.

Bergin grunted in disgust, and it was obvious by the expression on his weather-beaten face that it was directed at himself. "You know, out there, I thought he looked kind of familiar. But you know how that came up?" he said. "That chamber thing? He was out at the airport one day last week, wondering if it was staying light enough now for him to take flyin' lessons in the evening. One thing led to another, and I guess I told him that Tuesdays and Wednesdays were out. Got Chamber on the one, bowling the other. He said maybe weekends, then. Or maybe he'd wait until summer, when school was out."

"It could have been just talk," Estelle said.

"Obviously was," Bergin replied. "I've been thinkin' on it all the way in here from the airport. I know how he come to pick Jerry Turner's plane. He was there last week, all right. But a few times before that. I know that he hung around in early March, when I was puttin' a new ADF in Turner's plane. I had taxied her down there to the main hangar, and I remember that one day, Hector spent most of the afternoon there. Helped me clean up some."

"You're sure it was March?"

"Yep. I can look in the repair logs to get the exact date. But early March sometime. Just a kid hangin' out, as far as I was concerned," he said. "I didn't pay him too much mind, anyways."

"Did he talk about his father's business? The charter flying service?"

"Nope. He wondered with all this Homeland Security stuff if he was going to have a hard time taking flying lessons in this country. I remember that."

"He didn't tell you that he already had a license issued in Mexico?"

"Nope. I didn't know that. He really does?"

"He really does."

"Then the little bastard was just scopin' me out. That's the way it seems to me."

"So it seems," Estelle said. "It would be helpful if you could figure out when he first came out to the airport."

"I'd just be guessing. This year, though. Sometime after Christmas. The first time he talked to me, that is. He coulda snuck in anytime, far as that goes. But that don't mean he was planning to take an airplane back then. What's he say?"

"He doesn't yet. But we'll get there." She moved to her office door and opened it. "If you think of anything else, give me a buzz."

"You bet." He rose, hat crumpled in his hand like a little kid leaving the principal's office.

"Thanks for coming down, Jim."

"I'll get the locks changed today," he said, and grinned a brown smile. "Horse is long gone from the barn, but what the hell."

She could hear voices out in the hall, and stepped out after Bergin. She saw Bob Torrez escorting Gordon Urioste, with Tom Mears following, one hand on Pam Urioste's elbow. Deputy Jackie Taber followed, looking as if she needed a long nap.

"Take a few minutes with Gordon, all right?" Torrez said to Estelle. "Jackie will give you a hand. Me and Sarge will talk with Pam for a minute."

Mears steered Pam Urioste toward the sheriff's impossibly uncomfortable office.

"We can all…" Gordon started to say, but the sheriff cut him off.

"No, we can't all," he said ungraciously. "In there, please."

Estelle held her office door open. "This shouldn't take long, Mr. Urioste," she said. As Jackie passed, she added, "Have you been up on the mountain yet?"

"No, ma'am," the deputy said. She glanced at her watch. "The first riders were off at a little after nine. They'll all be on the course in about an hour."

"That'll keep everyone occupied," Estelle said. "Give us some peace and quiet." She indicated a chair, and Gordon Urioste sat down, hands clasped nervously over his gut as he leaned forward in the chair. Two doors down the hall, his wife would be sitting on a steel folding chair in the sheriff's office, comforted by the blank walls, government-gray office furnishings, and the unsmiling sheriff. Across the hall in the spacious conference room, Hector Ocate would not know that his host family was in the building. It would be interesting, Estelle thought, to see how the three stories puzzled together.

Her phone rang before she could close the door, and Gordon Urioste nodded as she excused herself. "We're in Grand Central Station at the moment," she said.

Out in the hall, she walked toward the rear exit of the building, out of earshot of any other room.

"Guzman."

"Ah, I am so glad I reached you, *señora*," Captain Tomás Naranjo said. "Is this a good moment? It is terribly early."

"It's a fine moment," Estelle replied. "It's good to hear from you."

"We have a name," Captain Tomás Naranjo's quiet voice said. Estelle had not been expecting to hear from the Judiciales so quickly, and she was stunned into silence. "A colleague of mine in Acapulco knows Rudolfo Villanueva—and his stepson, for that matter. Señor Villanueva is in, how do we say, the transportation business. People who need to travel discreetly from here to there—all entirely legal, I should think."

Or with the right people's palms greased, Estelle thought. "A charter business, then."

"Exactly. Nothing like what I'm hearing from you, however. That would be a new thing. But his relationship with the boy—Hector, is it? His relationship with this boy is obscure. It appears that *stepfather* is courtesy. He and the boy's mother are not married, you see."

"Really."

"But that aside, until now, at least, Señor Villanueva has been careful that his business is entirely legitimate and documented. But I must say, the friend standing beside the boy in the photograph…that would be a different matter. That was most interesting to receive that. I took the liberty of forwarding it to my colleagues, and they are *most* intrigued. His name is Manolo Tapia—and his relationship to the boy's mother is somewhat in question. Perhaps he is a brother…"

"That would make him Hector's uncle, then."

"Yes. It appears that Señor Tapia goes by several names, you see, depending on the circumstances. But we have reason to believe that is his name at the moment."

"And his significance?"

"Well, his *significance*," and Naranjo drew out the word, relishing each syllable, "is that of all the people with whom we would most like to speak about various…matters…Señor Manolo Tapia is certainly near the top of the list."

"Which matters might those be, Tomás?" Estelle asked.

"Ah. Just so. There is considerable evidence building that Señor Tapia may be involved in various *solutions* that his colleagues require."

"Tomás, please," Estelle said.

"Ah. *Lo siento.* You have become so *American,* Señora Guzman." He chuckled. "How can I say it? We have cause to believe that this man is responsible for a number of deaths, particularly in Oaxaca and Chiapas. Perhaps other activities in Guatemala and El Salvador as well. There are almost certainly others about which we are not aware."

"He's an assassin?"

"That might be accurate. Something of the sort," Naranjo said, as if loath to actually use the word. "I am surprised to hear that he is now in the United States. That is not his...turf? Do we say that?"

"It appears to be his turf now," Estelle said.

"Yes, it would," the captain said. "I may have something on the three victims before long."

"*Guillermo* is a name," Estelle prompted. "The boy says the older man's name was *Guillermo.*"

"Ah. I will forward that. There is word on that in some channels. But I am most puzzled. I can't imagine why Tapia would run the risk, the *considerable* risk, of flying with his victims to the United States. It makes something of a statement, of course. But..." He paused. "My guess is that other business calls him north. That is most unusual for this man, I should think. Most unusual. Find out his business, and you may well find him. That is what my colleagues say. Of course," and he laughed gently, "my colleagues have not been so fortunate in their own efforts. They are *very* interested."

"The boy has to be the link," Estelle said.

"I should think so."

"You'll get back to me if you hear anything else?"

"Most assuredly. And you must call us, should you hear anything further."

Estelle rang off and sat for a moment, staring at the phone. *The killer is Hector's uncle.* That explained the boy's confused efforts to protect the identity of the third man in the photo. And a favorite uncle, too…at least that's what the fold in the picture indicated.

If the three Salvadorans were fleeing north with money that wasn't theirs, she could imagine a man such as Tapia hired to resolve the problem. Traveling quickly, with contacts throughout the country oiled with generous payments, Tapia would overtake the family at his leisure. But why not just end it there, if that was the case?

In fact, this time, it appeared that he might have arranged the flight himself, baiting the three with what first appeared to be a quick, easy trip north, a flight directly to the safety of Socorro. But then what? Estelle ran a finger down the side of the telephone receiver, frowning. Why would Tapia hire his nephew, a mere youngster, to make the flight—and not without risk? Perhaps only because Rudolfo Villanueva would not, his high profile putting him immediately at risk.

And then, why Posadas? Why land at the gas company's primitive strip in the middle of the night, and immediately execute the family, leaving them to lie in the desert?

Had the observant Robert Torrez, ever the hunter, not observed the playing coyotes, the incident might have gone unnoticed for weeks, perhaps months. And then a little piece of metal hangar siding out of place in the glare of a spotlight had led them to Hector Ocate.

Estelle pushed herself out of the chair and returned to her office. Gordon Urioste looked up expectantly.

"Gordon," Estelle said, "I need to know who Manolo Tapia is."

"Who?" The blank look on his face appeared genuine.

"Manolo Tapia," Estelle repeated, enunciating the name distinctly.

"I don't know that name," Gordon said. "Unless you mean Mickey Tapia, the girls' volleyball coach."

"No. I don't mean him. It's *Manolo* Tapia."

"Nope. Am I supposed to?"

"I hope not," Estelle said, and abruptly left the room. She conferred briefly with Bob Torrez outside his office, then went in and repeated the same question, receiving the same blank response from Pam Urioste. A moment later, she sat down across from Hector Ocate—by now so worn and frazzled that he had difficulty keeping his eyes open.

"Hector, listen. When did your uncle first contact you?"

"My uncle?" The answer was unconvincingly evasive, and the sleepiness left his eyes.

"We know about Manolo Tapia," she said. "Your uncle." She laid the photograph down carefully on the table and tapped the image. "This man. Your mother's brother. When did he first contact you about making a flight like this?"

"He…" Hector began, and just as quickly chopped off the thought.

"Exactly," Estelle said. "He called you—or e-mailed you, didn't he?"

"Yes."

"When?"

"He e-mailed me some months before," Hector said cautiously.

"Before what?"

"I mean some months *ago.*"

"When was the first time he contacted you?"

Hector frowned at the empty soda can on the table in front of him. "It was during the winter," he said finally. "Some time ago."

"You don't remember when?"

"No."

"Did you save the message?"

He looked up quickly at her. "No. Of course not."

"Which computer did you use?"

"At home. At school."

"Which one?"

"I…I don't remember."

"Listen, Hector," Estelle snapped, "this is the time to see how smart you can be. Right now, you're being held on three counts of accessory to murder." She saw his eyes widen. "Three counts of conspiracy. Theft of an airplane. Illegal border trafficking. I can go on. Unless you cooperate with us, it will only get worse."

"If I cooperate with you, *agente,* I will be killed," Hector said, his voice a whisper.

She studied him for a moment, but he wouldn't return her gaze. "Out at the airport, you were eager for our protection, *hijo.* You have it now."

"I can't."

"Well, then, there's nothing we can do for you. You're of no interest to us." She straightened up and walked to the conference room door, where she turned and looked at Hector. "You can rot in prison. Get used to that idea." Opening the door, she regarded the boy. "And your *anfitriones,*" she said, using the formal word for "hosts." "I'm sure that Señor Tapia will have little trouble finding them...all of them."

"You must not," Hector said, and bit his lip in frustration.

"And of course, the two children, your friends. Marty and little Lorietta, is it? Let's draw them into this danger, too."

The boy's jaw bounced as if he were gnawing at his clenched lips, and then his head fell forward into his arms. Estelle felt a wrench of sympathy. She crossed back to the table and bent over, her lips close to his right ear. She kept her voice stern and unrelenting. "Is that what you want?" Hector pushed his head up and covered his face with both hands, elbows on the table. "Is that what you want?" Estelle repeated.

"No."

"Then talk to me. When did you first hear from Tapia?"

"In late January."

"How do you remember so clearly?"

"Because school had started again. I had just returned from home."

"You went to Mexico for Christmas, then?"

"Yes."

"Did you see your uncle when you were home?"

Hector hesitated long enough that Estelle knew his answer before he managed to voice it. "Yes."

"Did he ask you to do this thing then?"

"No. He asked only for my e-mail address. I gave it to him."

Estelle slid a pad across to him, along with the pencil. "Write it for me." He did so, and slid it back. She turned to Sergeant Tom Mears and handed him the pad. "I want the hard drive from the Uriostes' computer, and then I want the administrator for the school's system to open up that drive as well. If you have to go through Judge Hobart, get that process started. I want those messages."

Not knowing whether what she asked was actually possible or not, Estelle was gratified that Mears simply nodded and left the room, as if such requests occurred every day.

"Then what?" she asked. "When did your uncle next contact you?"

"It was in March, I think," Hector said. "Just before spring vacation. Yes. He wrote to ask if I was coming home for that vacation, too. I replied that I was not. He asked for my telephone number."

"The Uriostes' number, you mean?"

"No. My cellular phone."

Of course you have one of those, Estelle thought. "When did he call you?"

"That night. He told me to call him when I could be assured that I was alone. That is all he said."

"And you did."

"Certainly. Later that night. I went outside for a walk, and that is when I called him."

"What did he want?"

"He asked if it would be possible for me to secure an airplane. Without anyone knowing. He said that at small airports, there are always airplanes that sit unused for months at a time."

"And you knew of such an airplane, of course."

"Yes. But I told him that I could not do it."

"Apparently you could, after all."

"He said that my…my father had refused such a flight. And that it would be bad for him…and for me…" Hector nodded back tears. "If I could not do it."

"Why did your uncle want to come to Posadas?"

"I don't know if that's where he wanted to go," Hector said. "Maybe just because that's where I am living." He wiped his eyes. "He was most persuasive. He told of passengers at Culiacán who would pay a great deal for a short plane trip across the border. He told me how easy it would be. That I could fly right up the highway, and that if I remained…" And he held out his hand palm down toward the table.

"Low?"

"Yes. Low. The radar would not see us. It would be easy. And you see, I am a good pilot, *agente,* I know that."

"I bet you are," Estelle said. "I bet you are."

Chapter Twenty-one

As if the mention of Manolo Tapia's name had opened a flood-gate, Hector Ocate's recitation of events poured out in a babble of fatigue, and Estelle probed for something that would point her in the right direction.

"When you landed at the Posadas airport," she said, "in the early morning hours on Wednesday, your uncle was still with you?"

"Yes, he was," Hector said vehemently.

"But when you became engaged in putting the plane back in the hangar, he simply disappeared?"

"Yes. I turned my back, and he was gone."

"You never saw him again? Not since then?"

"No."

"And he hasn't contacted you?"

"No. Never."

Estelle fell silent, regarding the boy. He shifted uncomfortably and shrugged. In a rural county, Manolo Tapia's choices would be limited. He couldn't simply hail a cab. Stealing a car would be risky without urban cover. He could hitchhike, trying to blend in with the many strangers in town for the bike race. He might attempt to rent a car from Chavez Motors, if they had any left to rent. Or, he could simply find a place to stay and hole up until an opportunity presented itself to skip back across the border. There would be no rooms available at the two local motels, or at the one bed and breakfast, but an enterprising person could always find shelter.

"Where do *you* think he went?" she asked.

"I...I don't know." Hector didn't sound convincing.

"He could as easily be back in Mexico," Estelle offered, waiting to see if Hector jumped at the possibility. He nodded quickly. "During the entire time that you were with Tapia—beginning that night in Culiacán when you picked up the passengers and met with him—he never mentioned another destination or...job? Other than the passing mention of something up in Albuquerque?"

"Nothing." Hector rubbed his face again. His skin was pale and a sheen of sweat had formed on his face from the effort of trying to stay awake.

"Are you hungry?"

"No, I..." Hector began before the question actually sank in. "Oh, yes," he said. "I could eat something."

Without being asked, Eddie Mitchell rose and headed for the door. "How about you?" he said to Estelle.

"No, thanks." She turned back to Hector. "Tell me what you know about the Salvadorans."

"I know nothing," he replied. "Really. They talked, but in the airplane, it is not so easy to hear. The woman, she..." and he made a yak-yak motion with the fingers of his right hand. "I could not hear much of what was said."

"But each carried a money belt? You knew about that?"

"Yes, I think so."

"Your uncle paid you with one of them. That's five thousand dollars, Hector. A lot of money. And he promised the possibility of another payment?"

"If a return flight was necessary. Yes."

"You say *if*...Señor Tapia wasn't sure?"

"He did not say."

Estelle's cell phone chirped and she pulled it off her belt. "Guzman."

"Ah," Captain Tomás Naranjo said. "I am sorry for the interruption. But I thought you should know what we have discovered. Are you free to talk now?"

"Certainly," Estelle said, fascinated that the mere mention of Manolo Tapia's name had set the ponderous wheels of Mexican law enforcement in motion. That phenomenon, all by itself, told her that fortunes stood to be won or lost, depending on Tapia's actions and connections.

She held the door for Eddie Mitchell, returning with the box of not-so-fresh donuts that had graced the dispatch desk, then slipped out into the hall and stepped into her own quiet office.

"The three victims are from Santa Ana, a city of no particular distinction in El Salvador," he said. "Guillermo Haslán—the victim referred to by name—he is an accountant for PDC. Do you know of them?"

"I don't think so," Estelle replied. The world of corporate initials was so cluttered that any combination would sound familiar.

"Yes," Naranjo said. "Let me see." She could hear the rustle of paper. "A mining consortium with a regional office in Santa Ana. Most interesting. Ah, here it is. Pemberton, Duquesne, and Cordova." He pronounced each name slowly, as if he enjoyed the musical sounds. "Are you familiar with them? Construction, mining, and other undertakings."

"No. I'm afraid not."

"There's no reason you should be, I suppose. They are headquartered in New Zealand, but there are offices worldwide, I'm told. My sources profess to know little more than that, other than that it appears that Señor Haslán may have disposed of some funds that were not his. Certainly not an unusual story, I'm sure you'll agree. I suppose that the powers that be are perhaps justifiably irritated."

"Enough to send Manolo Tapia to retrieve the funds, minus administrative fees," Estelle said.

Naranjo chuckled. "Just so."

"PDC funds? Do we know?"

"We do not know that. The disappearance of Señor Haslán and his family was something of a local incident, I'm told. One day, they are home, well-regarded in the community, a pleasant family. The next day, their house stands empty. This happened sometime last week. The exact time of their disappearance seems to be something of a mystery."

"Who remains behind?"

"I will endeavor to find out for you. Perhaps there are more relatives. We don't know. Suppose I have someone from Santa Ana contact you directly?"

"That would be good, Tomás. I appreciate your assistance."

"Most assuredly. This boy pilot has no idea where Señor Tapia might have gone?"

"He says not. We're looking under every rock, believe me."

Naranjo sighed with commiseration. "I wish you well. This is a big country, of course. And we are so few. I have issued orders of my own. We will do what we can."

"We appreciate that." Estelle harbored no illusions about the efficiency of efforts—on either side of the border, for that matter. She wondered what Naranjo's orders actually had been, but had the courtesy not to ask.

Walking back to the conference room, she was reminded by the quiet ambience of the Public Safety Building of how tired she really was. Hector Ocate would be just about comatose, unable to think clearly, even with the sugar jog from the donuts. More important, he would be too tired to guard his answers.

When she pushed open the door, the young man sat with his head down on the table, and she could tell by the slump of his body that he was asleep. The donuts had not been enough of a boost.

She nodded at Mitchell and he reached across and shook the boy by the shoulder. His head rose slowly and he tried to blink, but his eyelids sagged to half-mast.

"Hector, listen to me," Estelle said. "We have to know where your uncle is. You must tell us. That is the only way that we can protect you and your family."

"Please," the boy murmured. "I do not know."

"He did not walk away at the airport, did he?"

"But of course he…"

"Please, *joven*." She let the heavy sarcasm hang for an instant. "We are not stupid. The airport is seven miles from town. What's he going to do, walk cross-country? Hitchhike?" She saw the look of confusion on his face, and she held out her thumb for explanation. "I don't think so."

"He…"

"You said that you put the plane away, and as if by magic, your uncle disappeared. That's what you want us to believe. But that's not what happened." The questions swirled in her own tired brain, and she turned quickly toward Eddie Mitchell. The captain had been waiting silently, and now raised an eyebrow in question. Estelle nodded toward the conference room door.

Out in the hallway, she lowered her voice to little more than a whisper.

"We need to check Reynaldo Estrada's place," she said. "I should have thought about that sooner. It's perfect. An empty house, and handy transportation whenever Tapia needs it."

"You think so?" Mitchell said. "The Uriostes next door wouldn't notice the truck being used?" He shrugged philosophically. "Of course, they didn't notice when Hector used it. Why change?"

"We need to ask them," she said. "But at night? Maybe not. Maybe they wouldn't notice. With curtains drawn, the television on, why would they? And," Estelle added with a weary shake of the head, "would they care if they *did* notice?"

"Well, it isn't night now," Mitchell said. His eyes narrowed. "Trouble is, the trail's most likely stone cold, Estelle. They flew back here when, Wednesday early in the morning? That's more than seventy-two hours ago. Why would Tapia be lounging around? What would he be waiting for?"

"It doesn't make sense that he would," Estelle said. "He's got work to do. That's what Hector claims. Maybe up north. But it'll fill in a square if we can find traces…if we know Manolo Tapia stayed in that house for a bit. Even one night. That's another little piece to all of this."

"Well, we need some clear thinkers," Mitchell said. "If there's any chance at all that Tapia is in that house, I don't want somebody who is half asleep busting in on him." He looked at his watch. "Let me round up some good hands, and we'll go check the place out."

"I'll go with you," Tom Mears said, but the captain shook his head. The sergeant had appeared out of the patrol office, a cup of coffee in hand.

"We need you here with the kid," he said, and turned to Estelle. "You're going to talk with the family again?"

"I'll call them in now," she said.

"We don't want to wait for that. I'll get things moving out at Estrada's. Give me a call if you find out anything I need to know." Mitchell paused. "A couple things don't jibe. The kid says that Tapia mentioned Albuquerque? If that's the case, he's long gone. Somehow, he got himself a set of wheels, or hitched, or caught the bus out of Deming. Any of that's possible. But if he didn't do that…what's the point of him staying around here? That's what doesn't make sense to me."

"We're missing something," Estelle replied. "It's as simple as that."

Chapter Twenty-two

Each time that she stepped out into the hallway, Estelle had glanced toward the foyer of the Public Safety Building, where Gordon and Pam Urioste had taken up residence as they awaited the fate of their houseguest. The undersheriff was convinced that the couple had no knowledge of Hector Ocate's escapades. Each time the Uriostes caught her eye, their expression were both hopeful and apprehensive.

Now, she beckoned them toward the conference room. "We need to talk," she said, but offered no other explanation as they entered. She closed the door behind them. Hector sat up a little straighter when his host family appeared. Sergeant Mears remained a fixture at the far end of the table, perched on the corner with his hands relaxed on his lap.

"Mr. And Mrs. Urioste," she said, "we will be detaining Hector on a variety of charges. This is complicated by his alien status, as I'm sure you can appreciate. I'm sure that the district attorney will be conferring with the Mexican consulate when we have a clearer picture of what has happened. But because he is over eighteen, and *was* over eighteen when the incidents in question occurred, he's on his own. He is legally an adult. As his host family, you are under no legal obligations to retain counsel for him, although you may do so if you wish—and I would recommend that you do. We'll be contacting his family and the various agencies involved later this morning."

That in itself was something of a conundrum, she reflected. A Sunday was never a good day to try and force bureaucracy to jump through hoops.

"Right now, our main concern is for his safety, and yours," she said, sure that the Uriostes were well-meaning, almost certainly innocent of anything other than an overdose of blind trust.

"*Ours?*" Gordon asked.

"We are quite certain that the killer of the three Salvadorans rode with the victims on the plane with Hector, and then flew on into Posadas with him."

Gordon Urioste sat down hard, jarring the long conference table. "Did you do what they're saying you did?" he demanded of Hector. The boy shifted slightly in his chair but remained silent. The face that stared back at Gordon was one of an exhausted, resigned teenager—hardly reflecting the steely nerved derring-do required of a pilot flying an overloaded plane at night through rugged country.

"Right now, it isn't what *he* did that really matters," Estelle said. "We think that he's just the taxi driver, so to speak. What more he might have done is still unclear." She let it go at that. Whether Hector had been a willing participant, or had been forced by threats against his family or his American hosts—or both—would come clear with time, she was sure.

"Mr. and Mrs. Urioste, at any time did you see activity at the Estrada place next door to you? We're talking about the period of time from early Wednesday morning until today. Did you notice lights, or activity around the truck? Anything that was out of the ordinary?"

Gordon Urioste grimaced, his rubbery face twisting into a caricature. "Look," he said, "I *knew* that Hec took the truck a time or two, but it was just when he was going over to see his friends. Stuff like that. See, when the old man was alive, he said that he was going to give that truck to my son when Marty was old enough to drive. In the past couple of years, old Ray didn't drive anymore. He couldn't see good enough to make it out of the driveway." Gordon shrugged. "I didn't see the harm in letting

Hec use it now and then. He's careful. Old Ray kept it licensed and all, so it was legal."

"So to speak," Estelle added dryly.

"Well, he's old enough to take care of himself. He's got lots of friends here now, you know. You can't keep a high school senior on a leash, for God's sakes."

"Much as we might like to," Pam said.

"I mean, there's a lot to see and do in this country," Gordon added. "This year is the chance of a lifetime for Hector." He stopped, and the righteous expression on his face told Estelle that he didn't realize how inane he sounded. That *chance of a lifetime* could offer itself in many guises.

"Three people thought that they had the chance of a lifetime," she said quietly. "Did you see lights on next door any time this past week? In the house?"

"Oh, no," Gordon insisted. "Hec wouldn't go inside that house." He turned toward the boy. "That's not what happened, is it? You weren't inside over there. No wild parties, nothing like that."

"We're not talking about wild parties," Estelle said. Hector didn't respond.

"You know," Gordon said, undeterred, and he twisted his head back to look up at his wife, who was standing behind him, hand on his left shoulder, "I don't even know where the key to that place is." He looked at Hector. "Do you? *La llave?*" he added unnecessarily.

"Yes."

The direct answer startled Gordon.

"It is hung by the back door. Up high," Hector said.

"You showed him how to get into the old man's house?" Estelle asked. "Is that where you uncle stayed?"

"It is possible," Hector whispered.

Tom Mears rose quickly. "I'll alert the guys," he said, and left the room, pulling his radio from his belt as he did so.

"It's *possible?*" Estelle snapped. She bent down close to the boy, close enough to smell his fatigue, his fear. "Hector, listen to me. You're helping this man. That makes you an accomplice. Do you understand what that means? *Un cómplice?*" She saw his eyes close a little, and saw the moisture at the corners. *"Un cómplice, joven. Un cómplice en todas cosas...los tres asesinatos incluidos."*

Once more, Hector's head settled into his hands. Estelle pulled one of the chairs over and sat down, so close that she could hear Hector's breathing muffled in the palms of his hands.

"Tell me, Hector," she whispered. "This isn't something that you're just going to walk away from, *hijo*. Tell me what we need to know. There must be no more killing."

"He will, you know." Hector's voice was so soft that she could hardly hear it. She rested a hand on his arm and turned to the Uriostes.

"Will you wait outside, please?" As if now anxious to distance themselves from Hector and what he might have done, the couple left the conference room without hesitation or argument. When the door clicked shut, she tightened her grip on the boy's arm. "Tell me, Hector."

A long silence followed, and Hector's breathing became so regular that at first glance he appeared asleep. "When we met in Culiacán," he said finally, "he said that he had some unfinished business here."

"Here? You mean in the United States, or specifically *here*, in Posadas."

"He did not say. But I think he went somewhere the next day."

"Do you mean Thursday? Or yesterday?"

He looked up, confused. "What is today?"

"Sunday."

"Then it was Friday. Yes, Friday. He helped me put fuel in the airplane when we were finished with it that night. The night of the flight." Hector snuffled what might have been a stifled laugh. "He thought it was funny, being able to take the airplane so easily—and then to be able to use the...tank? The gasoline tank at the school. After that, he spent the night in the home of the old man. I let him in."

"Did he use the old man's truck later on?"

"No. There was a motorbike in the shed behind the house. I never saw it, but he said it was there." His eyes flicked to one side as if to say, *I'm lying now.*

"Who said it was there?"

"My…my uncle. He said so. He explored the house after I let him in, and then he went outside, he said. Outside to look into the little barn. It is behind the house. I did not go with him. My uncle, he said he would use the motorcycle, if he could make it run."

"And did he?"

"I don't know." Again the sideways flick of the eyes intrigued Estelle. "He insisted that I go to school, each day—that I do not remain at home while he was there."

Estelle reached for her cell phone at the same moment that it buzzed, and the electronic noise was startling and harsh in the quiet room.

"Guzman."

"Estelle, we're seeing evidence that someone stayed in the house." Captain Eddie Mitchell's voice was clipped and businesslike. "Slept here, probably. Had a little bit to eat…looks like convenience store pizza and chocolate milk. Nothing else."

"Hector says that his uncle stayed there, Eddie. And he may have used a motorbike or motorcycle that's in the back shed. Will you check on that?"

"Been there, done that. It isn't there," Mitchell said. "Just some oil stains and tire marks on the dirt floor. The kid says the bike was still there last he remembers?"

"Yes. But he says that he never saw it." She watched Hector's face as she talked. It was hard to tell if he was listening, or if he had drifted off to sleep. "He doesn't know what condition it might be in. Or so he says."

"It probably runs just fine. You remember about Cody Roybal? The crash out at the old drive-in theater?"

"Ah," Estelle groaned. Mention of the bike hadn't stirred the memory immediately, but now the name brought the episode back to the surface. Cody Roybal had received the motocross bike from his grandfather, Reynaldo Estrada—perhaps for a birthday, maybe high school graduation. Estelle couldn't recall. But she did remember the tragedy at the theater, where Cody had been riding across the abandoned parking lot, lost control on one of the berms, and crashed.

The bike had slid harmlessly in the dust, barely scraping the paint, its knobby tires gouging the dirt. Cody had tumbled headfirst into the remains of one of the old drive-in's speaker posts, the helmet he should have been wearing left at home to protect the end post of his bed. That had been two years before. Old Man Estrada had kept his grandson's bike in the shed, unable to part with it.

"You there?" Mitchell asked as the silence grew.

"Yes." Her mind raced with the possibilities. "Tapia isn't going to Albuquerque," she said. "Not on a dirt bike." A myriad of doors opened, each one a new possibility. The motorcycle would open those doors for Tapia—and he had enjoyed three full days to find his way. "Who is with you, Eddie?"

"Abeyta and Taber."

"*Ay.*" She closed her eyes, running down the dwindling list of available deputies.

"State Police and the Forest Service are giving us all the help we need up on the mesa," Mitchell said. "I was going to send Taber back up that way for the time being. All the riders are on the course by now."

"We need a description of the motorcycle," Estelle said. "I'll get that from records."

"Lemme know," Mitchell said. "We've got some boot tracks here that might help. Tony and I will see what we can do with those."

She switched off. Hector slumped, head down so that his chin touched his chest.

"Why did he need a motorcycle, Hector?" Estelle asked. When he didn't respond, she rose, crossed around the table, and once more sat beside him. "The truck was licensed. No one would have noticed. Why the bike?" She gave him to the count of ten to answer, then said, "We can make all this go away, Hector. We really can."

Again, he remained silent.

"When did he contact you to actually make the flight, *hijo*? When did he actually set the date?"

Hector took a deep breath and sat up. "In April, I think it was early. He told me that he would visit this weekend. That is when I should secure the airplane."

"You mean he gave you specific dates for the flight?"

"He said that the opportunity should come during this week. That he would call with the specific time, if that was possible."

"What was so special about this week?"

"I don't know."

"And you made sure that it was possible when he called, didn't you?"

"Well, the airplane, *agente*—it was parked waiting. Any day was possible. I discovered that Señor Bergin had the meeting on his calendar, and I told my uncle. He agreed."

"For Tuesday night and Wednesday morning, then?"

"Yes. It happened that the weather was with us."

"And the route?"

"My uncle contacted me on the e-mail Sunday night. We made the final arrangements. I would fly to Culiacán on the night of Tuesday, late. Almost into the morning. If for some reason I could not, I should call him right away on the cell phone."

"The number," Estelle said, and slid the pad toward him.

"I do not know it now," he said. "It is on my computer at home. I can get it for you, of course."

"But you did not have to call, did you?"

"No. It was easy."

"How long is the flight to Culiacán, Hector?"

"Just three and a half hours. It could be done faster, but there was no need."

"Three and a half down, and three and a half back. You refueled at Culiacán?"

"Yes."

"Did your uncle arrange for that, too?"

"Yes."

"That's only eight hours at the most, *joven*. Mr. Turner says that the airplane was used for nearly eleven. Would you like to tell me about the other three hours?"

Hector shrugged in resignation. "That night…that night was not the first time I used the plane. I could not take that risk."

"Ah…you practiced."

The boy nodded. "On two occasions. It was easy."

Estelle shook her head in wonderment. "As long as you brought it back, no one would notice."

"That is true," Hector said, a trace of pride in his voice. "No one."

Chapter Twenty-three

Hector Ocate was too tired to appreciate that he was the sole occupant of the Posadas County Sheriff's Department detention facility—five small cells on the second floor. He practically dove onto the cot in the first cell. His eyes had been closed when he buried his face in the pillow, but when the door clanged shut, he rolled onto his side and his eyes flickered open, staring at the concrete block wall.

Estelle watched him for a moment, then turned away and walked back downstairs.

Dispatcher Gayle Torrez met her at the landing and handed the undersheriff a slip of paper. "That's the motorcycle," she said. Estelle glanced at the description of the late Cody Roybal's 2003 Yamaha dirt bike. Like a myriad of others, there was nothing unique about it—a bright red, high-fendered, knobby-tired machine designed for ramping up rough trails or sand dunes. "I put the information out."

"Thanks, Gayle. I don't think anybody is going to find Manolo Tapia motoring down the interstate," Estelle said. "But we never know. Maybe someone will notice a burly Mexican wearing a Rolex and Bermuda shorts riding a dirt bike." She could picture the bike headed south now, kicking up sand after vaulting the loose barbed-wire border fence, but she did not understand the point of that risk. Captain Naranjo was right—there was a good reason for not simply dumping the victims' bodies in the bleak Mexican desert. There was a reason for herding them north, other than the perverse joy taken in watching their excitement and hope evaporate in a moment of panic and desperation.

"I shooed the Uriostes home for a while," Gayle said. "I told them I didn't think there was much chance of Hector being released any time soon. I told them I'd call if there was anything they could do. They were going to talk to his parents in Mexico."

"There's no chance at all of him going anywhere," Estelle agreed. "We'll give him a couple of hours' sleep and then wake him up. Maybe he'll remember something that he wants to tell us."

"And the county manager is waiting in your office."

"Ah." It seemed like days or even weeks, rather than hours, since she had chatted comfortably with Leona Spears.

"And..." Gayle started to say, and hunched her shoulders as if in apology. "When the metro TV and newspaper folks call, I didn't mention that we have Hector in custody, or about the involvement of a local aircraft. Three dead illegals don't stir the scoop juices much anymore, it seems. It's right up there with a local mountain bike race in news ignored."

"Just as well," Estelle said. "But if we can avoid a circus for just a bit longer, that will help. No one asked about the airplane?"

"I told them that we're investigating the apparent theft of an airplane. The reaction is always the same—whoopee."

"Frank's on it?" The publisher of the *Posadas Register* would be sitting and sleeping with fingers and toes crossed, hoping that the story didn't break until his paper came out on Wednesday afternoon.

"Frank's luck is holding." Gayle laughed. "He wanted to know if he could take a picture of Hector, and I told him no—unless he happens to catch him when we ship him over to Judge Hobart's for arraignment tomorrow morning."

"*Happens to.*" Estelle smiled. "Be sure to tip him off," she added. "Sometimes we need Frank as much as he needs us."

Perhaps hearing their voices, Leona Spears appeared in the hallway outside Estelle's office. The large woman looked ready for the bush, with khaki trousers, dark green work shirt, and heavy hiking boots. Her long blonde hair was striking in a single, long Heidi braid reaching the small of her back.

"Perfect timing," Estelle said to the county manager.

"Oh," Leona said with a theatrical wave of the hand, "my goodness. For what? Are we making progress? You, my dear, look as if you've been up all night—which you have. I *don't* know how you do it."

"I've spoken with Captain Naranjo," Estelle said. "We know who the victims are now." The anticipation on the county manager's face couldn't have been more palpable, and she clasped her hands together under her impressive bosom as if preparing to sing an aria. Estelle said, "We think they're from El Salvador. One of them—the father, I think—was an accountant for an international construction company."

"Oh my," Leona said, her eyes narrowing slightly. "An accountant? There's lots of ways to go wrong there. But what's that have to do with us, for heaven's sakes. How are we so lucky?"

"I wish I knew," Estelle said. "Perhaps we're just a convenient dumping ground. That's happened before. And I don't know anything about the company, other than a name that Captain Naranjo supplied. I was going to ask you about them, but don't misunderstand. I don't know if they're somehow involved, or what. At this point it's just a name."

"What's the company? Do I know them?"

The question was more than idle curiosity. Leona's twenty-plus years with the New Mexico Highway Department, working in design and contracts, meant that she pretty much knew who was having tea with whom. There were few large construction projects in which the state agencies weren't involved somehow, however tangentially.

Estelle skimmed the notes she'd taken while talking to Naranjo. "Pemberton, Duquesnes and Cordova. And they're not Salvadoran…He says that the parent company is headquartered in New Zealand."

"Yes, they are," Leona said. "Multinational. Into *everything, everywhere*. Even once in a while on our shores. Anyone in the construction trades who isn't just a local contractor knows them, my dear," Leona said with satisfaction. "That's if we're talking the same PDC, and how many can there be? If you want a highway built or mine dug in the middle of the Congo or whatever that little country is called now, you arrange the bid so PDC wins it, believe you me. Or in El Salvador, for that matter. In fact," she warbled, "I know one instance where they built an *ice* road—can you imagine that? Up in Alaska by the Arctic Circle somewhere, for one of their subsidiaries. An ice road. Most remarkable."

"That's a long way from El Salvador or New Zealand."

The county manager held up an admonishing finger. "You just ask the former lieutenant governor about them, this PDC company. Remember our border fence highway…that grand master plan that never flew? Chet Hansen was stung by that particular bee."

"*You* worked on part of that, as I remember," Estelle observed. On paper at least, the idea of having a modern multilane highway paralleling the entire Mexican border, from the California coast to the southern tip of Texas, with a fancy and generally ugly security fence running the entire distance, had appealed to those folks who wanted a less porous border—and, Estelle supposed, to those folks who wanted to grow stinking rich on the construction of such a project.

One of many problems with the project was that the actual border—that thin black line on the map—passed through terrain that was hardly conducive to road building. Mountain removal was expensive. And perhaps that was the whole point, Estelle thought. *Expensive* put the money in the right pockets.

"Don't remind me that I wasted time on that project," Leona said. "But I'm sure that Mr. Iron Man wanted a share of those contracts as much as anyone else."

Estelle laughed. "*Mr. Iron Man.* I like that." If it could be biked, run, swum, or climbed for competition, Chet Hansen undertook the challenge.

"You should talk to him, if you catch him. He can tell you more, I'm sure." Chester Hansen, now two years out of office after a controversy-plagued brief stint as lieutenant governor, was the closest thing to a celebrity visiting Posadas for the race.

"That's interesting," Estelle said.

"The operative word," Leona said. "*Interesting*. I should look him up and talk to him myself," she added. "I don't know what he's doing now, other than racing, obviously. But whether our former lieutenant governor is in office or not, he's all in favor of hiring someone like PDC to complete the project in one mammoth push, someone with the contacts for this culvert and that bridge and this fence and that strip of pavement. And I think I agree with him."

"And put a bike path along the border at the same time," Estelle said. The former lieutenant governor's intense interest in all things physical had been in noted contrast with the habits of the governor himself, a dedicated couch potato.

"Well, you ask him about PDC—if you can catch up with him," Leona said. "There was a goodly contingent who thought the lieutenant governor was looking to line his own pockets with that highway deal. Even when he gave up his company to go into politics—not that *that* worked out very well, either."

"Of course they would think the worst," Estelle said. "That's the nature of things, not to trust politicians. And that's part of *our* problem. It's just that the politicians we may have to work with are Mexican, rather than our own." She turned at the approach of an older-model state pickup truck. Bill Gastner eased the vehicle into the Sheriff's Department parking lot and pulled into the spot reserved for the district judge. "I have to clear the cobwebs. Do you want to ride up on the mesa with me for a while?"

"Mercy, yes. I'd love that," Leona said. "I was hoping to catch a ride with someone." She held out her arms theatrically, modeling her clothing. "I'm ready for the wilds!"

"Let me talk to Bill for a minute. Maybe he'll come along."

The aging lawman wasn't in any hurry dismounting from his pickup, and he paused when he saw Estelle approaching.

"Hey," he greeted. "You had a long night?"

"Unending," Estelle said. She reached out and squeezed his arm. "I expected to see you out at the site."

They both knew what she meant, and Gastner shook his head. "Nah. You don't want more big feet walking over everything. And I sure as hell don't need any more of that." He straightened his shoulders and took a deep breath. "Quite a concert, by the way." He regarded Estelle speculatively. "Talk to the kid yet? You been home?"

"Oh, yes."

He grinned at her reticence. "Only seven years old, and it's starting," he said. "I noticed that Francisco was cozy with the Clarke girl—Rosy and Cameron's daughter?"

Estelle was impressed, as she frequently was, but not surprised by Bill Gastner's observations. 'That's about exactly right," she said. "For whatever teenaged reason, Miss Clarke has a grudge against Miss Mears. Maybe Melody is too cute, too talented, too much in love with the world to be sufficiently cool." Estelle shrugged. "Who knows why. Pitney tried to talk Francisco into some sort of musical practical joke at Melody's expense. *Mijo* didn't bite."

"I see," Gastner said. "What was the joke, do you know?"

"She asked Francisco to play the same selection that Melody was to play. Show her up, I suppose. Embarrass her."

"Jangle her confidence," Gastner added. "Gotta love 'em, these kids."

"Well, I was proud of Francisco. He was still up, sitting at the piano, when I got home. Still wound up like a little spring. Still composing in his head."

"So no one else got any sleep either." Gastner laughed.

"He wasn't playing. Just sitting and thinking, apparently." She tapped her own forehead. "It all goes on up here, anyway. Listen," she said, and took him by the elbow again with the urgent need to think about something else. "Ride up on the mesa with us?"

"Us? Brunhilde and you, you mean?" He waved at Leona, who waited by the sheriff's Expedition.

"I was thinking about going around on the back side, over by Jackman's Wells, to watch them come down off the top."

Gastner looked at his wristwatch critically. "I really should, but I really can't, sweetheart. I have an appointment with Herb

Torrance coming up here at one. If that doesn't take too long, maybe I'll swing up that way after a bit. You eaten anything yet today, by the way?"

"I think so."

Gastner barked a laugh. "We'll have to fix that."

"I'm not sure there's going to be time, sir. Let me tell you who we have in jail."

The older man leaned back against his truck, eyebrows arched in surprise. "I pick one night not to stay up all hours, and look what I miss," he said. "Who?"

She told him quickly about Hector Ocate, Manolo Tapia, and the night flight. Gastner listened without interruption. When she finished, he frowned at her.

"You and Bergin flew the same route in the middle of the night, just to see if it could be done?"

"Well…"

"Yes, *well*. And you guys landed out there on the unlighted strip?"

"Yes. But it wasn't just to see if it could be repeated."

"Remind me to talk some sense into you when we have a spare hour or two."

"It told us what we needed to know, sir."

"I'm sure. What's Bobby have to say about all this?"

"I didn't ask first, *padrino*. But as I said, it told us what we needed to know. In point of fact, it led us straight to Hector."

"And now you have some psycho riding around on a motorbike, who knows where, looking to do who knows what." He held up a hand. "Don't tell me—let me guess. Next *you're* going to borrow a dirt bike…"

"No, sir. Next I'm going to let my brain rest for a little while. Out in the boonies where the air is clear."

Gastner laughed again. "Last time you were out in the boonies, it seems to me you found a bunch of rotting bodies. But you suit yourself. I'd ride along, but Herb has fresh coffee and his wife said something about fresh pie." He held up both hands in surrender. "I can be bribed, you see. If you want to get together later, let me know." He opened the door of the truck. "If I get any brilliant ideas, I'll give you a buzz. Enjoy the Tour de Spandex with Brunhilde, there. You're braver'n me."

Her cell phone buzzed, and she pulled it off her belt.

"Guzman."

"They're all on the track," Sheriff Bob Torrez said without preamble or greeting. "Last rider went off a couple minutes ago. You do any good with the kid?"

"Some. I'm letting him sleep for a couple of hours. Leona and I are going up by Jackman's Wells for a little bit. Clear out the cobwebs. Mears is following up with the family. We sent the Uriostes home."

"Okay. You usin' my vehicle?"

"That's affirmative, unless you need it."

"I got my own. Keep the windows open so that woman doesn't stink up my truck." The phone went silent.

"You're up on the mesa now?" Estelle asked.

"Right about where that kid fell yesterday," Torrez said.

Yesterday. Yesterday seemed a month ago. "No other incidents yet?"

"Nope. Not yet." For an instant, the sheriff sounded almost wistful. "Pasquale went by a few minutes ago. He's pretty quick on that thing."

The sheriff was watching the riders from a spot less than an hour from the starting line. Ahead of them stretched five or six hours of tough, dangerous country.

"As soon as the last rider goes by, we're pullin' out of here," Torrez added. "I was going to wander on down to Fourteen, right about where they'll turn into Bender's Canyon. That ain't far from the airstrip, and I don't want a bunch of 'em settin' up a picnic there. I might take another look, see if we missed anything. Lemme know if you need something. Who's at the office?"

"Tom Mears will be there for a while."

"Okay. The county manager got any brilliant ideas?"

The question surprised Estelle, since Leona Spears was generally among the last people on Bob Torrez's mind. It had taken him months to grudgingly accept that perhaps the county manager actually knew what she was doing, but he was months away from including Leona in any inner circle.

"We'll see," she said. "She's familiar with PDC...That's something."

"Huh. Well, lemme know." The phone went dead as the sheriff switched off. Estelle had walked back to the truck, and Leona looked at her expectantly.

"Bill's not riding along?" she asked.

Estelle shook her head. "He's got work to do."

"You're sure you don't just want to go home and get some rest?"

The undersheriff laughed. "That's exactly what I want to do," she said.

Chapter Twenty-four

But instead of going home, Estelle sought the comfort of the high country north of Posadas, where Cat Mesa rose as a great, scarred buttress, its sawtooth rim running east–west for the better part of eleven miles. The mesa rim rose to nine thousand feet, and the sun-roasted scent of the earth and runty, parched vegetation would be a balm to tired nerves. Sharing the excitement of the bike race with her husband and the two little boys, who would screech like the jays when riders passed by, wasn't practical.

The race itself stood in the way. After the start at the Posadas Inn on south Grande Avenue, the course took the riders north on County Road 43, up the east mesa flank until the pavement turned to gravel and then to powdery dirt and rocks. Somewhere on the east side of the mesa, her husband would be watching with the boys, where the riders would be bunched together. To reach them, she would have to either trail the final riders, arriving at her family's vantage point when the race had passed by, or weave through race traffic with the large Expedition, more in the way than not.

The two boys didn't often have the opportunity to enjoy a full day with their father, and Estelle decided Francis might well make productive use of the occasion—especially with Francisco, now experiencing his own seven-year-old version of woman trouble.

The undersheriff drove west on the state highway, eight miles beyond the municipal airport to where a cluster of race officials' vehicles was parked at the intersection of the state highway and Forest Road 26. None of the riders had reached that checkpoint yet. When they finally hit the prairie after four or five hours on the mesa and in the backcountry, the remaining three hours into town would be a relief.

She slowed the Expedition to a stop as Howie Gutierrez, stopwatches hanging from his neck, rose from the tailgate of the pickup.

"Hey, sheriff," he greeted, and flashed a smile at Leona. "All the top brass out today, huh. What's goin' on down at the gas company? I heard they found some bodies out there?"

"Apparently so," Estelle said. Gutierrez worked as a salesman at Chavez Chevy-Olds, and once again, Estelle marveled at the efficiency of the grapevine. "How long will it be before we see the first rider down off the mesa?"

Gutierrez checked his board. "I would guess an hour, maybe? Once they're down here, it's pretty clear sailing. A spot or two on Fourteen headed south, but nothing like up there." He glanced "up there" almost with reverence. "You headed up?"

"I thought I would. Maybe as far as the Wells."

"Okay." He pushed himself away from the truck and put on his official face, looking at his watch at the same time. "I think you have just about enough time to get to the Wells before race traffic does. But keep an eye out. Remember they're going to be comin' down fast, and you'll be swimming upstream if you don't get out of the way."

"You bet. Thanks."

"Leona, you enjoy yourself," Gutierrez said, and Estelle wondered if the salesman was working on the county manager to replace her aging, colorful Volkswagen Vanagon with something that moved.

For the first mile, the forest road was smooth sand, but then the terrain angled up sharply. Leona grabbed for the panic handle as the Expedition lurched sharply, its fat tires walking over the rocky stairsteps that cut across the two-track.

"If you see any riders, let me know so we can pull off."

"But he said we had an hour."

"Unless a few of them are faster than everyone thinks."

Another two miles on, they reached Jackman's Wells, where not enough remained to qualify for ghost town status. A scatter of broken bricks, a few rusted pieces of metal roofing, a trash pile of busted bottles and corroded tin cans were all that marked Martin Jackman's dream of wealth and seclusion near the spot where a spring had once bubbled out of the mesa flank. As if in retaliation to Jackman's insulting clutter of trash, the spring had dried up. So had Martin Jackman's life as a prospector.

Any semblance of a road vanished as the trail headed up the mesa, switchbacking through the rocks.

Estelle reflected that, if there needed to be one at all, the bike race was the perfect use for this battered mesa. Every scar, every blemish became a potential and treasured racetrack feature for what Sheriff Bobby Torrez was fond of referring to as the "spandex crowd." It might be argued that, for a bunch of enthusiastic amateurs, the mesa portion of the race was far too difficult—too "technical," as Tom Pasquale was fond of saying. The terrain was rough, and there weren't enough spotters. The route was so rugged that even the motorcycle chase vehicles had to slow to an awkward pace no faster than a walk. But that was the lure of the challenge.

Estelle saw three other vehicles parked in various spots near the worn Forest Service sign that announced Jackman's Wells. One of the vehicles sported a race official's placard on the door. Half a dozen people stood near the trucks, two with clipboards and stopwatches.

She pulled the truck well away from the narrow two-track and backed it under a gnarled piñon. Movement up on the mesa face caught her eye.

"What am I seeing?" Leona asked, leaning forward as Estelle pointed.

"Just above the slag pile," Estelle said. "I saw a flash of color."

And sure enough, an instant later a lone cyclist appeared, his bike thrust forward with his weight over the back tire. He sailed down a particularly steep section of trail, deftly avoiding the strewn rocks and limb wood. A hundred yards behind him, three other riders formed a pack, locked in the chase.

"Well, we timed that just right, didn't we, dear?" Leona said. "I'm glad to be out of their way. And look at that. They started a minute apart, and still collect in bunches." She pulled out a glossy race program, ready to match numbers with names. "Who are you rooting for? Thomas?"

"That would be good," Estelle said. She leaned over and looked at the proffered roster. Thomas Pasquale carried number 58, just about halfway through the field. She'd seen the list before, recognizing only a handful of names. Number 8 had been reserved for Terry Gutierrez, the young rider from Socorro who had sailed off the cliff during a practice circuit. Terry's girlfriend, April Pritt, would have raced with number 121 on her back had the lacerated knee not ended her chances.

"Oh my," Leona said, beaming. "This is fun. What absolutely marvelous timing." Camera in one hand, race program in the other, she bundled out of the truck, then turned to rummage her floppy safari hat out of a voluminous handbag.

The cyclist, face gaunt with effort, shot by without a glance at them or a nod to the other spectators, despite their encouraging cheers.

"Number 18," Leona announced. "That's somebody something from Belen...I can't read this without my glasses." She extended the program toward Estelle, who waved it off good-naturedly. "Wow. That means that he's passed the first seventeen riders!" the county manager chortled as she watched the cyclist disappear into the trees.

Seconds later, the chasing pack shot by, and it became even more apparent that, with the race now three hours old, the starting order had little to do with placement. Number 6, a chubby young man in bright yellow with thighs so thunderous that they threatened the integrity of his spandex, led numbers 37 and 78, and Estelle was impressed that the third member of the trio sported silver gray hair sprouting out from under his blue plastic helmet.

"He started almost an hour and a half behind the leader," she said. "And still caught him."

Both Estelle and Leona leaned against the warm grill of the Expedition, and as the trio of bikers raced away down the mesa, the mountainside near Jackman's Wells grew silent, even the piñon jays puzzled mute. After a moment, she heard voices high above near the mesa rim, too far away to distinguish what was said. The metallic sounds of jounced bikes drifted through the trees.

Each time she saw a cyclist plunge into sight, Estelle held her breath, searching for the husky figure of Tom Pasquale, riding under number 58. She knew that expecting a top finish was wishful thinking. Tom was no pro rider. The young deputy had taken up bicycle riding less than two years before as a way to shed some weight and counter the cumulative effects of eight-hour shifts spent on his butt in a patrol car. A powerful young man, true enough. But the kind of endurance needed for this race was new to him, tempered by only a few practice sessions on the mesa when he could steal the time.

Forty-five minutes later, she watched with mounting apprehension as number 115, a girl with a bloody right elbow, trotted down the trail, her bike jangling along beside her. "Ouch," Leona remarked. "We should be seeing young Thomas pretty soon now."

"Long ago," Estelle said. The girl stopped by the small cluster of race officials and spectators. One of them took her bike to examine the front wheel while another tended to the elbow, and in that space of time, half a dozen more riders clattered down the trail, far off the pace and content to enjoy the bike ride.

"In a minute," Estelle said to Leona, and she walked over to the group, one of whom she recognized as Richard Overmeyer, the new principal at the middle school. He glanced up and greeted her.

"Sheriff," he said. "Amazing event, huh?"

"Yes it is. How many more to go?"

Overmeyer had a clipboard with roster, and it appeared that he had checked off the riders as they passed. He consulted his list. "We've seen about a third of 'em," he said. "Race radio says there's a big crowd just coming off the rim." He flashed a smile. "This is a tough course."

"How about number 58?"

"That's..." And he scanned the numbers. "Pasquale. One of you guys. He hasn't come through yet."

"Can you check up the hill?"

"Sure." He pulled the small race radio out of the pocket of his jacket. "Benny," he said, "status check."

"Go ahead," a disembodied voice replied.

"Number 58. That's five eight."

"Copy. Just a sec."

"If he abandoned up near the top, it'd be quicker just to hook a ride back down to town on the east side," Overmeyer said. "A lot of riders will do that. It's a nice ride up from the village, but once you go by the halfway mark, there ain't no easy return." He grinned. "Although I don't guess I need to tell *you* that. You guys know this mountain as well as anybody." He rested the clipboard on the hood of his pickup. "How's that boy of yours doing?"

"That's 58," Estelle said, and Overmeyer shook his head.

"No, I meant your little boy. What, he's in second grade now?"

"The boys are fine," Estelle said, wondering in what context news of her son, or sons, had reached the middle school already. "I think they're up the hill watching the race with their father."

"Dick, you there?" the voice asked.

"Go ahead."

"Fifty-eight went through check station three about fifty minutes ago, and through station four at eleven thirty-two." Estelle glanced at her own watch. At twenty-five minutes after noon, Tom Pasquale should have roared down the hill long ago, becoming a checkmark on the Jackman's Wells list just ten minutes or so after passing station four. Timers at that point were perched on the rim of the mesa, just before the road started its torturous route down the west mesa face.

She easily pictured half a hundred ways that the young man could have vaulted off into space somewhere, dashing his fancy plastic helmet against the rocks.

"Dick?" the voice asked.

"Go ahead."

"We just had the last rider check through on stage one," the voice said, referring to the first mesa check station where paved road turned to dirt. It had taken that competitor three hours just to pedal from downtown Posadas up the paved road to the turn-off, a distance of only twelve miles. "That's number 111, and he's abandoning. We'll clear out here in a bit. You counted 58 yet?"

"Not yet."

"They'll be along. We're hearing that a couple of 'em are working on flat tires. Just a sec."

They waited patiently, and then the disembodied voice said, "Yeah. Fifty-eight is headed down now. He and a couple others got tangled with some rocks and had to change a front tire. That ravine just below the rim is a real bitch."

"Ten-four."

Richard Overmeyer consulted his list again as a rider shot by. "About half of them are going to end up walking down," he said. "*That* will take some time." Estelle couldn't imagine Tom Pasquale walking. Crawling if he had to, but not walking.

Overmeyer read the touch of concern on Estelle's face correctly. "We got about eight guys riding down on sweep when it's all over," he said. "Nobody's going to be left up there."

"I'm sure not," Estelle said. She turned and looked up the mesa. "How far is it from checkpoint four to here?" Estelle asked.

Overmeyer didn't need to consult his race literature. "Six point two K," he said. "That's a little under four miles."

That was an easy hour's walk, absent broken bones.

"And I tell you, Sheriff, there aren't very many spots where we don't have somebody within eyeball distance. One or two spots, maybe. At the most. And we'd know if there's a problem. He'll get that tire sorted out. Probably half of 'em have flats before they're done."

Every time a rider went by—and in one instance, fourteen riders formed a cluster that hooted and laughed its way down the mesa, in no hurry to record a competitive time—Estelle searched the colorful jerseys for number 58.

"Does he have his phone with him?" Leona asked.

"I think so. But that's the last thing he needs." She envisioned Tom trying to talk on a cell phone while he negotiated the difficult trail. The undersheriff waited as one more group jangled by, this time five riders, all high-numbered late starters. In just a few minutes, the last competitor would have passed through the upper checkpoints.

Just as she spoke, three riders appeared, two close together and the familiar figure of Tom Pasquale fifty yards to the rear.

"Ah," Estelle breathed. Number 132, the last to start, was a rangy young man whose left arm was now bloody from shoulder to elbow. Jaw set in ferocious determination, he led number 109, former lieutenant governor Chet Hansen, by a bike length. Hansen, a small-framed man sporting a ponytail that was a recent addition after leaving the formality of state government, rode slack-jawed, his breath wheezing in high-pitched gasps. One knee was bloody.

As he passed, Tom Pasquale sat back, making use of the only smooth patch of ground, and lifted both arms in salute. He grinned, dropped his hands to the handlebars, and shrugged.

"Better than last," he shouted as he shot by.

"He'll surely gain ground down below," Leona said, taking video clips with her small camera as Pasquale vanished around the turn. Another noisy group appeared above them, and Estelle glanced at the time.

"If we wait about half an hour, we can slip out of here without running over anyone," she said.

"Well, don't rush on my account," Leona warbled. "This is heaven for me, believe me. Sunshine, excitement...I only wish I'd remembered to bring a nice bottle of wine, some cheese, and some crackers. Wouldn't that be elegant?"

"That's all I'd need," Estelle said. Now that the apprehension of waiting for Tom Pasquale had been released, the long hours settled heavily on her eyelids. The drive back to town, lulled by the sweet smells of the desert, was going to be a challenge.

Chapter Twenty-five

Now that Tom Pasquale and the other riders had survived the mesa, Estelle's mind drifted back to other, more pressing concerns. The Expedition thumped onto the pavement of the state highway, and the undersheriff turned away from the race, back toward the airport and the village of Posadas. From this point on, race competitors faced miles of undulating prairie—not much of a spectator sport.

"That's enough excitement for *one* day," Leona said almost wistfully. "I thought Thomas looked pleased with himself, don't you think?"

"Not too much blood yet." Estelle grinned. "He's been working hard on the organization for this race. I'm happy to see it working out. So far, so good, anyway."

"I think I got a good picture—and one of Mr. Hansen as well, looking exhausted." She stretched languidly. "I think I'll e-mail him a copy. He'll get a kick out of it."

"He probably would—just him and the bike and the rocks and the blood," Estelle said. "No politics out here."

"Well, he's not into politics much anymore. I think that when his brother died, he kinda shrank back a little. And I'm not surprised."

Estelle glanced over at Leona. "I didn't remember that's what happened."

"Sad, sad. You spend your life building roads, and then drive off a bad one."

"Really?" Estelle asked, but Leona needed little prompting.

"Apparently so. He and his wife." She frowned. "And *I* can't remember their names. Anyway, it was one of those little narrow roads down in Chiapas, with no guardrails." She sighed. "I never did hear the details, but it's sad nevertheless. They didn't even bring the bodies back. Terribly burned, I suppose."

"*Ay.* That's right. That rings a bell. I remember there being some talk about how odd it was that they settled for burial in Mexico."

"Well, dead is dead," Leona said almost cheerfully. "Just a nasty, nasty thing."

"That's the brother who took over Hansen's construction company while Chet was in office?"

"That's the one. After Donnie's—*that's* his name—after Donnie died, Chet got the company back, but that's a tough way to do it. I think the two boys were quite close. That's what I'd heard, anyway." She held up both hands in resignation. "But that's ancient history. So, are we headed home now?"

"I wish I knew," Estelle sighed. "I suppose so." She took a deep breath. "You know, this youngster puzzles me." She glanced across at Leona. "Hector, I mean. I don't understand him."

Leona frowned. "An impressionable young man, perhaps," she said. "Easily talked down the wrong path."

"He knows more than he's telling us. I'm sure of that. He brings this Manolo Tapia into the country without knowing a thing about the man's business? I don't think so. And then we discover that the man is actually his uncle. We don't know how much he confided in the boy, but we do know that Tapia stayed in the abandoned house next door to the Uriostes. Hector set him up with that little convenience. At any time, Hector could have tipped us off. Instead, this boy claims that he doesn't even know how long his uncle hid next door."

"There's some trust there, though," Leona said. "This ugly Tapia person trusted Hector enough that he must have figured the boy wouldn't turn him in."

"Sure there's trust. And that's the question. How much did Tapia keep Hector in the dark? Hector's story seems to be that Tapia *might* come back. That the boy *might* be needed for another round of air taxi service."

"And that door has been certainly and most definitely closed," Leona said. "Thank heavens for that. This Mr. Tapia may not even know about Hector's arrest yet."

"But he just as easily *could* know, if he's in the area. If he went up to Albuquerque as Hector suggests, then no, maybe not. It depends on how much of a spread the media gives it all when we finally open the door to reporters."

"Well," Leona said philosophically, "we can always hope that he *never* returns. And I can think of a very good reason why this man might not confide in the youngster, beyond the necessary basics. We're dealing with a mere child, after all. I mean really... he is, is he not?" Estelle didn't remind Leona that many of the world's most accomplished thugs had never turned eighteen years old, and Hector had passed that milestone.

"He flies a mean airplane, that's for sure," Leona continued. "But Hector is a child. And you know, look where he ended up. Hmm? Clever as a little rat, but look where he ends up. In the clink. So there you are. I can empathize. The less the boy knows, the safer for this Tapia fellow, nasty as he is." Leona's eyes widened. "And he's *not* in the clink. Not yet, anyway." She reached over and patted Estelle's shoulder maternally. "*I* think he's back in Mexico...for what it's worth. I think he accomplished his nasties, and now he's back home."

"His nasties," Estelle said, amused at Leona's quaint turn of speech. "They're certainly that. Unless we're very lucky, I think we can expect another trail of bodies showing up...somewhere, sometime. We're missing something. It's that simple. That's what I think."

They rode in silence as they approached the airport from the west. "Why would he *fly* into Posadas, and then depend on a motorcycle?" Estelle asked. "That doesn't make sense, except that it happened to be there. Hector knew about it, maybe even told his uncle beforehand that it was there. The little weasel might even have borrowed it for a joyride himself from time to time. But Tapia? Steal a car, yes. Rent a car, sure. *Borrow* a car. Why not? But a *motorcycle? A dirt bike?* What sense does that make? What's more obvious than a bright red dirt bike, ridden by a fat middle-aged man?"

"Oh," Leona corrected. "Burly. I don't see fat. And it's only obvious if the motorcycle *happens* to cross the path of someone who's looking for it, or someone who cares. But you'll piece it all together," Leona said. "I'm confident of that." She let out a sharp gasp and reached out a hand to the dashboard for support as Estelle braked hard. The undersheriff swung the Expedition off onto the shoulder, then cranked it around in a hard U-turn. As soon as the truck was squared away and accelerating hard, she reached for the mike.

"Estúpida, Estúpida," she said, and keyed the radio. "Three-oh-eight, three-ten."

For a moment the radio was silent, and then Sheriff Torrez's quiet voice responded. "Three-oh-eight."

"Ten-twenty?"

"At the airstrip, headin' north."

"Ten-four. I'm headed that way. Look, Chet Hansen is number 109. He just came off the mesa with Pasquale right behind him. They'll be on the prairie by now, headed south on fourteen."

"Okay."

"I think we need a close escort for Hansen."

"Ten-four. I'll be twenty-one." Torrez didn't elaborate, but in a moment Estelle's phone buzzed. With the county truck charging westbound at well over eighty miles an hour, she took her time finding and opening the gadget.

"Guzman."

"So what's going on?" Torrez asked. Estelle could hear his vehicle in the background.

"The three victims were involved somehow with Pemberton, Duquesne, and Cordova, Bobby. At least one of them worked for that firm. They were headed for Socorro—that's what Hector tells us. Coincidence or not, the lieutenant governor is from

Socorro. On top of that, Leona just reminded me that Chet Hansen's brother was killed in a car wreck last year in southern Mexico, along with his family. Hansen took his construction company back after that."

"Huh." The sheriff's grunt was noncommittal. "So what?"

"It's the only thing we have," Estelle said. "And this has been bothering me—why would Tapia want a *dirt bike* if he was headed to Albuquerque, like Hector claims he was? He wouldn't. He'd want the bike if he's going into the rough, if he's going out in the boonies. And that prompts coincidence-or-not number three. Why did he come to Posadas this particular week? He made that very clear, Hector says. This was the correct date. So what's going on this week? A cyclo-cross bike race. Our ex-lieutenant governor is in a well-publicized race right through the heart of our finest boonies. That's opportunity, Bobby."

"Yeah, well," Torrez said, and he still sounded dubious. "There's a hundred and thirty riders in the race, though. Might be a hundred and twenty-nine other targets. Might not be Hansen—if it's anyone."

"All I'm going on is the Mexican and PDC connection, Bobby. If you can look down the list of names and come up with someone else more likely, have at it." She glanced at Leona, who was scanning the list as she spoke. The county manager looked at her and shook her head.

"I don't recognize anyone else," Leona said.

"We're on the list right now," Estelle continued. "Look, suppose that for whatever reason, this assassin is after Chet Hansen...or someone else participating in this race. Think about it. The race is a well-publicized convenience for him...close to the border, lots of hubbub."

"And lots of opportunity," Torrez interjected. "If a rider is the target, he's got a nice big number pinned on him, front and back."

"Absolutely." She pulled into the passing lane to shoot past traffic. "But it's too rough up on the mesa, and there are too many witnesses. Not hard to hide, or ambush, but way too hard to make a getaway. He's too smart to let himself be trapped."

"Huh. Everybody's off the mountain?"

"Yes. Off and accounted for. At the same time, we don't have much coverage all the way down County Fourteen. That's thirty-one *miles* of opportunity, with plenty of escape routes. And in the country, a dirt bike is just the ticket. The terrain is open, and it's just minutes from the border."

The phone was silent. "Bobby, there's evidence Tapia stayed in the house next door to the Uriostes. That's saying he had some business here, *not* up north in Albuquerque. He might have told Hector that just as insurance—in case the boy was caught and decided to talk."

"Makes sense."

"Yes, it does. He didn't even need the boy to feed him information beforehand. Anyone with a computer can find race information online, starting in February, when they posted the route map and started registering riders. The story Hector tells us coincides with all of that. And anybody can get a race program online, with the riders' names and numbers. Like you said, a number front and back—that makes for a handy target."

"Shit," Torrez muttered. "He could just as well be after any name on that list. They're strangers, most of 'em."

"That's right. They are. I'm going by only one thing…. Make that two. Number one, Hansen has had dealings with PDC in the past. Number two, his brother died in Mexico in odd circumstances. His body wasn't even brought back to the States for burial. Why didn't Hansen insist on that? It just doesn't jibe. I might be wrong. But it makes sense to me."

"We got nothing to lose," Torrez said. "If it's a hunch, follow it up. If you're wrong, all we've done is waste a little gasoline."

"Look, I'm coming in from the north," Estelle said. "I'm probably closer to him than you are."

"I'm on my way." Torrez switched off, and Estelle dropped the phone on the seat beside her. She braked hard as they reached the check station. Six riders were guzzling fluids, and Estelle had time to see the expressions of surprise as the Expedition turned off the highway onto the dirt, red lights flashing, fishtailing as she applied power.

Leona murmured something and grabbed the panic handle.

"Keep a sharp eye," Estelle said. "We're going to be overtaking riders, and this road doesn't give us a whole lot of room."

"I'm watching when I don't have my eyes closed," Leona chirped.

For a mile, the county road ran arrow-straight, the prairie so dry that traffic had pounded the red soil into fluffy dust that billowed up behind the truck like a jet's vapor trail. Just beyond a windmill and a large stock corral, the route jogged left around the base of a low mesa, cutting through the jumble of rocks that over the eons had calved off the mesa rim.

Estelle slowed. She didn't want to roar up behind Pasquale and punt the deputy and his bike off into the piñons. At the same time, she saw that opportunity for ambush abounded, with harsh shadows making it hard to identify individual shapes under the trees or behind boulders. There would be a fair amount of traffic, but an ambush would take only seconds.

With the windows down despite the dust, she drove up and around the small mesa, then braked hard as they dipped across an arroyo, clawing and chewing rocks up the other side. A helpful sign, riddled with generations of bullet holes, announced: COUNTY ROAD MAINTENANCE ENDS, .5 MI.

"I have to ask," Leona said, hanging on tightly as they charged up and out of the arroyo. "Why ever not just come into the country like a normal tourist, this assassin person? Why all the risk with this night flying business?"

Estelle didn't answer for a moment, instead concentrating on avoiding a series of frame-bending ruts that yawned eighteen inches deep in the prairie. Once more on sharp rocks as the road took on a steep rise dead-on, she replied, "For one thing, border checks are tighter than they used to be. If a weapon turns up, he's dead meat. Anyway, we're *assuming* that he has business north of the border. Otherwise he *wouldn't* show up here. But it works for him. If he killed the PDC accountant and his family in Mexico, he runs the risk of having those authorities on his tail. This way, everything is in the United States. He finishes his business here, skips south, and he's home free."

"Ah. I'm not smart enough for this."

"And maybe just because it suited his sense of fun," Estelle added. "And it gives him a tie to Hector. Another bond. That might be of use later. Who knows, maybe he's *training* the little weasel."

"Oh, my goodness." Leona sighed. "We're talking about a different species here."

"I hadn't thought of it that way," the undersheriff said. "But you may be dead-on right."

Driving as quietly as a jouncing two-ton vehicle could manage on a dirt road, they crested the top of the rise. She had slowed to thirty miles an hour, with emergency lights off. As she drove and listened, Estelle tried to recall the intimate details of the country—how the road twisted, how the sweep of vegetation flowed up on the high ridges where the cattle rarely strayed.

For a hundred yards, they drove along a low ridge. They could see all the way south to the San Cristóbals, and to the north, Cat Mesa. The road then swept down in a graceful, fast curve to an abandoned windmill and the remains of a stock corral.

Twisting left, the county road left the meadow and skirted a conglomeration of old fence lines that converged from several directions. Turning to hard gravel and emerging limestone outcroppings, the route climbed back into the scrubby trees. The next two turns were so tight that Estelle slowed to a walk, keeping the Expedition away from the jutting rocks on the passenger side, and the growing drop-off on hers. She glanced at her watch. The cyclists would be flying on this section of the race, rougher for a four-wheeled vehicle than for a bike.

Out on top again, the road ran along the spine of the little wrinkle in the prairie and, craning her neck, Estelle could see back down to the windmill. For a hundred yards or so, they drove straight north, and then the road turned sharply to the left and downhill, switching back to slope down toward the next meadow. As she rounded the right corner, mindful of the drop-off once again on Leona's side, she caught sight of a figure wearing the colorful garb of the race. Not leaning against his bike, not sitting on a rock or a stump, Tom Pasquale was collapsed awkwardly in the dirt at the very edge of an arroyo, the drop-off directly behind him. His legs were buckled under him, his back leaning against the fresh dirt cut where a road grader's blade had trimmed the road two weeks before, cutting a ditch to the arroyo.

The county truck slid to a stop and it was only when Estelle opened the door that she saw Pasquale's right hand lift. He didn't look up, but his signal for her to stop was clear enough. For just an instant, he held his hand palm toward her; then the fingers curled, his index pointing up the hill behind him.

Estelle froze, eyes scanning the sparse and runty timber. After a few seconds, she leaned back into the truck. "Stay in the vehicle," she said as she tripped the shotgun release.

Chapter Twenty-six

As she slid down out of the truck, Estelle saw that Tom Pasquale was slumped sideways, supported by his left shoulder ground into the dirt. He tried to stretch out his right leg, but his left was crumpled under him. There was no sign of his bike. She wanted to sprint across to him, but at the same time couldn't shake the feeling that other eyes were watching.

She scanned the scrub undergrowth around them, trying to separate forms from shadows. Farther on, the county road curved out of the scrubby trees, sweeping back out into the open prairie to parallel the arroyo whose cut grew until it could engulf a full-sized truck and still leave room for thunderstorm runoff. It was the sort of jumbled terrain that offered a good vantage point to watch passing traffic from a dozen places.

Slipping her phone in her pocket and unsnapping her automatic, the undersheriff crossed the road and approached Pasquale. His eyes were now closed. At one point, she froze in her tracks as she heard the clanking of bicycle chains. Above them, three riders appeared, cycling along the ridge. She knelt beside Pasquale and saw that blood soaked his left hip, staining his spandex shorts to the knee. His left hand was pressed tightly into the pocket of his hip, just below the beltline.

"Damn, that hurts," he murmured. "The son of a bitch shot me." He opened his eyes and tried to lean to the right, looking down at himself. The motion drained his face to pasty gray.

"Let me see," Estelle said, and he let her lift his hand, grimacing as she did so.

"This is embarrassing," he whispered.

"Oh, *sí*," Estelle said. "I'm deeply embarrassed. You just sit still." The hole in the bright blue polyester of his shorts was tiny—it would have been unnoticeable had it not been marked by oozing blood. "Ooze is good," she said. "No gushers. This is it?"

"That's it," Pasquale said dubiously. The "it" was enough. There was no way to tell what damage the bullet had caused inside, but there were no spurting arteries. Shattered bone, most likely. It didn't take a howitzer to mangle a hip joint.

Sitting back on her haunches, she kept one hand on top of his, feeling the shaking in his body. With her free hand, she hit the auto-dial on her phone, and was relieved when Gayle Torrez answered promptly.

"Gayle, we need an ambulance on Fourteen, six miles south of Seventy-eight, just a half-mile beyond Torrance's abandoned windmill. And send backup."

"Hang on," the sheriff's wife said, and Estelle waited while the efficient dispatcher made sure the rescue unit was rolling before she asked more questions. "Okay. There's an emergency unit at the checkpoint on the state highway. They're on the way. What have you got?"

"I think Tapia shot Thomas," Estelle said. "It looks like the bullet is lodged in his left hip. That's all I know at the moment. I don't know where the shooter is."

Pasquale clamped his other hand over hers. "Hey, I *know* Tapia shot Thomas," he said. "And check behind us. Down in the arroyo. I think Hansen's dead."

Estelle stood up and in two steps could see down into the deep arroyo cut. Two bikes and one body lay on the rough arroyo bottom, bare rock where rains had washed away the loose sand and gravel.

"Can you hang on a minute?"

"Yes."

Estelle turned and beckoned to Leona. "Bring the kit that's in the back," she called. Making no move to plunge down into the arroyo, she scanned the terrain all the way to where the arroyo skirted the buttress of the hill to the east, and then to where the cut in the prairie circled around where they now stood, following the road.

"I saw Tapia swing at him first," Pasquale said. "I was just coming down the hill, around that corner back there, when I saw him swing. Hansen went off the bike, and Tapia was headed toward him when I tackled 'im. Maybe he didn't see me comin', maybe he just didn't care. I hit him pretty hard, and he went down. We went at it pretty hard. Damn, he was strong. I thought I had him, and I heard his ankle pop. That's when he got me off-balance, and I went off into the arroyo. That was that."

Pasquale heaved backward as a bolt of pain shot through him, then slowly relaxed. "Christ." He panted for a moment, and his grip on Estelle's hand was like a vise. "Didn't hurt at first. Fallin' in the arroyo knocked the wind out of me. And then he had the gun on me. He shot Hansen, then me. He tossed the bikes in the arroyo. To someone ridin' by, it'd be all cleaned up."

"Which way did he go then?"

"Up this road, behind us. I heard him start the bike. He went the same way you guys came down."

"We didn't pass him," Estelle said.

"Dozen routes he could have taken," Pasquale said. "There's that fork down by the other windmill; there's trails all over. He could see you coming and just pull off into the trees until you went by. One thing—he isn't going to ride hard. I think he's got a busted ankle." He grimaced and then tried a smile of satisfaction. "I hit him pretty hard. Knocked him right over the motorcycle. That had to hurt."

Far in the distance, the thin wail of a siren cut the air.

"Three-ten, three-oh-eight."

Estelle pulled the handheld out of its holster. "Three-ten."

"I'm about eight south. What's the deal?"

"Ten-fifty-five, Pasquale is down. Be advised that he thinks the suspect fled north. He didn't pass us, so he's either cut off on back trails or took shelter somewhere to let us pass. He's on the dirt bike, but I don't hear it, so he's not pushing it. And Tom says he may be hampered by an ankle injury."

"What about Hansen?"

"He's here in the arroyo. I'm headed that way now. Hang on."

"Ten-four. Lemme know ASAP."

"You gotta be kiddin'," Pasquale murmured as Leona knelt beside them.

"Hush," Estelle said. At the sight of the blood and torn shorts, Leona's heavy blond eyebrows furrowed into thunderclouds. In short order, she had a hefty pad of gauze, and deftly pressed it into place. "Can you move the hip?" the county manager asked Tom, and the young deputy made a face.

"Hurts too much to try," he said.

"Do you think it's broken?"

"Don't know. I think so."

"Can you feel your toes?"

"Sure."

"Well, then, that's good."

"Can you stay with him for a few minutes?" Estelle asked, and Leona nodded.

"Surely."

"I'm going to check down in the arroyo," she said. "The ambulance will be here in just a few minutes." As she stood, the bike racers appeared, clattering around the switchback. She stood up and as they began to slow, waved them to a stop.

"Did any of you see a man on a dirt bike?" she asked. "Headed northbound? A red bike. Older guy."

All three shook their heads in unison, eyes glued to the fallen Tom Pasquale. "Is he going to be all right?" one of them asked.

"We're fine," Estelle said, motioning for them to pass by. "An ambulance is on the way. Be careful and stay on the road."

In a moment, the riders disappeared, taking advantage of the relative smoothness of the open meadow down below.

Even a single stride from the arroyo edge, the sides were so sheer that Estelle could not see the bottom. Careful to avoid the scuff marks in the dirt, she stepped past Pasquale and Leona and carefully approached the edge. Ten feet deep at that point and twice that wide, the arroyo had started from the smallest head-cut up on the flank of the hill, and only a single storm would have been necessary to wash out the soft earth.

Chet Hansen lay in the arroyo bottom, flat on his back, staring sightlessly up into the blank blue sky. He still wore his helmet, but the wreckage of his lower face canceled out any expression. His fancy bike, apparently undamaged, lay in the arroyo bottom a few feet beyond, invisible from the road. Tom's machine had been hurled a dozen yards upstream.

Without taking another step, Estelle turned in place, and a dozen paces to her right saw a hefty piece of piñon limb wood, about a foot longer than a baseball bat and uniformly steel gray. Swung hard at a bike rider, it would have been lethal.

The undersheriff walked along the arroyo's edge until she found a spot where she could slide down, then walked back along the bottom. Reaching Hansen, she knelt and placed a finger on the side of his neck. As she did so, she noticed the single hole just above the bridge of the victim's nose. The strike with the limb wood had caught Hansen flush in the mouth, shattering teeth and jaw. The blow would have been so incapacitating that he would never have seen the final bullet coming.

She keyed the phone again, and waited for three rings until Gayle could answer.

"Gayle, we'll need the ME out here," she said. "And I need anyone else you can spare."

"Okay. Stand by."

"Affirmative." But standing by was the last thing she wanted to do. Tapia was cunning. She granted him that much. That Pasquale had taken a bullet in the hip was no accident. Tapia knew that a wounded Pasquale required more manpower than a dead man. One shot, just enough to put the young man out of commission, and requiring another person or two to care for him.

Estelle stood up, turning in place. And where had Manolo Tapia gone? Bob Torrez was northbound on the county road, but Tapia could have seen his vehicle approaching and hidden with ease. She had been southbound. Tapia had avoided them. But to what end? The Mexican border lay twenty-five miles south. Any of a dozen routes would take him there, but no matter which way he went, pavement or dirt, there were only two gateways through the San Cristóbal Mountains to Mexico—one over Regál Pass directly south of her current location, or through the flimsy, barbed-wire border fence at María, on the east side of the county. They could slam those two doors shut easily enough.

How much did Tapia know? Estelle squatted silently by Hansen's lifeless body. "What did you do?" she whispered. There had been a violent settling of accounts here. In a terrifying instant, Hansen might have recognized Tapia—maybe not. He would have seen the cudgel hefted and swung so swiftly that ducking away was impossible.

Had Tom Pasquale not seen the incident, Hansen's corpse might have lain in the arroyo for hours, perhaps even days. Tapia was an opportunist, but as cunning as he might be, what did he know about Hector Ocate, the boy in custody? Would Tapia head back to the village? Back to old man Estrada's house? Was he assuming that the boy would fly him to Mexico?

Estelle's pulse hammered in her ears. For days, they had assumed that the killer was putting miles behind him, that the trail was growing colder by the hour. And now those days and miles had been reduced to a scant handful of minutes. She found herself holding her breath, listening for the high-pitched snarl of a dirt bike.

Chapter Twenty-seven

It began to feel as if everyone else was trudging slowly toward her position. She was trapped in this patch of sunshine while Manolo Tapia motored blithely away. For the first time since the discovery of the three shooting victims, the killer had proved that he was still in Posadas County—and just as obviously, Estelle knew that in minutes, their small advantage could evaporate.

Not about to leave the injured Pasquale, nor willing to abandon the crime scene, Estelle chafed at the delay—and knew that was exactly what the killer wanted. She had retrieved a blue tarp from the Expedition and covered Hansen's corpse, then unreeled a length of yellow tape to protect the area along the roadway—not that there was much to see, other than gravel and a few crunched grass clumps.

Tom Pasquale had not moved, marking the minutes with his eyes shut while Leona murmured comfort, unable to do anything else but keep him in the shade. The county manager had taken a quick look down into the arroyo herself, turned pale, and concentrated on Pasquale.

All the while, Estelle tried to imagine Tapia's progress. Her guess was that the killer would ride carefully, perhaps even slowly. If Tapia had an injured ankle, as Pasquale thought was the case, that would take some of the starch out of his effort. But even fifteen minutes' head start would change the game.

"He was on the bike when you charged him?" Estelle asked.

"Just going to it," Pasquale said. "I saw him hit Hansen when I was fifty yards away, maybe more. I shouted, but he ignored me. Tapia did, I mean. Then Hansen crashed right by the lip of the arroyo, and Tapia just sort of kicked him in. Just that fast," Tom whispered. "I bailed into him, and down he went. I didn't see the gun right away, or I might have given...I might have given the situation more thought."

"He could head for the border now," Leona said. "Taking any number of routes."

"He's not going to make it across," Estelle said. "You're okay?"

"No," Tom Pasquale said. "But that ain't going to change."

"I need to look at the map," Estelle said. "I'll be right back." She jogged to the truck and dug a county map out of her briefcase, folded it so that their patch of prairie was in the center, and returned to the arroyo edge. She knelt and flattened the map on her thigh.

"He could have cut off to the east," Leona said. She sat beside the injured Pasquale, a protective hand on his shoulder. "There are two-tracks and ranch trails all over out here."

"And most of them not on the map," Estelle said. Tapia could wind across the prairies, dodging this way and that, always out of sight of the main routes, always able to keep an eye out for dust trails thrown up by chasing vehicles.

"We need a chopper," Estelle said, and a moment later had Gayle Torrez on the phone. "If a State Police unit isn't available," she said, "see if you can find someone else. Even Channel Eight is better than nothing."

"They'd like that," Gayle said. "I'll see what I can do. How's Thomas holding out?"

"He's tough," Estelle said. "I think he'll be all right."

"Linda's here," Gayle said. "She wants to know if she can head out there."

"*Ay,* "Estelle said, and glanced at Pasquale. He and Linda had lived together for nearly three years. "Tell her no. We need her camera out here, but if she comes out, she'll miss him. He'll be inbound in the ambulance here in just a minute. Have her meet him at the hospital. And will you reach Lieutenant Adams and ask if we can have some help from his mobile unit? We don't know what Tapia's intentions are at this point, or if he knows about Hector. Make sure you have a couple of people there with you." When Gayle was hesitant in acknowledging, Estelle added, "I'm serious. Right now, Hector is the only witness to what happened out at the airstrip."

"Eddie was here just a minute ago," Gayle said. "We'll be fine."

"No, not *was*, Gayle. I want him in the building with you *right now*," Estelle insisted. "And whoever is free needs to stay central. Let's keep our eyes open."

Gayle acknowledged, sounding as serene as ever.

"And here we wait," Leona said; putting her finger on the pulse of things with her usual unerring accuracy. As crime scenes went, this one was pretty simple. But some dark corner of Chester Hansen's life had been ripped open, and the repercussions no doubt would reach far beyond this spot. The investigation would have to be meticulous and thorough.

Estelle felt a chill thinking about Tapia. *Calculating* was an understatement. Wounding the deputy was a perfect touch, effectively hog-tying their pursuit efforts until the wounded were cared for. Everyone else, all of their other personnel, were splattered about the county, watching bike riders sweat themselves pounds lighter, closing sections of highway and intersections as the riders approached.

Estelle looked up from the map. Pasquale opened his eyes and grimaced at her, disgusted by his incapacity.

"Tell me again what happened," Estelle said, more to keep him occupied than anything else.

The young man tried to shift position and groaned miserably. "I came around the curve just in time to see this guy swing a chunk of wood and catch Hansen right in the face." He closed his eyes again, trying to stretch a little. "That old guy can really move on a bike, and he was goin' so fast down this hill that there was no way he could avoid it. He went off the bike hard. Wobbled and swerved first, but then he went off right up here."

He pointed behind them, toward the road. "I'm comin' down the road toward 'em, and I see the guy kick Hansen's bike into the arroyo, then he starts to drag the guy over here."

"Toward the arroyo?"

"Yes. I thought first that it was some guy who had passed us earlier, or something like that. Someone with a beef with Hansen. It didn't even snap that it could be the guy we're looking for." He stretched again, trying to find some relief, and hissed through his teeth.

"Bike riders normally don't take off after each other with baseball bats, do they?" Leona asked.

"You never know," Pasquale said, attempting a grin. "I just rode straight at him, and we went down in a tangle. Shit." He stopped, shaking his head. "That guy is *strong*, Estelle. I got to him a little, though. He's got a hurt ankle. I heard it pop. Then he threw me and next thing I know *I'm* in the arroyo. That's when he pulls the gun."

"He hadn't shot Hansen yet? Not when you tackled him?"

"No. He points the gun at me and says, 'This is none of your affair.' And then he shoots me in the hip. Real careful and calculated. Then he takes his time and shoots Hansen in the face, just like that. The old guy didn't even move or nothin'. I think he was out cold already…Maybe he was already dead. Then Tapia pointed the gun back at me and I thought, *Now, this is it.* But he just says, 'You stay right there,' and then he's gone. A second or two later, my bike comes flyin' into the arroyo. Then I hear his motorcycle start, and he rides off that way." Pasquale pointed back to the north. "And that's it." He sat up a little straighter.

"It was a semi-auto, Estelle," the deputy said. "I think it was a Beretta, with a suppressor. Casings are off to the left, there. I figured that my hip was going to start hurtin' pretty bad, so I concentrated on climbing out." He pointed upstream a bit, where the edge of the arroyo was caved in, providing a ramp out. "I pulled myself out, and that's as far as I got when you showed up."

"You did good," Estelle said. "How many minutes' head start does he have?"

"Maybe ten by now. Maybe fifteen."

"Company," Leona said.

A clump of five cyclists was speeding down the hill toward them, kicking up dust. Since the riders couldn't see down to the carnage in the bottom of the arroyo, they had no reason to do more than glance at Estelle, who rose and walked back to the truck where she leaned against the front fender as if this remote spot was somehow the choicest race seat in the house.

After another couple of minutes, Estelle heard a vehicle and turned to see Bob Torrez's aging pickup truck vault over a rise, almost putting daylight under its wheels. To the north, the thin wail of the ambulance siren grew louder.

Estelle met the sheriff as his truck slid to a stop on the road. "Hansen," she said urgently. "He's dead. Tommy's okay, but took a 9mm through the hip. He can't walk. I think Tapia is headed back toward Posadas. Tom said he took off back to the north."

Torrez jammed the gear lever into neutral, set the parking brake, and got out. He strode to the arroyo, glanced at the footing, and then slid down the bank a dozen feet west of Hansen's corpse. Flipping the corner of the tarp to one side, he looked impassively at the dead man. After a moment, he dropped the cover and climbed back out of the arroyo. He looked down at Pasquale.

"You makin' it?"

"I'll be okay. I mean, maybe I'll be okay."

"Did you see this happen?"

"Yes, sir."

"It was Tapia?"

"Yes, sir. He matches that picture you circulated to all of us."

Torrez looked back up the dirt road. "He was waitin' for him here, or what?"

"Yes, sir. I was far enough behind that I didn't see where he actually was standing before he swung. When I first saw him, he was already out by the road. But I *saw* him swing, just like a big baseball bat. He stepped out into the road real quick, and just like that. *Wham.* Right in the face. He threw the stick over there," and he pointed upstream. "I can see it from here."

"Huh. How long ago did this happen?"

Pasquale moved his hand with great care, and looked at his watch. "It's goin' on about fifteen minutes now."

Torrez looked quickly at Estelle. "He didn't pass you on your way in?"

"No one's passed us," Estelle said. "Not on the road."

"He must have seen you comin'," Torrez said. "That's if he stayed on the road. Enough trails around. And he sure as hell didn't pass *me*. You sure he went back north?"

"Yes, sir," Pasquale said.

"Huh. Mexico's the other way," Torrez said. "So where's he goin'?"

"He may know that Hector is in custody," Estelle said. "It would be important to spring him out. Or shut him up."

The sheriff looked sharply at her. "Who's central?"

"Eddie's at the Public Safety Building. I told Gayle to round up some others."

"Okay. I'm going to head that way, then. Who else you got comin' out here?"

"I've asked for Adam's team, and a chopper."

"Fair enough." He rose and started back toward his vehicle without further comment. He stopped with a hand on the door handle, turning back toward them. "I'm goin' straight back in. The kid is the only link we have to all this shit, and there's no way we want anything to happen to him. You're all right with that?"

Estelle nodded. The ambulance siren wailed louder. "As soon as Tomás is headed in, and we have some coverage here," she said.

Torrez nodded and swung up into his truck. "I'll make sure the border is buttoned up," he said. "Keep in touch."

The approaching siren was not the ambulance, but a State Police cruiser, and Torrez swerved his truck off the road without slowing, passing the cruiser and then the ambulance that lumbered behind.

"Well, thank heavens," Leona breathed.

"Do you want to head back into town with them?" Estelle asked. "You picked a great day for a ride-along."

Leona shook her head emphatically. "My goodness no," she said and managed a brave smile. "I'm having all kinds of constructive budgetary thoughts. I find myself wishing that some of the county commissioners were with us now. What's our next step?"

"The village is covered. We've got coverage here, and Tom will be in good hands. Now we can go hunting."

Chapter Twenty-eight

"The lieutenant said whatever you need," the young state officer called from his black and white. He didn't step off the roadway, and turned to flag the approaching ambulance to a stop. "Where do we want things?"

Short of a sky-hook, there was no way to remove the wounded Pasquale without causing him great distress, or without further disturbing evidence, but that was the trade-off. Chester Hansen's body would remain in place awhile longer, until the scene had been thoroughly documented.

In a few moments, the two EMTs had the deputy bandaged and then secured, white-faced and panting with pain, on the gurney. In another minute, Matty Finnegan had the IV running, and before long the big diesel ambulance pulled away, heading back north.

"The CSI team will be out here in a few minutes, Rick," Estelle said to the state policeman, Richard Black.

"A few *long* minutes," he replied. "I heard them saying that the van was over in Hocico. They had a multiple drowning somehow in one of the irrigation ditches." Estelle shot a glance at the officer. "I don't know," Black added. "That's what they were saying."

"They'll be here when they're here," Estelle said.

"What happened, do we know?"

"Tom came upon the killer just as Tapia knocked Chester Hansen off his bike. When Tom tried to apprehend him, they scuffled, and Tapia managed to shoot Tomás in the hip. He cleaned things up by dumping everybody and everything in the arroyo, out of sight of the road, and made sure Hansen was dead by shooting him in the head. We think that Tapia is on a motorcycle, and he may be hurt. We don't know more than that. He headed out north, and that's where I'm going right now."

She put a hand on Black's shoulder and turned him while she pointed. "The scuffle happened right over there, where you can see that trampled greasewood? That whole area. Tomás was thrown into the arroyo, and that's where he was shot. Tapia was standing on the arroyo edge when he shot them both. We need those two empty casings from his gun, so be careful where you step. We think it was a 9mm, so the brass is easy to miss in this grass. While you're waiting, you can scour the area carefully and find those. Just mark them with evidence flags. Don't pick them up. Okay?"

"Got it."

"Linda Real will be out here after a bit for pictures, so give her any hand she needs. I'm going to snap a quick couple before I go."

The trooper nodded. "Her and Pasquale are livin' together, aren't they?"

"They are. She's apt to be distraught, so be helpful. She's going to want to get back into town as quickly as she can."

"Sure."

"The ME will be out as soon as *he* can, but we're really short-handed today."

"You ain't just a-kiddin'," Black said.

"What can I do?" Leona asked.

"I wish I knew," Estelle replied. "Feed me good ideas." She made her way to her vehicle, and with camera in hand returned to the edge. As she was taking the third photo, she saw the wink of sun on brass. The casing nestled in a clump of bunchgrass. "We need a flag on this one," she called, and waited until the trooper had placed the thin wire securely in the dirt. "The other one won't be too far."

When she was finished, she returned to the Expedition to find Leona mulling over the county map.

"Look at this," the county manager said. "If I wanted a discrete route back into Posadas from here, this is how *I'd* go." She traced the route with a pencil, not touching the point to the paper. "Back up this road about a mile, and there are all these spiderwebs." She indicated dotted lines that represented nothing even as grand as an established two-track. "One of them wanders over toward the Salinas arroyo, another to the windmill on the back side of Cooper's ranch, and then…" She paused and leaned forward, pushing her dark glasses up into her hair.

"Remember that grand plan a number of years ago for that housing development south of the airport? If my memory serves me correctly, Hardy Aimes almost talked the county commission into that one. Close enough that he graded a whole bunch of access roads and lanes and such. This whole block here."

As Estelle leaned forward to examine the map, Leona added, "The point is, with a copy of the county map from the Chamber of Commerce, or off the Web, or a dozen other places, we can go where we want." She dragged a finger across the paper. "He can wend his way back to State Seventy-eight, where one of the development 'roads' comes out across from the airport, or he can meander south and east and eventually, he'll come out on North Flat Street, right behind the high school. Voilà."

"And with the race going on, no one is going to see him," Estelle said. "He'll be mistaken for one of the support team." She nodded. "Maybe so." She walked around the front of her truck. "Rick, keep your eyes open," she said. "If you see a stocky Mexican guy with a broken ankle riding a bright red Yamaha dirt bike with no plates, your excitement is about to begin."

"I got the picture of him off the computer," the trooper said. "But it don't make sense that he'd come back here."

"We hope not," Estelle replied. "Keep the bikers on the road and moving. Don't let anybody congregate here. We've lost enough evidence already." She started the truck and backed carefully away, turning around on the road. As they wound back up the hill, she kept the pace steady, mindful of the sporadic appearance of bike competitors and occasional official race vehicles.

Just beyond one of the dilapidated windmills that dotted this portion of the county, Leona leaned forward, pointing.

"That's it," she said. The turnoff could have been mistaken for an attempt by a sun-struck road grader operator to cut a bar ditch. Estelle stopped the truck and got out, scanning the ground. It would be impossible to hide a motorcycle's tracks in the red earth, even through the gravelly sections. One recent set of vehicle tracks cut a crescent across the trail where someone had pulled over, perhaps to let cyclists pass. And off to the side, cut deeply in the soft soil, was a clear track showing the imprint of both front and back tires, and then doubled as if either there were two motorcycles or someone had driven in here and then retraced the route back out to the county road.

Estelle walked two dozen paces away from the truck, until the scrub growth closed in on either side of the path. The tracks showed that the motorcycle had veered in here and then, forced to a halt by the narrowing window of vegetation, had turned around. For a moment, the undersheriff stood and gazed at the tire prints. They could have been cut ten minutes before or a month ago. In this protected spot, with no rain or snow since January, the tracks might as well be petrified.

A series of shoe prints were indistinct beside the tire tracks, and Estelle could imagine Tapia, grimacing with the pain, putting down his good leg to support the bike as he horsed it around on the narrow trail. She knelt and took a quick set of digital pictures, forcing herself to take her time, then returned to the truck feeling an odd combination of relief and regret. Now that she knew something of his route, Estelle wanted nothing more than to charge after an escaping Manolo Tapia, running him to ground. But the big county vehicle was no match for a nimble motorcycle, whether the rider had an injured ankle or not.

"Next plan," she said. "Someone on a bike went in a ways, then turned around."

Leona was undeterred. "Now, Bobby is the inveterate hunter," the county manager said. "I'm surprised he isn't dashing about through the brush in hot pursuit."

That image brought a smile from Estelle, since Bobby never "dashed" anywhere. "He's thinking Posadas," she said. "For all he cares, Tapia can bake out in the sun all day. He wants to be sure that Hector Ocate stays put and safe."

"Not to mention that his Gayle is back in town and would be in some jeopardy," Leona added.

"There is that."

"Now, your man made the same mistake I did," Leona replied. "I don't think this is the right turnoff." Waving ahead, she added, "Just a bit farther."

A bit farther was an obvious two-track, and as soon as she turned off the main road, Estelle recognized the route. She didn't spend a lot of time touring the back byways of Posadas County, but she knew this particular path, knew that it ran almost due east. Clearly, the tire prints showed that the motorcyclist knew that, too. The tracks swung off the county road in a smooth arc, no hesitation, no slowing. The undersheriff turned into the narrow lane and stopped.

"He came back out," Leona said, seeing the double tracks.

"Or there was more than one," Estelle said. "Or Tapia was out here yesterday or the day before, practicing his setup."

"I hadn't thought of that possibility—a man *practicing*. That makes sense. Risky, though. Surely he would want to be careful not to be seen."

"Who's going to take a second look at a man on a motorcycle?" Estelle asked. "Especially this weekend. Illegals don't jump the border on dirt bikes. Ranchers use them and four-wheels all the time. So do hunters. And kids."

"But a stolen, unlicensed vehicle…" Leona persisted.

"Number one, we didn't know it was stolen until just hours ago. Number two, Tapia might not know that we *do* know… now. And as long as he doesn't cruise the streets and state highways, the odds of us seeing him are slim to none. Under normal circumstances, if an officer were to see him out here in the boonies, odds are good he would never be stopped."

Estelle eased the county truck along the rough trail, trying to avoid driving on the motorcycle tracks whenever she could. They had traveled less than a hundred yards when her phone buzzed in her pocket.

"Guzman."

"Estelle," Gayle Torrez said, "Channel Eight is offering their chopper. They're over in the motel parking lot right now."

"Accepted," Estelle said instantly, fully aware of the risks of involving civilians in an emergency operation. "We're just east of County Road Fourteen. Tell them to pick me up at Cooper's windmill. There's a good wide meadow there. They'll see my vehicle. I'll park at the base of the windmill, out of their way."

"You got it. Jessica Duarte and her cameraman are here in the office right now. I'll give them a map for the pilot. She says they can be in the air in about five minutes. That's maybe ten out to you at the most."

"We'll be there," Estelle said. Cooper's windmill, two miles east of their current position, hadn't pumped water in ten years, since the day that Jim Cooper had climbed up the wooden tower to service the transmission. He had ignored the modest dark clouds so far away that the thunder was just a faint rumble. The lightning bolt flicked out and swatted the rancher. He fell, probably already dead, his skull hitting the water tank so hard that the dent was still visible in the steel rim. When Estelle had responded to the incident, the sky was a blank blue, innocent of any wrongdoing, the homicidal clouds having retreated beyond the San Cristóbals.

For much of the distance to the windmill, the road was no more than a scuff on the rough table of prairie. Here and there, Estelle could see the motorcycle tracks. On a few low humps, the sort of things that would have vaulted a bike into the air had the rider been a rambunctious youngster enjoying his freedom, the tracks showed this biker had stayed firmly, and patiently, on the ground.

As they approached the windmill, Estelle saw that the lop-sided fan had frozen in place. Enough remained of the tail, with the faded Aeromotor logo still visible, that the mill head drifted this way and that, ruined fan facing into the breeze.

The stock tank below the windmill was empty, one side caved in by the back bumper of a careless woodcutter's pickup. Bullet holes dappled the metal. Estelle slowed the truck to a crawl, scanning the area around the mill. After passing the stock tank, the lane turned and circled left, up a gradual rise to the north. She picked up her binoculars as she braked to a halt. Focusing carefully, she examined the road ahead.

"Nothing," she said. The road up the grade was facing them, in bright sunshine. She should have been able to see the tracks left by a passing motorcycle as Tapia accelerated up the hill, away from the meadow and the windmill.

"Is that..." Leona started to say, pointing toward the tank. Where it wasn't crushed inward, the steel tank rim was four feet high. It now cast a hard, sharp-edged shadow on the prairie on the east side—a shadow that humped outward at one point into an amorphous shape. Estelle trained the binoculars and immediately saw what appeared to be the back wheel of a motorcycle.

Chapter Twenty-nine

The stock tank was a hundred yards ahead, and Estelle hesitated. Manolo Tapia was a cunning man. Where he might be, or what he might intend, was anyone's guess. It made sense to flee to the border, or perhaps to the relative anonymity of a major city, like El Paso to the east or Tucson to the west. The border was close, within striking distance via back roads. In many spots, the border fence was nothing more than a few strands of barbed wire, sometimes not even that much. The large metro areas presented an immediate risk for a fugitive, reached by traveling on the interstates, where he would be exposed to sharp eyes.

Tapia had killed in the most calculating, cold-blooded fashion—it appeared that both the Salvadorans and Chester Hansen had gone from exhilaration to death in an instant, with no time to plead for their lives. Then, Tom Pasquale had been neutralized as efficiently as circumstances permitted—that Tapia hadn't killed the young deputy when he had the chance was a surprise.

Estelle lifted her foot off the brake and let the Expedition creep forward a few yards. If what appeared to be a motorcycle belonged to Manolo Tapia, there could be any number of reasons why he might have abandoned it—mechanical breakdown, flat tire, even lack of fuel. If that was the case, the injured man was on foot somewhere—or resting on the far side of the tank in a patch of shade. And he had to know that they were there. The undersheriff picked up her binoculars again and methodically began a scan of the runty vegetation—mostly low juniper, greasewood, and black sage.

Twisting around in her seat to her left, Estelle searched the trees across the meadow. Shadows moved a hundred yards away and materialized into three mule deer, curious about the intrusion. They looked placidly at her, but their attention was drawn nowhere else. Wherever Tapia was, he hadn't spooked the wildlife.

"I don't see anything," Leona said, then just as quickly added, "Oh, yes, I do."

At the same time that she turned back toward the county manager, Estelle felt the truck jolt. Leona recoiled back in her seat as Manolo Tapia's face appeared in her open window. A black semiautomatic rested on the windowsill, the blunt muzzle of its silencer pointed unwaveringly at Leona's throat. His left elbow was thrust into the truck, tight against the window post, almost close enough to elbow Leona in the face. He stood on the running board, bracing a leg against the vehicle.

"Now," he said, breathing hard, "we must think very carefully." The gun didn't waver away from Leona, but his gaze was locked on Estelle.

She sat quietly, right foot on the brake, the truck in gear and idling. Her right hand was full of binoculars, her left hand on the steering wheel. In a heartbeat, she could stab the accelerator to the floor, and the big V-8 would jar the truck forward in a shower of rocks. She could see that Tapia was braced for such a maneuver, and nothing she could do would dislodge him quickly enough to protect Leona. A trigger pull was just a few ounces away.

"You must know that I will shoot if I have to," Tapia said, his voice almost courtly with its gentility. "This position in which we find ourselves…It can all be resolved so easily if we don't indulge in heroics."

Estelle didn't move, and thankfully neither did Leona. The county manager's eyes were huge, focused on the gun barrel.

Tapia's face was pale and sweaty, the only indication that he might be hurt. He had positioned his body in such a way that his crooked left arm, besides locking him to the truck door, protected the gun. Leona was a large woman, and no doubt stronger than average. She could slam forward, trying to bash the threatening muzzle forward. But Tapia's beefy arm blocked that, even if she were inclined to attempt it.

"Put down the binoculars," he instructed. Estelle did so, freeing her right hand. Her own service automatic was tight in its holster, blocked by her seat belt. The shotgun rested in its rack, tantalizingly close but absolutely useless.

"Put the vehicle in park," Tapia continued in flawless English. "Be oh-so-careful now." There was no threat in his voice, just quiet patience—and somehow all the more deadly for that. He grimaced as he shifted his weight. The muzzle of the silencer ticked upward toward Leona's chin. "Just into park."

"What do you want?" Estelle said.

"Ah, a beautiful voice as well," Tapia said, and nodded his approval. "What I want is that lever," and this time he shifted the gun to point at Estelle, "pushed gently into park. At this moment in time, that's all I want. Can we accomplish that much without bloodshed?"

"I hope so," Estelle replied, at the same time calculating the odds if she went for reverse, lurching Tapia away from his braced arm. But that could force the gun back toward Leona. She placed the binoculars on the seat, then with the tips of her fingers lifted the gear lever and pushed it up through the gates. In at least one respect, Manolo Tapia was a known quantity—he had plenty of experience pulling triggers, but he *hadn't* killed Tom Pasquale when he had the easy chance.

"Ah, good. Now turn off the key, if we please. Just that. No more."

She released the gear lever and switched the key back to the first detent, not far enough to lock the steering wheel or free the key. The deep murmur of the engine quit and for a brief moment, their breathing was the loudest noise in the cab. Tapia shifted his position, leaning more weight on the door as he dropped his good leg to the ground. He pushed himself away from the truck, making it impossible for Leona to make a grab for the gun.

"Now," he said. "It is very simple what we must do, and you may help me do it. I think that is the best thing, no?" Estelle didn't respond, since Tapia clearly would understand her two priorities—to prevent more bulletholes in people and to see him behind bars.

"You will drive me back to the village. That is a most simple thing, I think. So," and he shifted backward another fraction of a step, left hand on the truck door, right hand still holding the pistol on Leona. "You do not appear to be an officer, *señora*. Are you with the race?"

"I am the county manager," Leona said matter-of-factly. "And you must know that you're not going to get away with any of this."

Tapia laughed gently. He swung the muzzle of the pistol toward Estelle. "You will remain exactly where you are, with both hands on the steering wheel. Are we agreed?"

Estelle rested both hands on the wheel. There would be opportunities, but at the moment, nothing balanced the risks.

"Now," Tapia said, but stopped as he heard the characteristic whupping sound of a helicopter approaching.

"That chopper is coming here," she said, without moving her hands. "I need to call them off. They're with the television station." The last thing she wanted was a spray of bullets involving civilians—particularly Channel 8, "More News at Ten."

"Yes, indeed you do," Tapia said. "Be careful."

"It's just a television news unit," Estelle said. "I have to call my dispatch in order to reach them. We don't have their frequency on our radios."

"Of course you don't. Be very careful."

The undersheriff found the cellular phone without taking her eyes off Tapia, and auto-dialed dispatch. She watched as Tapia reached into the truck and locked one hand on Leona's right shoulder, at the same time swinging the gun so that it pointed directly at Estelle's head.

"Gayle," she said as soon as the connection when through, "I need the Channel Eight chopper to clear the area. Tell Ms. Duarte that I'll meet with her back at the office in a few minutes."

"Affirmative," Gayle replied. "Tom Mears is heading up the team out at the site. He should be there by now. Linda's on her way."

"That's good," Estelle said. *The farther they stay away from here, the better.* The chopper appeared, flying along the top of a low rise, skimming no more than a hundred feet above the ground. It banked sharply toward them, then appeared to hesitate. It slowed and turned broadside to them a thousand yards out, hovering nose high.

"They want to know what the ambulance is for," Gayle asked. "They can see it from their position now."

"I'll talk to them in a few minutes," Estelle said. "If they want to fly over west of the location, there's an open field there. Tell them they'll see an old broken-down homestead off the road a ways. They can land there. Sergeant Mears will talk with them. But tell them that we don't want that chopper near the crime scene. The last thing we need is the rotor wash sweeping everything away."

"Roger that," Gayle said.

Estelle switched off the phone. Tapia was watching her with something akin to amusement.

"Very good," he said. "I am much impressed." In a few seconds, the helicopter's nose dipped and it headed past them toward the southwest. "Now, let us do what we must do. There is little time," Tapia said. He stepped closer and braced one hand against the door as he touched the muzzle of the automatic to the county manager's right ear. She flinched and said something that Estelle couldn't hear. "Now," Tapia said, "give me your telephone."

"Why would I do that?" Estelle asked.

Leona yelped as Tapia jammed the silencer's muzzle into her skull. "Because I ask of you," he said pleasantly. Estelle extended the phone toward him. "Take it," he said to Leona, who did so instantly. He released his grip on the door and she placed the phone in his hand. "Now," he continued. "You have a radio, I believe."

"Of course."

"I mean the small one on your belt." He nudged Leona again, but his eyes never left Estelle. "You will be careful not to trigger the emergency call button as you hand it to me." He had slipped the phone in his pocket, and once more extended his hand. "And now," he said as he took the small radio, "the gun."

Estelle didn't move.

"The gun," he repeated. "Now is not the time for heroics. After all," he added pleasantly, "pop, pop, and I am free to take your fine truck without arguing with you. That is so, is it not? I am offering you an opportunity, *señora*, an opportunity to avoid blood all over that nice upholstery. You must see that."

With one finger, Estelle released her seat belt, then popped the holster snap. Moving slowly, she withdrew the pudgy .45. It took conscious effort to do so without snuggling the grips into her palm, the thumb safety so easily released. But she understood clearly that no matter how practiced the maneuver, it was just that—an orchestrated series of coordinated movements, none of them as instant as the single twitch of Tapia's trigger finger: in point of fact, a far more practiced trigger finger than her own.

"Give it to him, Leona." She held out the pistol and Leona took it, holding her hand flat like a platter.

"Very good," Tapia said. He grimaced again and shook his head. "Ah, well. Now, on the back of your belt, young lady. There are handcuffs, I assume?"

Estelle said nothing.

"You will remove them now."

"You don't need handcuffs," she said.

"Ah, but that would be something that I must decide," he said. "If you please."

Estelle leaned forward and reached around behind herself, slipping the set of cuffs off her belt.

"Secure your right wrist," Tapia said, and when Estelle hesitated, he ground the muzzle of the silencer into Leona's ear once again, so hard that she yelped. "I have been as patient as I intend to be," he added. Estelle snapped one side of the cuffs around her wrist, keeping the latch well back from her hand. "The other on the steering wheel." As she started to move her hand toward the bottom of the wheel's arc, he said sharply, "Above the center." When she was tethered, he nodded with satisfaction and withdrew the gun from Leona's face.

"And now, madam county manager, you will step out of the truck. With the utmost care. Things have gone so well up to now. Don't do something foolish to ruin our day."

He stepped back a pace, and Estelle could see him wobble clumsily on the bad leg. "Come. Do not be afraid."

"I'm *not* afraid of you, young man," Leona said, lying expertly.

"Ah, I suppose not. But thank you. I haven't been called a young man in a long, long time." He beckoned with the gun. "Out, now." An eyebrow lifted with surprise at Leona's size as she slipped out of the truck. "Give me your telephone," he commanded. Leona pulled her phone from her pocket and he waved toward the truck. "Just toss it on the seat." As she did so, he said, "Now, listen to me. It is a beautiful day. Pleasant sunshine, a gentle breeze." He chuckled softly. "Almost poetic, don't you think? A pleasant day for a walk. It is not far back to the main road. And as you walk, you will remember that I have your friend with me." He motioned away from the truck with the gun. "You will remember that, I'm sure."

Leona looked at Estelle, eyes pleading. "You will be careful, won't you?" she said.

"A wise woman," Manolo Tapia said. "Of course she will be careful." Moving painfully, he swung himself up into the truck. "Let us do what we must do."

Chapter Thirty

The effort to climb into the truck cost Tapia considerable agony. Estelle watched him and saw his eyes go wide with pain as he pulled himself into the high seat. Through it all, he never took his eyes off her. A handcuffed right wrist was effective, she granted him that. She couldn't reach him with her left without performing ridiculous gymnastics, and the massive transmission tunnel and center console corralled her legs. She forced herself to relax, to wait for opportunity, to seek ways to *make* opportunity.

At the same time, a laconic comment made years before by Bobby Torrez came to mind. A dog had bolted out of a driveway, madly chasing the sheriff's cruiser in which they were riding. "What's he gonna do when he catches us?" Torrez had joked as the dog snapped at the cruiser's tires. Chasing Tapia, Estelle had hoped to see him in the distance, to have time to plan and coordinate. But her fatigue had blunted common sense. Tapia's work brought him up close and personal. It was even possible, with the broken ankle, that he had known someone would see his tracks and follow him.

Once in the passenger seat, Tapia slammed the truck door and immediately leaned toward Estelle. His polo shirt was soaked with sweat and dust, and his odor was pungent. With his left hand he crunched the cuffs even tighter on her wrist, sliding the shackle forward of the wrist bones so she had no chance of sliding her hand free. He held the silenced Beretta so close that she could see the rosette of burned powder on the blued steel of the muzzle. Despite some confidence that Manolo Tapia was not going to just shoot her out of hand, her mouth went dry as he allowed the blued steel of the silencer to slide almost seductively down her arm.

"If you behave, you lovely creature, you'll be home to your family by dinnertime. You understand that, don't you?"

Estelle didn't reply. Tapia sounded too much like Tomás Naranjo for comfort. The two of them could have cooperated to present a workshop on how Mexican men could sound gentle, suave, and self-assured all at the same time—no matter how dangerous they might be.

"When you passed by on the road earlier, I thought certainly that you had seen me. But," and he waved with the gun toward the narrow two-track that wound up the slope, "let us be on our way. You must drive me to the airport."

Estelle twisted in the seat until she could see Leona Spears in the rearview mirror. The county manager stood helplessly, both hands on top of her head as if she meant to tear out her braid. Finally realizing that there was nothing she could do by standing alone in the sun and dust, she turned and began a determined jog back the way they had come.

"Now," Tapia said, tapping her right arm just ahead of the elbow with the silencer. He then pointed ahead. "Go."

Estelle didn't move. "You're going to leave Hector to face authorities all by himself?" The question jolted Tapia, and the wink of uncertainty in his expression told Estelle that for all his self-assurance, Manolo Tapia had no idea what events had transpired in the past twenty-four hours. "You think you're just going to take the airplane again and fly home? That's not possible."

So you know, his expression said. "There is no purpose in discussing this with you. Now go."

"I'm not 'discussing' it, *señor*. The boy is in jail, and that's where he's going to stay. He may have flown you in to Posadas County, but he's not going to fly you out."

Tapia frowned and for a moment he was silent. "We will see," he said. He twisted in the seat, watching Leona's retreating figure.

"She will do you no good," Estelle said. "You can take all the hostages you like. The simple fact remains that your nephew will remain in jail, and will face charges as an accessory to multiple counts of murder. The only way you can help him now is to testify that you forced him to accompany you—if that's true."

Tapia laughed with genuine amusement. "Really now," he said, and then his face twitched as he tried to shift his leg, lifting it clear of the floor and then finding no place to rest it that was comfortable. Estelle saw the swelling above his expensive tan trainer. He pointed with the gun. "Go. I am growing weary of arguing with you."

Estelle leaned as far from the steering wheel as she could, left side against the door. "And if I don't?"

He heaved a heavy sigh. "You have forgotten the two men in the arroyo?" He thumbed the hammer back on the Beretta, and having carried exactly that model handgun for a decade before switching to the heavier .45, Estelle knew how little force was required to drop the sear. Her bulletproof vest suddenly felt five sizes too small.

Tapia cocked his head and reached across carefully with his left hand. He drew the corner of her light jacket to one side, exposing the county shield on her belt. *"Undersheriff,"* he read. "Most impressive. I'm sure you are popular with the troops, no? I'm sure they would not wish for anything to happen to you. But if you do not cooperate with me, well then." He shrugged expressively. "A bullet for you is simple enough. And I take the truck and go on my way, uncomfortable as that would be considering my condition. So you see? I have been most generous up to this point. I have not harmed your large friend. I really do not wish to harm you. But it is your choice. And it is one you must make quickly."

He lifted the muzzle of the Beretta and squeezed the trigger. Despite the suppressor, the gun was surprisingly loud, a vicious sharp sneeze coupled with the clatter of the slide slamming back and then forward. The hot gases scorched Estelle's forearm, and a chip of something stung her left cheek as the bullet slammed into the door panel just below the windowsill. The empty shell casing cracked against the windshield, bounced off the dash, and disappeared down one of the defroster vents.

Estelle realized she was holding her breath, and she tried to force herself to relax. Somewhere deep inside the door mechanism, something tinkled and then clattered to the bottom of the door frame.

"Go," Tapia repeated. "No more discussions."

By sliding the cuffs down to the crossbar of the steering wheel, Estelle could reach the ignition key, and she started the Expedition.

"Up that way," Tapia said, pointing with the gun. She touched the gas and the truck jarred forward. He gasped and she glanced across at him. It was clear now why he had taken such a risk in abandoning the motorcycle rather than pressing on. Perhaps at first, he had intended only to rest for a few minutes. But riding the bike must have been agony, with no way to support the injured ankle. He had seen the white Expedition blundering along on his path, and he had made his decision.

They cleared the hill, and Estelle scanned the prairie before them. Four miles ahead as the crow flew lay the state highway that passed by Posadas Municipal Airport. Their route, winding across the rumpled terrain, would eat up the better part of twice that. It would be impossible on foot with a shattered ankle, and sheer torture idling a motorcycle along.

As if reading her mind, Tapia reached out once more with the Beretta, tapping her arm. "Think self-preservation now, as I do," he said. "Without this fine truck, I would be nearly helpless in this country—easy hunting, perhaps. But you would have a hole in you, no matter how very brave you might be." He paused, then pointed where the rough two-track teed into a wide swath cut years before by the developer's bulldozers now nearly overgrown by desert brush. "Go left," he instructed.

"You've practiced," Estelle said, and Tapia shrugged. The truck hit a hummock and lurched hard enough that Tapia put his hand up on the roof, bracing himself.

"Why Hansen?" she asked, and Tapia waved the gun again.

"Slow down here," he said. A shallow arroyo had channeled across what the developer had envisioned as a street, a rough and gravelly channel. Estelle could see a set of single tracks. Tapia had made good use of his time planning the attack on Chester Hansen, right down to scouting the best getaway route.

He reached across and touched the four-wheel-drive button on the dash. "Like so," he said, nodding in satisfaction as the little icon on the dash illuminated. The truck waddled across the cut, dropping first one tire and then another, like an old, overweight horse picking its way. The front bumper pushed gravel as they surged up and out, back onto the flat prairie.

When it became obvious that he had either not heard, or chose to ignore, her question, she repeated it. This time, he looked balefully at her. "My business is just that, *señora*. It is my business. There is nothing you need to know."

"You've left four dead bodies for us to clean up," Estelle said. "And you shot one of my deputies. And rest assured that it's not over yet. It most certainly *is* my business."

Tapia shrugged expressively, and his grin was genuine and warm—it would have been appealing under other circumstances. "Then we must agree to disagree, my dear *señora*," he said. "What this man is to me is of no consequence."

"And an entire family dead in the desert—they're of no consequence either?"

"None. None whatsoever. What happened was of their own choosing, not mine."

"You're only the instrument, is that it?"

"Just so. That is a good way to put it. Only the instrument." He whispered something in Spanish that she didn't catch.

"For whom?"

He laughed gently and stretched out a hand to the dashboard as the truck surged over another hummock.

"Captain Tomás Naranjo of the Judiciales tells me that you work for corporate interests in Mexico and El Salvador. Do you think we won't discover who sent you?"

"Please, *señora*. At this point, I do not really care *what* you are able to discover about me, or anyone else. You are in no position. In a few moments, I will be nothing but a memory for you. Your jurisdiction—your *importancia*—ends at the borders of your little county. It would be best that you remember that."

"How poetic. You are a confident man. Almost as if the modern radio and telephone don't exist."

"It must be so. Without confidence, we simply become motionless, no?"

"PCS, three-ten." The radio was jarringly loud, and when Estelle made no move toward the mike, Tapia pulled it off the radio clip and extended it toward her. Leona Spears had been left to find her way out on foot a mile and a half from County Road 14. She would have strode along at a good clip after the initial burst of speed, perhaps even breaking back into a jog when she could. Had it taken her ten minutes? Fifteen?

"Now you must choose," he said. "If there is no response, they will worry." He winked at her. "I know what I would do."

"And what am I to choose?" Estelle asked. She could picture Gayle Torrez on the radio, counting the seconds until she repeated the message. Tapia draped the mike's cord over her arm, and she took it with her left hand. A word or two, and every cop in the county would descend on them, enough weapons to start a small war. Odds were good that Manolo Tapia would die, and there was a good chance that he might take some of them with him, even though his only weapons appeared to be two handguns and now the pump shotgun in the rack.

"Ten-six, ten-eighty, ten-eighty-five," she said, keying the mike. Tapia's eyes narrowed, but he made no move to take the mike. She handed it back to him, Maybe it was a grimace, perhaps a grin, but he shrugged philosophically.

"So now they know," he said.

"Now they know."

She watched as he shifted the pistol and lowered the hammer. She took a breath, relieved that the threat had been reduced, seven or eight pounds now required to snap the double-action trigger. For a long time, he rode in silence, one hand holding the Beretta, the other arm crossed in front of him, hand grasping the molded assist handle on the windshield post.

"Is Hector well?" he said after a moment.

"Why is that important?" She regarded him with interest. "How is your nephew somehow worth more than the three Salvadorans you left dead in the desert? Or more than Mr. Hansen, whom my deputy says you killed without an instant's negotiation? Or my deputy, whose hip you ruined?"

"I had no choice with your deputy, *señora.* I did only what I had to do for self-preservation. He fights like the lion. You can be proud."

"Anyone fights for his life, *señor.* And that is exactly what your nephew is doing. Hector will tell us what we need to know."

"Do you think so?"

"Yes."

"Ah. Then you do not know the boy. He may steal your heart, but beyond that, my *son* is like the tempered steel. And he is so eager to learn."

Estelle looked across at Tapia sharply. "Your son?"

The assassin ducked his head in self-deprecation, and let his left hand slide down his leg. He leaned forward, the Beretta still focused on Estelle, and lightly touched his ankle. "Ah. My wits are not as sharp as they should be. I tell you more than you need to know. But yes." He straightened up and sat back, pulling himself upright in the seat, taking the weight off his leg. "Hector is my son. And I cannot simply leave him now. I am amused that he referred to me as merely an *uncle.* Clever."

He reached for the microphone, and as if his touch had triggered the signal, Sheriff Robert Torrez's quiet voice floated from the speaker.

"Three-ten, three-oh-eight."

Tapia looked quizzically at Estelle.

"Now what?" she asked, and he frowned, his eyes going hard. He rapped her smartly on the forearm with the silencer, and she flinched.

"Who is this?"

"That would be the sheriff," she replied. She gripped the steering wheel hard, flexing the fingers of her right hand, feeling the deep ache of the bruise.

"Reply to him," Tapia said, once more handing her the mike. "He must keep his distance."

"Three-oh-eight, three-ten, go ahead."

"Ten-twenty?"

Estelle hesitated. There was a certain safety in keeping Tapia isolated out in the desert. The killer leaned toward her, obviously making his own decision. "Give it to me." She did so, and he palmed the mike expertly, as if he'd had considerable experience. "You must have children?" he asked Estelle, not yet keying the mike.

"That is no concern of yours."

"If one of them is threatened, imagine how you would feel, you see," he said. "If someone were holding your son, you would do anything you could to see his release. You know that."

"My son is not a killer. He doesn't steal airplanes and cross international borders. He doesn't chauffeur professional hit men."

Tapia laughed. "*¡Caramba!* Such fire," he said, and lifted the microphone. "But he is still my son. Now, what is the sheriff's name?"

"Robert Torrez."

"He is the person who can make decisions?"

"Of course."

"Good. Señor Torrez, can you hear me?"

"Go ahead." The sheriff's tone was guarded.

"Good. This is what you must do." Tapia released the transmit button for a second as he collected his thoughts. As he broke in, Torrez's tone was blunt and unequivocal.

"Ten-twenty-one. Three-oh-eight out."

Tapia looked across at Estelle quizzically. "He wants you to use the phone," she said. "You have mine in your pocket." He fished the small phone out and opened it. "Press auto-dial, then eight," she instructed. He did so, and in a moment the connection went through.

"Señor Torrez? Are you there?" Estelle could not hear Torrez's reply, but she knew it would be monosyllabic. "What I want is very simple. I have your delightful undersheriff with me." He glanced at Estelle again. "And you have my son, Hector. There is nothing more simple, no?" The sheriff said something cryptic, and Estelle found herself straining to hear his voice. "So," Tapia said. "I don't think you understand. Perhaps you can imagine that someday a hiker might find the bleached bones of your undersheriff somewhere in the Mexican desert. No? You care so much about keeping my son that you would allow that to happen? I don't think so."

Tapia listened briefly, tapping the muzzle of the silencer on his thigh.

"This is what *you* will do," he interrupted. "Now listen to me. You are familiar with the small private strip, I'm sure. The one owned by the gas company? I believe you already have had some business there. So. You will leave the boy standing by himself on the east end of that runway, right by the dirt road that passes by. You will leave him there, and clear the area. If I see anyone as we approach, anyone at all, that will close the agreement. You know what will happen. When we have picked up the boy unharmed, and are well away, I will release your undersheriff unharmed. But only then."

He listened for a moment, a slight smile touching the corners of his mouth. "There is high country to be used, I know," he said. "By both you and I. But I hope you will be intelligent in this, *señor*." Torrez said something, to which Tapia merely shrugged. "As we are both aware, there are innocent bystanders, Sheriff. You will allow this bicycle race to continue…There is no reason for any of them to become involved."

He's going to fly. Estelle slowed the SUV to negotiate another dry wash, her mind racing ahead. Of course the assassin planned to fly out of Posadas County. He could not cross the border at the Regál crossing—there were too many agents, too many cops swarming. A single vehicle was too easily stopped. He could wind his way east beyond the village of María and find a remote spot, but that route was too easily blocked, too. He'd be traveling with a crowd of officers at his heels, awaiting the opportunity for a well-placed shot.

"That way," Tapia said, pointing again. He kept them heading roughly north, taking the trails that eventually would bring them out on the state highway just west of the Posadas Municipal Airport—and a selection of airplanes.

"You will free my son immediately," Tapia said into the phone, "and proceed to the spot that I described." His features brightened as a thought occurred to him. "I'm sure that in the next few minutes you can find two things: a convertible automobile and your wonderful county manager. She…" And he turned to Estelle. "Her name?"

"You don't need her," Estelle said.

"Ah, but I do. Her name? It is merely a courtesy. She will be in no danger. You have my word."

"Leona."

He nodded and once more spoke into the phone. "The *señora* Leona," he said. "She will drive the convertible. Only she with my son as a passenger in the front seat. Is that quite clear?" He looked at his watch. "It is now one fourteen, Sheriff. I will pick up my son at two o'clock. That gives us both sufficient time to get there."

Apparently Torrez protested, because Tapia said, "Oh, yes it is. I'm sure you can move efficiently." He snapped the phone closed and dropped it in his pocket. "So," he said, as if waiting for Estelle to voice her thoughts. When she said nothing, he asked, "Your sheriff. He is a creative man? I suppose we shall see."

"You don't really want your son back, do you?"

He looked at her in surprise. "But of course I want my son returned to me."

"Then why all the theatrics? You know that what you ask is not possible in forty-five minutes."

"Ah," he said, nodding. "By now, they know exactly where this county manager is, yes? They have a helicopter in the vicinity. They can pluck her away, return to the village, and by then, your sheriff—who must surely know everyone in this small community—will have secured a convertible automobile. And then they drive that automobile to our rendezvous."

"It's a thirty-minute drive," Estelle pointed out.

"Ah. Then I hope they waste no time." He laughed. "But no one drives the speed limit these days."

Chapter Thirty-one

Estelle heard the helicopter before she saw it, and although she was sure that Tapia also heard it, he showed no reaction. For a few minutes, it paced them from behind, out of sight. Then, it drifted off to the right, paralleling them. Once, when it sounded as if it were descending dangerously close, Estelle ducked down and caught a glimpse of it. The garishly painted flanks announced *Channel 8 FirstNews.*

"So, we have an audience now," Tapia said finally. "This is unfortunate, I suppose. Perhaps your sheriff is having trouble making up his mind."

Not likely, Estelle thought, and almost added aloud, *but he doesn't do well with ultimatums.* And now that they were pinpointed by airborne observers, she hoped that the sheriff both had gained an advantage and would put it to good use. At that moment, Estelle supposed, Channel 8's big zoom lens was focused tightly on the dust-covered Expedition, hoping for a good profile shot of Tapia in the passenger seat. If they were lucky, they might even win a network feed. The narrator of *America's Wildest Cop Chases* would have to figure out how to make a dirty SUV, lurching along on desert two-tracks, exciting for viewers.

The radio crackled.

"Three-ten, chopper eight ETA a minute or so." Gayle's voice was steady, and the television station's Jet Ranger banked sharply away from them, angling back toward the original crime scene.

"Ah, you see?" Tapia said, and flinched as a slight change in position shot agony up his leg. "Now, go." The two-track flattened out, and far ahead she could see the flat black line of the state highway and, to the east, the low buildings of the air-port. If they could stall long enough, one of the Border Patrol's Blackhawk helicopters might be brought within striking range, but the Mexican counterparts certainly were not a factor. Manolo Tapia knew as clearly as she did that although he might be paced by ten dozen officers and half a dozen helicopters on the north side of the border, once across that imaginary line etched in the desert, he was a free man.

"Tell me something of yourself," Tapia said conversationally, as if they were engaged in a leisurely Sunday drive.

Estelle ignored the request and slowed the SUV to avoid a wash of rocks that a careless road grader operator had left when he pulled his blade out of the bar-ditch cut. For a moment, she considered a sudden swerve, crashing the truck's suspension into the rocks. The outcome of that was unattractive any way she looked at it.

"You have young children," Tapia persisted. "What…two? Three?" When she didn't answer, he reached across with the gun and once more aimed a quick, hard rap at her right forearm. Estelle saw the black barrel coming and more out of reflex than anything else, intercepted the blow with her left hand, grabbing the weapon by the silencer and twisting up and away as hard as she could. Tapia was caught off-guard. As she saw his weight jar forward, she stomped the brake pedal and yanked the steering wheel with her shackled hand.

The SUV swerved right, surging over a hump just before its front wheels plunged down in the bar ditch. Estelle ignored where the vehicle was headed, concentrating instead on twist-ing the pistol with all her strength. As the truck crashed down into the ditch, she floored the accelerator, the tires spraying dirt and rocks.

Tapia cursed and with astonishing strength lashed out in two directions at once. He yanked his right hand away from her, so hard that the front sight of the Beretta raked a trough across the palm of her hand. Chopping with his left at the same time, he struck Estelle with the back of his fist, the blow smacking her in front of her right ear.

The SUV burst through a thick grove of creosote bush and with the gas pedal still mashed to the floor, began a long, almost lazy power slide to the left. As skilled as a rodeo rider on a plunging bronc, Tapia grabbed the back of Estelle's neck, using her as support as he drove his good leg against the firewall.

"Stop," he commanded. His hand clamped her head, and he pulled her toward him, tight against her shoulder harness. The gun's suppressor dug into her cheek. "You will stop." Still spraying rocks, the SUV vaulted back over the bar ditch, crossed the two-track once again, and slid to a halt, its front wheels cocked sideways in the prairie gravel.

For a moment their harsh breathing was the only sound other than the idling engine. Tapia did not release his hold, and his viselike grip forced Estelle's head toward the side window. He was smart enough to know that, alone in the desert without Estelle as a shield, he would be easy prey. Slowly, Estelle lifted her left hand in apparent surrender. Blood trickled down her wrist.

"You must be smarter than this," Tapia said. The pressure on her neck increased, and Estelle panted, trying to keep her vision clear, waiting for the cervical vertebrae to pop. For emphasis, he jerked his hand sideways, smacking her skull against the glass. "Now go. There is nothing to be gained by your heroics." He touched her forearm with the gun again, this time gently. "Only much to be lost. Now go."

"Hit me again and we'll both be without a vehicle," Estelle whispered through clenched teeth.

"Spectacular," Tapia said with good humor. He released her neck, the powerful clamp becoming a caress with his fingertips that ran up the back of her skull to the top of her head, a gentle touch that a patient parent might use on a child—or one lover to another.

She guided the truck back onto the two-track. The blood from her hand was a sticky mess on the steering wheel, but she ignored it. Tapia pulled away, and now sat well away from her, his back against the door. "You have not answered my question," he said pleasantly, as if they hadn't struggled, as if he had not struck her, as if her neck would not carry the bruises of his grip. "You have children, no?"

"I will not discuss my life with you," Estelle whispered through clenched teeth.

He regarded her with interest. A quarter mile ahead, where State Highway 78 cut its swath across the prairie, she saw two State Police cruisers parked along the shoulder of the highway. If Tapia saw them, he didn't react.

"You must care for them," he said instead. "The children. I can see that you do."

"Do you now," she replied coldly.

He actually chuckled. "You must put this all into perspective. What is done is done. The three? Four? *They* are nothing to you. What do you gain by putting your family at risk for them?"

"My family is not at risk." She glared at him. "They will not *be* at risk."

"Ah, but you see," Tapia said, "they expect you to come home this evening, ¿verdad? You can assure that will happen, at this very moment you can assure it, by your cooperation. That is what I am saying." He tapped the muzzle of the silencer on the dashboard, the gun aimed ahead at the police cars that could so easily block their path.

"What do you want?" Even as she spoke, she saw the wink of lights coming from the east as yet another cruiser, this time one of the county's own, headed west on the state highway to intersect their route.

"Make sure the airport gateway is open," he said, and picked up the radio mike and draped it over her arm once again. This time, his touch was feather-soft.

She took the mike, and for just a moment she held it, the transmit button untouched. Every law enforcement officer in the county—and surrounding counties—would know by now exactly where she and Tapia were. That Tapia had allowed County Manager Leona Spears to simply walk away was interesting. It was clear that Manolo Tapia firmly believed that Estelle would make an effective shield, and that they would release Hector in exchange for her safety.

"What was Chester Hansen to you?" Estelle asked, the mike still ignored.

Tapia laughed. "Ah. You are wonderful," he said. "How many children do you have? A fair trade."

"Two," she said instantly.

He tapped the dash again, watching the white county police unit pull across the highway, blocking both lanes. "Two. They are beautiful children, beyond a doubt. Your husband—what does he do?"

"What was Chester Hansen to you?" Estelle repeated. Tapia shifted, his posture almost casual, right elbow on the windowsill. His eyes twinkled with amusement.

"A man who refused to pay his debts," Tapia said. "That is all. I entered into an agreement two years ago to eliminate a family problem for him and his company—and then he refused to pay after professional services were rendered. So." He shrugged. "A question of honor, perhaps. Or just good business. In any case, what is done is done. Now you know a little more. It will make no difference. And your husband? He is delightful, I am sure. What does he do?"

"A physician."

Tapia's heavy eyebrows shot up. "Really so? Such a tiny village, deserving such grace." He straightened a little, twisting in his seat to scan the country to the side and behind them. "Tell them now," he said, nodding ahead.

"Three-oh-three, three-ten. We'll be to the cattle guard in just a few minutes. Ten-eighty, ten-eighty-five."

Deputy Jackie Taber's voice was subdued. "Ten-four."

"Make sure the troops understand," Estelle said. *Watch from a distance.*

"Ten-four." Now three hundred yards away, she could see one of the State Police officers outside his vehicle, watching them through binoculars. He held a short black assault rifle in his left hand, the butt resting against his hip. Sheriff Robert Torrez had headed back toward town when Tapia's position was not yet known. Where was he now? Had he acted on Tapia's demands?

"Three-oh-eight, three-ten," she said. "Ten-twenty?"

Manolo Tapia reached across and took the mike from her. "Your sheriff has but one mission," he said. "Perhaps we will discover how much he appreciates you. Do you think so?" He glanced ahead at the waiting officers. "We don't need to know what he might invent as his location, *señora*. What matters is that he does as he is told. Otherwise, we must begin to worry about you."

"Three-oh-eight is one mile out." The sheriff's tone was clipped and impatient, and he didn't elaborate "out" from what. He would have heard the exchange with Jackie, and Estelle had no trouble envisioning the sheriff turning around abruptly to intercept them on the highway, rather than tending to Tapia's demands.

A second state officer appeared out of the car, and Estelle could see that he held another of the short AR-15's, this one fitted with a telescopic sight. At the same time, Jackie's Bronco pulled forward to the shoulder, clearing the highway.

"Roll up your window," Tapia said, and Estelle complied. The dirt two-track turned abruptly to the right before once again curving to cross the cattle guard on the state highway right-of-way. When she reached the highway, two of the state officers would be on her side of the vehicle, exactly where Tapia would want them.

"When you reach the highway, turn right," Tapia ordered. Once more, he leaned toward her and his left hand encircled the back of her neck, not a clamp, but a promise.

Now we find out how patient everyone can be, Estelle thought.

Chapter Thirty-two

As they neared the cattle guard, Estelle could look east, down the state highway. There was no traffic. A roadblock would have been established between this point and the village. There had been no radio traffic, either—Sheriff Torrez was sticking to the phone, refusing to give Tapia any more advantage than he already held.

The two State Police officers made no move away from their vehicles, but the rifles tracked Estelle's vehicle every inch of the way. The officers were the first of what would eventually become an army, and she knew that with every player added, the odds of a peaceful resolution diminished.

Deputy Jackie Taber stood by the right front fender of her Bronco. Estelle lifted the fingers of her right hand off the steering wheel in acknowledgment as they slipped by.

"You see?" Tapia said. He ignored the two state troopers, but watched Jackie Taber closely. "When we behave, there is no problem."

"And now?" Estelle asked as they pulled out onto the pavement.

"Now to the airport." He pointed with the pistol. "Just ahead. And promptly."

Instead of accelerating, she slowed the SUV to a crawl, and he looked at her sharply. In her rearview mirror, she saw the three officers reenter their vehicles. "I want to clear the airport. There may be people there that will only get in the way." She didn't know what airport manager Jim Bergin would do when they drove blithely onto his turf and stole an airplane—and it appeared certain that was what Tapia had in mind, even though he would be surrounded by enough firepower to start a small war.

"That is not necessary," Tapia said. He rocked her head gently, never releasing the grip on her neck. "As long as you are with me, there is not problem, *¿verdad?*"

"And if I'm not?"

"But you are. Now go," he said, pointing down the highway. "Stop the delay. You *are* with me, and that is that." He stroked her right forearm with the muzzle of the silencer again, and she snapped her arm away to the limit of the handcuffs. He chuckled. "In other circumstances..." he began, then finished the thought with a shrug. "I know people who in your circumstance would be no more than..." He groped for the right word. "Is it *jello?*" She didn't give him the satisfaction of knowing that her stomach had been tied in knots for the past hour.

"You will drive to the airport now. Drive directly to the hangar where niner two Hotel is kept." The hand on her neck tightened. "Quickly now." His use of pilot jargon opened another door in Estelle's mind.

She accelerated down the empty highway, the other police units trailing behind.

He twisted in his seat without releasing his hold on her. "I want them to stop," he said. "Tell them so." He handed her the mike.

"Three-oh-three," she said, "stop at the mile marker and block the highway. I don't want anyone through." She saw the Bronco slow immediately, then turn sideways on the highway, the two state cars flanking it from behind. "If the sheriff has the highway blocked at the village, have them stay in place."

"Ten-four. Are you okay?"

"Ten-four." She dropped the mike, and Tapia gathered it up.

"Very good. What is the saying here? I heard another American police officer say it once years ago...Our goal is that we all go home at night." He released her neck and transferred his hand to her headrest. "That is what we must keep in mind, no?"

"Maybe it's not the same 'we' that *you* have in mind," Estelle said. "Did Hansen know the Haslán family?" Those were pieces of the puzzle whose edges refused to mesh. Guillermo Haslán, his wife, and son had fled north, allegedly with cash belonging to someone else. Was it their intention to meet with Hansen? Was he to provide their safe house? Estelle doubted that. Chester Hansen's mind had been on the race, not on wondering where the Hasláns had gone after their disappearance.

He regarded her curiously. "Now why do you think that I would tell you my life story?" he asked. "Of what advantage is that to me? And that is what we are about, is it not? Advantage? I think that it is better that you do *not* know, *señora*. I think perhaps that is ground where you do not need to walk."

"We must not interfere with the business of the rich and powerful," Estelle said. "Is that it?"

Tapia laughed heartily. "That would be it, exactly. You are very good." Ahead of them, another set of winking lights approached. He handed her the mike. "Make sure there is no interference."

"PCS, three-ten."

"Go ahead, three-ten."

"I want the area both east and west of the municipal airport cleared. You have an emergency vehicle westbound on Seventy-eight. Have them stop."

There was a second's hesitation on the radio. "Three-ten, be advised that unit is an ambulance. They're responding to an assistance call from the race officials west of your location."

Estelle looked across at Tapia, who nodded. "Be careful," he said.

"Tell them to go ahead," Estelle said. "Three-oh-three, did you copy?"

"Affirmative."

"And Gayle," Estelle continued, "call Jim Bergin and tell him that we're on the way in. Tell him to remain in his office and not to interfere." Tapia's hand reached for the mike, and Estelle added quickly, "There's nothing he can do."

Almost gently, Tapia took the mike from her hand. "Very intelligent," he said. "We must hope that the sheriff is now doing *his* part."

"Why did you pull your son into all this?" Estelle asked. "He is a boy with so much promise. So much talent, so gifted." *A gifted little liar*, she thought. "And yet you ruin his life. You had no right to do that."

"We all gamble in different ways," Tapia said.

"That is not a gamble. And what is to win? A few thousand dollars? His life is worth only that? *Your* life is worth only that? What did Hansen ever do to you that makes killing *him* so necessary? And the three Salvadorans—what did they do? Did the father embezzle a few thousand from the wrong people, and the entire family is *killed* for that?"

Tapia grinned at her. "Such passion, *señora*." He sighed and watched the highway as she slowed for the airport entrance. "A few thousand is one thing. When the number is millions, that's another thing, you see."

"Why not just have the boy brought here?" she asked. "To this airport? Where the airplane is?"

"Ah, well," Tapia said, and let another shrug suffice. "A little isolation is helpful, sometimes, no?"

"Three-ten, three-oh-eight."

The sheriff's voice was tight and his delivery uncharacteristically rapid. She could picture Robert Torrez hunched over the steering wheel, jaw clamped tight, his square, handsome face set with determination as he sought a way out from under the ultimatum. Tapia handed her the mike.

"Three-ten. Go ahead."

"Two subjects will be southbound here in just a minute. Be lookin' for a yellow '64 Mustang. You know the one. Two occupants."

"Ten-four." What Sergeant Tom Mears jokingly referred to as his "pension," the classic convertible saw the outside world in the evenings, when the sun wouldn't blister its paint, or on an occasional weekend run. A yellow convertible, driven by a large woman with a flying yellow Heidi braid, accompanied by a darkly handsome Mexican youth—that would set tourists to gawking, Estelle thought.

The airport gate was open, and she drove in and turned hard right, skirting the FBO office. Jim Bergin stood in the doorway holding a cell phone. Estelle lifted a hand in greeting. The airport manager's face was grim, and he pointed the phone at her.

Stay put, Estelle whispered.

"To the hangar," Tapia ordered, and then a moment later, as they rolled down the tarmac to the last hangar, "Stop here." Once more, his left hand encircled her neck, not hard, but a constant reminder. He twisted in his seat, surveying the area. No one could approach from across the airport without being seen—across taxiway, runway, and prairie, where the tallest cover was scrub creosote bush. When they had driven into the airport, the back of the hangars were visible, but Estelle doubted that anyone had secreted themselves there. Tapia's plans were only now becoming clear, and no one had had the time to mobilize.

Satisfied, he turned back to Estelle, leaning so close that she could smell his breath. "Listen, now. And listen carefully. If you cooperate with me, no one will be hurt. I think you know this—*I* do not want to hurt you. But *they* are another matter. Do you understand me?"

"They?"

"There is always the temptation to do something heroic," he said. "But you must think carefully. If you cooperate, my son and I will be gone from your lives in just a few minutes. That will be that. If you do not cooperate, then someone else will die. There is no doubt. You are all hoping that will be me." His smile was tight. "But you must know that I will do all I can to assure that is not the case. You can choose which one of your associates will *not* go home to his family tonight. You will decide who, no?"

Keeping one hand on her neck, with the other holding the Beretta at a comfortable distance, he lowered his voice. "Let us do this without incident. You have a son as well, so you must understand." He hesitated. "If mistakes were made, this is the time to make rectification." He pronounced the word with heavy emphasis on each of the five syllables. Reaching across, he turned the ignition key and pulled it out of the lock.

He examined the ring thoughtfully for a moment, isolating the small handcuff key. Then, with a final look behind them to make sure that the police escort had not followed them into the airport, he opened his door and slid out of the truck. At one point, as his weight touched the bad ankle, he hissed between his teeth. Working his way around the truck, the hand with the Beretta on the hood for support, Tapia didn't take his eyes off Estelle.

She watched him make his way around the front fender, and as he hopped awkwardly a sheen of sweat broke out on his forehead. He stopped in front of the windshield post, left hand on the spotlight for support.

In the rearview mirror, Estelle saw one of the State Police cars ease around the FBO office and stop, three hundred yards away.

"There's no reason for me to go with you," she said. "You don't need me."

Tapia laughed gently. "Would that were so. Get out of the car now. And be careful." He moved past the Expedition's door, away from its range as a battering ram, and opened it. "Slide out now. As far as you can."

She did so, right hand still shackled to the steering wheel, her body stretched awkwardly. He slid behind her, forcing her forward against the door. With one hand tethered, she was helpless to strike out in any effective way. He reached around and held out the keys so she could take them with her left hand. "Now is the time to think carefully," he whispered, the bulk of his body pressed against hers. Even as she reached out with the cuff key, his right arm slid past her and he grasped the chain link of the cuffs. His left hand pushed the automatic into the back of her neck. "Open only the side on the wheel," he said. "Leave them on your wrist." He had covered her wrist and the lock on that side with his hand.

As the cuffs came loose, he held them securely, a slight twist sending the message to her right wrist. He didn't move, but stood still, blocking her against the open door. The gun was gone, replaced by his hand clamped on the back of her neck.

"Do you understand me?" he said.

"Yes."

Tapia had not snapped the loose end of the cuffs to either himself or anything else, and she knew that if she could break free from his grip, she could outsprint him easily, leaving him alone and vulnerable in the open. Would he shoot her if she broke away? Probably not. There would be no point. A wounded or dead hostage was of little value at this point.

"Now," he said, still not moving. "Come with me." He pulled away, a little more twist on the cuffs bringing her right arm behind her, canceling her ability to strike out, left hand braced on her neck. She could feel him using her as a crutch, his weight shifting with each painful step. She could feel his breath on her neck, and every time he winced with pain she could feel his hands clench.

Ten shuffling steps brought them to the hangar door. He pushed her against it, arm wrenched behind her. An instant later, breathing hard, he reached past her with his left hand and inserted a key into the lock. "The owner is most accommodating," he whispered. The door yawned open, the interior air of the hangar musty and oil-tinged.

Jim Bergin had not had the time to replace locks—nothing had spurred him to such urgency—and Hector or his father had had the foresight to make a duplicate when they discovered the original hanging from the Cessna's ignition.

Tapia pushed her inside, hand once more on the back of her neck, but the twist in the cuff chain relaxed just short of discomfort.

"Come," he said. The hangar was dark, the shape of the Cessna cut by sharp lines of light from the open door. "Give me your left hand." His moves were quick and practiced, and before she understood what he actually intended to do, he had cuffed her around the smooth sloping wing strut. Always, his body was pressed close to hers. "You will excuse my discourtesy," he said. "But I find this leg all but useless."

With a flick of the other key, he unlocked the airplane and in a moment appeared with a slender plastic fuel sampler. He hopped with one hand against the airplane, sometimes both, and by the time he had completed only half a circuit, Estelle could see that his face was soaked with sweat. Doggedly, he found a way to stop at each wing fuel drain, and once under the engine cowl. He drained a small sample from each, scrutinized it closely, then flicked it out on the hangar floor. She watched him exam-ine the airplane, hand stroking down the leading edge of each propeller blade, then a stop at each control surface. The tour took several moments, and more than one gasp of pain when he failed to find the support he needed. He finally returned to where she stood, manacled to the strut.

"So," he said, and shrugged. "You may ask what is the point of checking the airplane at this moment. And you are right. If it works, it works. If not, well…" He shrugged again. "Old habits, you know. Sometimes they cause us trouble. But now, we see."

He pulled himself past her and half-limped, half-hopped to the hangar door. The bolt shot open with a loud clang, and he leaned against the door, rolling it open on its coasters. He stayed behind the heavy framework, protected by the shadows and the rolling wall of steel. As he guided the door, he looked east toward the airport's FBO office. Satisfied, he lurched back to her. "Do I trust you?" he asked. With him standing close to her now, she could see that his face was ashen from the pain.

"To do what?"

He grinned, despite his obvious discomfort. "I could leave you so, you understand." The image of her cuffed to the wing strut, first jogging along beside the plane on the taxiway, and then dragged down the runway, to hang like a broken rag doll as the plane lurched into the air, was not the finish to this day that she would willingly choose.

"When my son steps into the airplane," Tapia said, "you will step out. That is my word. That is why I choose the other runway, *señora*. There will be less of an audience, fewer complications."

"And if your son is not there?"

"Ah," Tapia said, moving toward her wrist with the cuff key. "Let us hope that does not happen. If that is the case—if I do not see him standing alone on that deserted runway—then we go on to Mexico, you and I. What happens to you there, I cannot guarantee." He popped the lock of the cuff around her right wrist this time, holding the link securely. The gun was out of sight, perhaps stuck in his belt behind his back.

"The sheriff said there would be two people in the convertible. Let us hope it is the *correct* two people, no? From the air, it will be very easy to distinguish. I'm sure they will do the right thing. They will want you back, no?"

Twisting hard on the cuffs, he spun Estelle's left arm behind her, the force making her gasp. His right hand now clamped on her neck, he pushed her to the airplane. The grip of his large, beefy hand on her slender neck was paralytic, and spots danced in her vision. "Open the door." She reached out and fingered it open, and once more he used his entire body to block hers. With almost a negligent swat, he yanked her left arm down, swung the empty cuff and caught the bottom seat bracket, then snapped the cuff ratchet closed.

"You don't need to do this," she said.

He laughed and stepped back. "Ah, but I'm afraid I do." He paused, his grip on the back of her neck almost gentle once again. "At one time, I had the opportunity to hold a jaguar kitten," he said. "Perhaps no more than a month or two old. So beautiful he made the heart ache. But intent on doing damage unless held just so." He released his hold on her neck. "Get in the airplane."

To do so, she was forced to turn around, backing close to the fuselage, then pushing and pulling herself up onto the narrow, plastic-upholstered seat. With her left hand cuffed to the seat frame, she could not straighten up fully, nor could she launch any effective assault on the right-seat occupant.

With gentlemanly care, Tapia made sure that body parts were not caught in the door, then slammed it closed. He then limped around the airplane to the aft cargo door on the right side. She felt the aircraft lurch as he pulled himself inside. In the cramped confines, there was no easy way, no graceful way, to move forward between the two front seats. With a broken ankle, the performance must have been torture. When he finally slumped into the right seat, he leaned his head against the window, but for only an instant. He reached around, brought out the automatics and slipped it into the door boot, within easy reach.

Taking a deep breath, he regarded the instrument panel for a moment.

"I realize that even with only one hand free, you can cause no end of trouble," he said. "Another pair of handcuffs would be useful, but…" He shrugged. "I will break your right arm if I have to. You understand that? If you endanger the aircraft, you endanger yourself. You must balance this, you see. Do you want to return home this evening to your family? I'm sure you do. Is it worth it to sacrifice yourself, leaving your family to suffer your loss, merely to apprehend me? I don't think so." He gazed at her thoughtfully and when she said nothing, he slipped the Beretta from the pocket and pointed it at her right forearm. "Decide quickly."

The bullet would shatter the arm bone, or bones, and then if she was unlucky, the deformed slug would punch into her right leg. "You have my word."

"Good. You are as intelligent as you are beautiful." He slipped the gun back into the door boot. He flicked the master switches on, and something deep inside the aircraft began to spool up, a high-pitched whine of electronics. With practiced skill, he set the mixture and throttle, and then paused. Estelle realized that he was searching for a comfortable way to rest his left foot on the rudder pedal. She knew, from several hours riding with Jim Bergin over the years, that the brakes were integral with those pedals—Tapia would be working with a serious disadvantage, unless he wished only to turn right once the engine started.

With a quick glance at her, he turned the key, and the big prop jerked into life. The engine caught, and as the prop became a blur of motion, the aircraft shifted and moved forward toward the door. Tapia pulled the throttle back to idle and let the airplane ease out of the hangar, a foot clearance at each wing tip. Estelle heard his right foot shuffle on the rudder pedal, at first pushing, then dancing to the opposite pedal to guide the plane. As the nose cleared the door, sun flooded into the interior, and Estelle turned to look down the tarmac. The State Police cruiser that had been parked by the FBO was driving slowly toward them.

The instant the aircraft's tail cleared the hangar door, Tapia pushed hard on the right rudder. Estelle felt the pedals saw back and forth at her feet, and the Cessna headed for the taxiway.

A flick of the finger and the flaps spooled down, and then Manolo Tapia's intentions became clear. He firewalled the throttle, and the big engine bellowed, the turbo a shrill whistle. He spun the trim wheel and continued to dance his right foot first on one rudder pedal and then the other as the plane charged down the taxiway, using the full width of the macadam surface. The natural assumption was that, on taxiways, airplanes taxied. That was unnecessary, as unnecessary as flying thousands of feet up in the air to clear low bushes and fences.

It didn't matter that the state trooper was following them. His Crown Victoria was fast, but it couldn't fly, and Tapia used the taxiway to full benefit. Two hundred yards before the donut turnaround at the end, he pulled back hard on the yoke and the ground dropped away.

Chapter Thirty-three

The Cessna roared off the end of the taxiway but rose only a dozen feet over the prairie scrub before leveling off. As it accelerated to well over a hundred knots, Tapia let the plane drift right, remaining north of the state highway and closing uncomfortably close to the flank of Cat Mesa.

Under other circumstances, flashing across the prairie just over the tops of vegetation might be exhilarating, but handcuffed to the seat and having to trust her life to a man with a broken ankle was terrifying. Sitting awkwardly anyway, Estelle could not pull herself upright to see over the massive, arched dash cowl. She turned and looked out the side window as the airport faded behind them. If Tapia didn't change course, their route would take them north of the intersection of County Road 14 and the state highway.

His left hand outstretched to the dash cowl for support, and with only his right hand on the yoke, Tapia flew the airplane with a light touch. They continued to accelerate, and then with a glance to the left, Tapia curled his right wrist, bringing the yoke back. Estelle felt her stomach sag under the mild G's, and the plane climbed steeply, banking south.

They flashed diagonally across the state highway, climbing toward five hundred feet. Estelle's view west toward County Road 14 was blocked, but from his side of the airplane Tapia would be able to look out and in the distance see the crime scene where he had left Chester Hansen and Tom Pasquale. Tapia continued his turn to the south, and Estelle saw that their route would take them across State Highway 56, the southwestern route to Regál and the border crossing. Without another course correction, their route would also take them straight into the boulder-strewn northern flank of the San Cristóbals.

Satisfied with his vantage point, Tapia allowed the Cessna's nose to lower. His left hand dropped to manipulate the trim wheel, and then balance the throttle, mixture, and prop for a smooth, fast cruise. With a twist of the yoke and five minutes, they could be across the border and into Mexican airspace, away from State and Border Patrol aircraft—if that threat should materialize.

If a person knew where to look, the Broken Spur Saloon and its parking lot would be visible for miles from the air. Obviously Manolo Tapia knew exactly where to look if he wanted to see a yellow Mustang convertible.

He turned to her and shouted over the loud engine. "Now we will see."

What he referred to, she couldn't tell. Her view out the left side of the airplane was the vast, rumpled northern flank of the mountains separating Mexico from the United States. She leaned toward him. "Give me the cuff key now." The noisy cockpit wasn't the place for nuance.

He grinned at her, dismissing the demand. Estelle slumped, trying to relax her back. Deputy Jackie Taber came to mind. The deputy had established the habit of wearing a handcuff key around her neck on a fine gold chain, the cop's version of a crucifix. Estelle's handcuff key was on her key ring, lying on the front seat of her Expedition parked back at the airport. She kept another in her wallet, now out of reach, and another on her utility belt for those rare times when she wore a department uniform.

She pulled gently on the steel tether. Tapia had locked the cuffs tightly on her right wrist, but when he'd transferred the lock to the left, he'd left more slack. Pulling her thumb in tight, she eased her weight back against the shackle, twisting her hand. The combination of bone and steel produced pain, but no progress.

The Cessna banked sharply again, dipping the right wing. Estelle could see the Broken Spur Saloon, and farther on, County Road 14 twisting north from the state highway. A bright yellow spot winked, and as they drew closer, she could make out the blocky lines of Tom Mears' Mustang convertible. Tapia kept the plane south of the highway, paralleling it.

The saloon's parking lot was full, making the place look like a watering hole for cops. Far to the north, she saw two dust trails as vehicles headed down the dirt road at high speed. Estelle felt a sinking feeling, and it wasn't an air pocket. Most of it was apprehension at not knowing what Sheriff Torrez had planned.

Manolo Tapia held the vantage point, that was certain. There was no way to approach the airport without announcing the arrival from miles away. The saloon was two miles by road from the gas company's airstrip—far less by foot, but still a significant trek over rough ground, far more than what might be possible in the narrow time window.

On County Road 14, the first southbound car pulled to a stop at the brow of a low hill north of the airstrip. Farther on, a second joined the roadblock at the county road and its intersection with the Bender's Canyon Trail, the race route that wound and twisted northeast, roughly paralleling the state highway to emerge at Moore, an abandoned village site halfway between the saloon and Posadas. That was one less concern. The race cyclists would turn on the canyon trail, heading away from the airstrip.

A third vehicle, this one a white SUV, headed north on the country road until it met the other two vehicles, joining the roadblock there.

Tapia kept the Cessna south of the state road, the flank of the San Cristóbals looming off the left wing. His hand reached out and turned the trim wheel forward. The nose of the Cessna dropped and the airspeed accelerated. A mile beyond the west end of the gas company's runway, Tapia banked hard to the right, the Cessna's descent increasing as they swung north. In a moment he pulled the plane level four or five hundred feet above the scrub.

The yellow Mustang had stopped at the airstrip gate, and a large figure emerged from the driver's side.

The plane turned to parallel the runway, heading due east now, back toward County Road 14. Looking out past Tapia, Estelle saw the gate open and the figure return to the Mustang. By the time they had flown the length of the strip, the car had pulled forward onto the apron of the narrow runway.

As far as Estelle could see, no vehicle was within a mile of the runway. There was no way for anyone to approach the west end of the runway, the direction from which she assumed Tapia planned to land. Once he had touched down, he had but to turn around and take off, away from any threat—a maneuver that took only seconds. With no Blackhawk chopper on the horizon with lethal firepower, nothing blocked his route south.

The passenger climbed out of the convertible, and Estelle recognized the figure of Hector Ocate. The boy trudged straight down the center of the macadam strip, away from the car and Leona Spears. Manolo Tapia said something, more to himself than to Estelle, and the Cessna banked sharply again, this time to the east, taking a tight circle that afforded Tapia another look at the saloon parking lot, at the county road, and at the threshold of the airstrip. They had a large audience, but save the county manager and Hector Ocate, no one was near the airstrip.

Estelle searched the prairie on either side of the airstrip, looking for breaks in the shadows. At one point, a jackrabbit broke cover and flashed away, and Estelle scanned the area from which the rabbit fled. Without pulling the throttle, Tapia let the plane sink in the turn until it appeared he intended to buzz the three vehicles on the rise. The Cessna shot over them, no more than fifty feet over the surprised faces. Estelle had a clear view, and saw Eddie Mitchell, Tom Mears, and a State Police officer.

She felt the ache of tension in her spine and tried again to settle back. Sheriff Robert Torrez would not stand back with his arms folded, simply allowing this event to happen—while

Estelle wanted to believe that the sheriff wouldn't take an unnecessary gamble, he would try something. She had no clue what.
In the best of all possible worlds, one did not simply let a killer
escape—or his son.

As they thundered over the top of the hill, she scanned the
brush and rumpled landscape surrounding the airstrip. South
of the macadam, the ground dropped away a bit, then rose in
a series of rills. Although the scrub vegetation rarely grew more
than four or five feet high, it provided plenty of cover.

Estelle twisted, trying to look behind them. Hector Ocate
continued to plod down the center of the runway, approaching a
point a third of the way along the tarmac. Without a glance at the
dash, Tapia reached out and manipulated the throttle, mixture,
and prop, and Estelle felt the aircraft sink. The flaps spooled down
a notch, and Tapia pulled himself upright, shifting in his seat.

They paralleled the runway, and then as they sank toward
the prairie, Tapia smoothly fed in power. This time, the turn
was uncomfortably tight, the plane practically standing on one
wing, engine bellowing. If Manolo Tapia could fly this well with
a broken ankle, it was easy to imagine that under less trying circumstances, the trip across the border was simplicity itself. And
what had he needed his son for? When the plane rolled out of
the turn, the nose was pointed down the center of the runway.

Ahead of them, Hector Ocate had stopped walking, and now
stood quietly. *Follow in your father's footsteps,* Estelle thought.
The boy had proved he could steal an airplane, had proved he
could fly with the best of them. Maybe that was all he had ever
wanted—to prove himself to his father.

More flaps wound down, great rattling barn doors that
produced as much drag as lift. Shedding speed as Tapia bled
off power, the Cessna sank toward the strip. For a moment, it
appeared that they were going to sink right into the vegetation
short of the runway, but a burst of power brought them to the
pavement not a dozen feet from the two little yellow marker
cones at the verge of the asphalt. Tires smacked the pavement
hard and smooth, without a trace of bounce.

Tapia let the aircraft roll without braking, the slight uphill gradient serving to slow the aircraft. Estelle extended her feet, touching the set of rudder pedals on her side. She could slam one to the floor now, and the plane would in all likelihood careen off the runway, perhaps ripped off the landing gear—and then just as likely go cartwheeling in a pile of junk before exploding in a fireball.

With a roar of pain, Tapia braked hard, this time using his bad foot on the left brake. He let the airplane drift toward the right side of the runway, and as he did so, Estelle saw Hector walk away from the center, toward the opposite side. Tapia pounded his left fist on the dash cowling so hard that he left dents, but the smooth braking didn't waver. When the Cessna had slowed to a fast walk, he swerved to take up the last inch of macadam, then shifted feet and pushed the left rudder/brake pedal to the floor with his right foot, toeing the brake hard.

The aircraft had enough momentum remaining that it spun in a smooth circle, once more facing southwest. Hector ran to the plane, ducked under the trailing edge of the wing, and opened the cargo door on the right side. At the same time, Tapia reached across with Estelle's keys.

"Thank you," he said, and it sounded as if he meant it. Estelle took the ring and maneuvered the small key. The cuffs came loose and she straightened up. The Beretta eyed her, no longer in the door boot. Still, she hesitated to open the door.

"You are free to go," Tapia said. "Get out of the airplane. Now." Without wavering the muzzle of the gun away from Estelle, he turned to his son. "You will fly." Ready and willing, Hector moved to a position between the front seats, one hand on each, ready to vault into place in the left seat, behind the wheel. Estelle opened the door, immediately feeling the strong wash of air from the windmilling propeller. Even though the engine was at idle, the thrust was strong enough that opening the door required effort.

As she started to slide out, the airplane jerked a little as Tapia shifted his feet. Not wasting a second, Hector was already wedging himself forward toward the pilot's seat. Her feet touched the tarmac and Estelle felt the airplane begin to drift forward. She took an awkward step to catch her balance, waiting for an instant of opportunity. It came as the boy shifted his weight forward so he could maneuver into the pilot's seat. Estelle drove toward his extended left arm with the loose end of the handcuffs. The steel connected with his wrist with a sharp crack but he jerked backward before the ratchet could snap closed.

Estelle lunged back into the plane and grabbed the front of the boy's shirt with both hands. He flailed wildly as he lost his balance, trying not to crash forward into the control yoke or instrument panel. She pulled backward with all her weight. He tumbled toward Estelle, striking out at her with one hand while the other made a wild grab at the control wheel.

A burly arm shot around the boy's body as Manolo Tapia tried to grab him. Hampered as he was by his own seat belt and shoulder harness, he could not equal Estelle's attack. Instantly realizing that, he brought the Beretta around, the barrel danger-ously close to Hector's head. Even as the boy lost his grip and was hauled headfirst and flailing out of the airplane, Tapia fired.

Estelle did not hear the oddly muted snap of the gun, so concentrated was she on the boy. The round struck her squarely in the center of her vest, a sharp blow that only added momen-tum to her backward struggle and knocked the wind out of her. As her body twisted away, a second blow struck her, but now, disregarding the airplane or the boy struggling on top of her, she concentrated on only one thing. Grabbing his right arm as he aimed a punch at her face, she smashed the handcuffs on his left wrist and crunched them closed.

Scrabbling wildly, Ocate shouted for his father, and his right hand grabbed for the landing gear strut as they crashed to the ground.

For an instant, they were an awkward heap—both of them fully out of the airplane, with Estelle trying to rise to her hands and knees, slipping on the pebbles of rough asphalt while Hector Ocate tried his best to hold on to the landing gear strut. With a cry, Tapia stabbed the brakes, and the plane lurched sharply to a stop.

Something struck the passenger window above Estelle's head at the same time that she heard a sharp pop, like someone clapping his hands, or slapping a ripe melon. She flinched down, assuming that Tapia had fired at her again, this time through the thin aluminum skin of the airplane. Hector lost his grip on the landing gear and tried to regain his feet.

Estelle scrabbled hard as the airplane once more started to drift forward, and she lurched toward the approaching horizontal stabilizer with the sole thought of putting distance between herself and the aircraft. But her body refused to obey, and she dropped to all fours again, unable to move the anchor of the boy on the handcuffs.

The Cessna's engine pitch didn't change, and the airplane continued its slow amble diagonally across the runway. The stabilizer passed over her head. She grabbed at Hector's right wrist as he threw an ineffectual punch at her. It should have been easy to throw him facedown, twisting his left arm hard behind him. But she couldn't move, and instead her body sank to the asphalt despite her best efforts. She heard running footsteps and vehicles approaching. Hector stopped his struggle, and lying together in a heap, they both watched the Cessna cross the runway, lurching as its nose wheel dug into the soft gravel on the other side. As soon as the mains ran off the pavement, the airplane slowed. Its prop burst through a thick, stout bush, sending an eruption of plant matter, dirt, and rocks in all directions. Finally the plane stopped, engine burbling in idle, prop windmilling. Estelle could see only a small portion of Manolo Tapia's slumped body in the cockpit.

The boy cursed in Spanish, crying at the same time. But he was trapped, and knew it.

Estelle felt the cuffs released from her wrist. It was Jackie Taber's quiet voice that she heard next. "Be smart now," the deputy said to Hector. "It's over."

It felt good to relax and let her face touch the warm asphalt. She could see a line of police vehicles swerving onto the runway, pulling past the Mustang. Moving as little as possible, she looked west and saw the tall, powerful figure of Sheriff Robert Torrez. He walked quickly through the runty vegetation that grew south of the runway, the scoped rifle cradled in his left arm, right hand relaxed on the stock near the trigger. He circled the airplane warily, then disappeared behind it.

"Tapia has a handgun," Estelle tried to say, but the words came out as little more than a whispered burble.

"You just hold still," someone said. The aircraft engine ran rough and then died, the propeller ticking to a stop.

Estelle pushed herself up, astounded at the weight of her own body. "I'm okay. Really," she said. Other hands took custody of Hector Ocate, and Jackie knelt close to Estelle. "I'm okay," Estelle said again.

"Sure you are," Taber said gently. She barked instructions into her handheld radio, and in a moment Torrez loomed over Estelle, face grim. "He's dead," he said.

"*Ay,*" Estelle murmured. She tried to take a breath. "That's too bad." She tasted copper, an odd, pervasive sensation that was as much a smell as a taste. She knew the first round from the Beretta had caught her flush on the vest, and she tried to turn her head so that she could look down at the single small tear just below the third button of her tan blouse. "Bruised me pretty good," she managed to say.

More faces and hands appeared and she found she had difficulty keeping them in focus. Jackie Taber leaned close, a hand on either side of Estelle's face. "I want you to lie back a little," she said. "We have help on the way."

"Shit," Estelle heard Sheriff Torrez say. "Where's that comin' from?"

In her fog, Estelle found the question absurdly funny. *Help came from Posadas, Robert. Where else?* The asphalt was warm on her back, and it felt good to lie quietly. "I'm okay," she said again, but the faces and voices ignored her.

"Like that," she heard Jackie say, and when shade fell across her face, she opened her eyes and saw Leona Spears. The county manager's large hands took over from the deputy's.

"We'll get you fixed up," Leona said.

"I don't need fixing," Estelle said. What might have been a weak chuckle erupted in a single violent cough. She struggled against the lack of air.

"Get them down here now," Torrez shouted, and off in the distance, toward the end of the runway, Estelle heard more sirens. "Use this," he said, apparently to Jackie. She felt hands fussing with her blouse, her vest, her belt.

"Disrobed with an audience," she whispered, and then the world shifted out of focus and light.

Chapter Thirty-four

Three times Estelle drifted up toward the surface, and her mind linked the moments together and remembered them as an incomprehensible mix of light and sound. When she finally distinguished her husband's voice, she couldn't remember if she had already had conversations with him.

"Can you hear me now?" he asked.

She might have said something, or only thought a reply. He continued to talk to her, quiet and insistent, and the flow of sound gave her a point of focus and comfort. She allowed time to march on, drifting in and out. Oddly, it was a single sound somewhere outside her room—a dropped clipboard, perhaps a clanged mop bucket—that started her into consciousness. It felt as if someone had lowered a concrete slab onto her body.

For a time, she lay absolutely immobile, except for her eyes. She could move those without effort or pain, and she took advantage of that, counting the ceiling tiles, examining the way they were cut and trimmed around the electrical conduits that fed the machines that tended her. She concentrated on the simple task of bringing all the sharp edges into focus. The earlier events that had brought her to this place remained indistinct and confused.

Francis Guzman moved back into view at the right side of the bed. At the same time, she became aware of a thin, bony hand that firmly clamped her left hand. She tried to turn her head and was greeted by a sharp stab of pain whose epicenter erupted in her right armpit, coursing down her arms and up through her shoulder, finding its way to her neck and then down the other side.

"Don't do that," Francis said, and he leaned closer so she could see him without being tempted to shift position. She looked into his dark brown eyes and saw nothing hidden there. "Your mom is here. She's going to make sure you do what you're told." He straightened up, adjusted something, and bent back down, watching her closely. "Is that better?"

"Drugs are wonderful things," she whispered as she felt the odd buzz of the morphine drip.

"Oh, *sí,* they are. Lie quiet and let them do the work."

"Where's *Mamá?*" The tiny hand that held hers didn't feel attached to anything, but it squeezed again.

"She's sitting right beside your bed, *querida.* Don't be moving around, now."

She heard a chair and cautiously shifted her eyes. Her mother's tiny form moved into view, so short and bent that her shoulders were even with the bed.

"You can rest now," Teresa Reyes said, the command absolute.

Tricks of time blended things together again, and when she was able to focus on her husband's face once more, her vision had cleared another click, like sitting behind an optometrist's gadget as he spun the little pinhole wheels and asked, "Which is better, this…or this?"

"I need to talk to Bobby," Estelle said, or thought she said. Her husband leaned close again.

"There's a whole crowd of people who want to see you, *querida.* They're all going to have to wait."

"*Padrino?*"

"Of course."

"You'll tell them for me that they all need to go home?"

"Sure. Maybe you can have some company tomorrow. Maybe Thursday."

That made no sense. She searched his face. "What time is it?"

"A little after three."

She closed one eye in an expression of skepticism, careful not to move anything else. "Come on, *oso*."

He grinned and looked at his watch. "Three-oh-five a.m. This is Tuesday. You're in Presbyterian in Albuquerque."

"Ay." None of that computed. There had been no passage of time in her world. Just an instant ago, her face had rested on the asphalt of the gas company's airstrip…sometime early Sunday afternoon. She could still feel the warmth of the pavement, the sharp bite of the little pebbles against her cheek.

"Tell me," she said.

He bent down close, brushing her cheek with his lips. "Tell you what?"

The thought was easy to consider, but for a moment the words wouldn't form. Eventually she whispered, "Am I going to die?"

The grip of the bony little hand was ferocious, but her mother said nothing. "No," her physician–husband said. "No, you're not. The docs here did a first-rate job of putting you all back together. You're going to hurt a lot, *querida*. But you'll be okay."

"Just okay?"

"You'll be fine."

"You're not lying to me?"

He looked askance, and his touch on her right hand was light but insistent. "When did I ever do that?"

"I'm sorry. What happened? I need to know."

"The first bullet hit your vest and gave you a nice bruise. The second one missed the vest."

"Tell me."

"You just need to concentrate on resting and healing, *querida*."

"Tell me. Every gory detail."

"What's the benefit of that?" the physician asked. "There's time for that later."

"Now is fine. I have nothing to do."

"Caramba," her husband sighed. "A 9mm slug found a way past the edge of your vest just under your right arm, right at

the back of your armpit. You must have been twisting away somehow."

"I need to know," she whispered. For a moment he didn't move, then he gently touched her forehead. "I'll be right back." In less than a minute he returned with a large X-ray sheet. He held it horizontally over her face so she could study it without moving, the ghostly images floating against the ceiling tile.

"Clouds," she said. She'd seen enough X-rays to know what should or shouldn't be there. She could see small fragments where the bullet had punched two ribs, the clouds of hemorrhage along the bullet's path, and more fragments where the slug had busted out through the ribs in front.

"Nasty." He lowered the X-ray. "Like I said, my guess is that you were pivoting away. Do you remember that?"

"I don't remember any of it."

Francis regarded the sheet of film. "Well, it hit you right where your vest wasn't," he said. "The path was across and down a bit. Some lung damage, some liver damage. Busted ribs coming and going." He looked at her affectionately. "You're a mess."

He put the X-ray somewhere out of her sight, then returned and rested his right hand on hers. He touched a strand of hair away from her eyes. She concentrated on reading his expression and concluded that he was telling her the truth.

"*Ay*, that's nothing, then," she said.

"Absolutely nothing," he said. "What were they always saying in the old movies? *Just a flesh wound.*"

"But I'll be okay?"

"Yes, you will. They spent seven hours patching your insides together to make sure of that."

"*Ay*. I'll be a little bit ugly, then."

He grinned. "A few dramatic touches, maybe. You'll have a long scar that follows the body contour, more or less."

"You didn't do the surgery?"

"No, but you had a team of the best."

"Not if you didn't do it." She squeezed his hand. "Tell me about Manolo Tapia."

"He's dead."

She remembered the image of Sheriff Torrez walking across the prairie, rifle in hand. "Bobby?"

"One long-range shot, I'm told. He took it the instant that he was sure you were clear of the airplane."

Ten seconds sooner would have been nice, she thought, and then dismissed that. Robert Torrez would have entertained exactly the same thought, she was sure, and no one needed to dwell on it.

"Hector?"

"INS has him in their custody now."

"Okay." She closed her eyes, and felt the drug-induced fog move a step closer. *"Los dos?"*

"We're all enjoying a big-city vacation," Francis said. "They'll be in to pester you in a little bit. But not right away."

"Soon, though. I need to see them soon."

"Sure. Soon. Francisco wants to bring in his new practice keyboard so he can play you his latest creation."

"Practice keyboard?"

"Padrino has been keeping them busy. Apparently they found this wonderful gadget at a music store. It allows fingering and it's got the touch of working keys, but doesn't make any noise. *Thunk, thunk."*

"The best medicine," she said.

"He wants another recital, of course," Francis said with a laugh. "He's working on his own composition for it. That's what he wants to play for you, so the sooner *you* heal, the better, because the kid is impatient." He let his left hand rest motionless on her forehead. "But we gotta give all those tiny little sutures time to do their thing."

She gripped her mother's hand with her left, and his with the right. Just that simple muscle twitch woke up the demons, and she said nothing for a long time, waiting for the war to reach an uneasy peace.

"I'll wait right here," she whispered.

Chapter Thirty-five

A major triumph came when Estelle could turn her head enough to find the window—without bracing for the blinding stab of pain that lurked somewhere in the cavern under her right shoulder. The blinds were drawn, but she could see edges of bright light drawn around the periphery. Her room was quiet. She vaguely remembered being transferred to this room, the transfer from the rolling bed to this one the most memorable event. When that had happened, she wasn't entirely sure.

"It's twenty minutes after six," her mother's voice said. Estelle felt the tiny hand on hers again. "And you know, it's Saturday. You're getting to be a real lazybones."

"Maybe that's my true calling," Estelle said. Her voice was soft and husky, little more than a whisper after the assault of the various tubes and drugs. She shifted her feet with care. From the waist up, she felt wooden. "Can you open the blinds a little?"

"I don't know." Teresa Reyes made her way to the window, taking her time to maneuver her walker. Estelle watched her mother's tiny figure, aching for her as one gnarled, arthritic hand reached out in slow motion to find the pull strings for the window blinds. "Maybe we'll ask one of the nurses. They'll be along any time now." She persisted until she found the right combination. Light blasted into the room.

Estelle flinched, and the sudden motion brought reminders. She turned away, and saw for the first time that another hospital bed shared the room. It was lower, and she recognized one of her mother's wraps lying at the foot. "You've slept here," she said, but it came out as a gurgle, and she carefully cleared her throat and repeated herself.

"What do you think I would do?" Teresa said. She turned from the window. "One of those doctors says that you have to get out of bed today sometime. They're not going to let you rest, you know." That was exactly what she wanted to do, and understood the conflict of opinions that irked her aging mother. Teresa was old school—rest until the bad humors all went away, perhaps driven off by sheer boredom. Modern surgery's method of convalescence often was the opposite: "Up and at 'em, you slacker."

"That'll be memorable," Estelle said. "I feel like my insides will fall out if I move too fast." A week gone. Just like that. Like turning a clock ahead in the spring. The hour is gone as if it had never been.

"Then move slowly, *hija*." Teresa chuckled. "Take a lesson from this old lady." She reached out a hand to the lower bed beside Estelle's, guiding herself to a slow-motion landing on the edge.

Estelle's eyes ached from the bright light, and she lifted her left arm, hoses and all, and rested her forearm across her eyes.

"You want it closed now?"

"No. It's fine." She turned her head without moving her arm and peered across the room. On a small table, a single vase overflowed with two dozen deep-red roses, the only bouquet in the room. "Those are pretty. I can smell them from here."

"I sent all the others to geriatrics," her mother said, sitting with both hands on the walker. "I couldn't breathe, there were so many." One hand lifted in a dismissive wave, but she smiled at her daughter impishly. "Some of those old people, though. They like a little bouquet now and then."

"Thank you. Who are the roses from?"

"You want to read the card?"

Fogged as she was, Estelle still was amused by her mother, who deftly avoided the question. "Sure. Or you can read it to me if you like."

"I don't think so. You just wait." Something as simple as crossing the room, picking up an envelope, and delivering it was a major undertaking for Teresa Reyes. "You're going to have a crowd today," she added. "They moved you out of that ICU place, where no one could visit."

"I want to see everybody," Estelle said. "All these drugs are funny. I can remember that I had company, but I don't remember what anybody said."

"Not much to miss," Teresa said. She reached the bouquet and stopped, collecting some energy. "They all talk too much."

"I want *los dos* to be here," Estelle said.

"They've been in and out all week. Right now, *Padrino* has them out to breakfast," Teresa said. "These are interesting." She regarded the roses critically. "I've never seen ones so dark."

"I can't stand the suspense," Estelle said as Teresa laboriously removed the envelope from the bouquet.

"This is sealed," she announced.

"Ah, maybe we're not supposed to open it, then."

Teresa sniffed. "*You* open it, *mija*. That will give you something to do." She walkered back across the room and placed the envelope in Estelle's right hand. For a moment, she didn't release her grip on the paper. Instead she leaned as close to her daughter's bed as she could, looking deep into her eyes. She reached out and placed her left hand on Estelle's forehead.

"I'm sorry that you go through all this," she said.

"*Yo también,*" Estelle whispered.

"There are many people thinking of you right now," Teresa said. "When you want to see the cards, there's a whole big box over there on the table with the roses. They just keep coming. And you should see the newspaper. The one from home."

"*Ay.*" Frank Dayan would have had a field day, no doubt. "There will be time for that." Teresa released the envelope, but kept her other hand on Estelle's forehead.

By flexing her elbow with infinite care, Estelle was able to draw her hands together without pain, and she was delighted with that progress.

The envelope was heavy, expensive paper, perhaps even handmade. Most interesting was that Teresa had been correct, in an old-fashioned sort of way. The envelope *was* sealed, its flap secured with a single wax seal that featured an ornate crest. *"¡Qué elegante!"* she said.

"I'm not sure that I trust this man."

"Mamá, por favor." She turned the envelope over, but the address side was blank. She rubbed her thumb on the elegant paper. "How did this arrive?"

"How do you think," Teresa grumbled. She gave Estelle's hair a final affectionate pat and pushed herself away from the bed. "He brought it here."

"Really." Not only was Capitán Tomás Naranjo's office in Buenaventura a *long* way from Albuquerque, it was an *awkward* long way. "When?"

"He came one day."

Estelle turned her head so she could see her mother more clearly. *"Mamá,* I love you. You know that?"

"Of course I know that."

"Which 'one day' was it?"

"Friday, I think. After he called—and not just once. That afternoon, he stayed until he had the chance to talk to Dr. Francis. You were in ICU recovery. He and your husband spoke at some length. And he talked with others, too, I think. Then he left you these roses and the card."

"Did he say that he planned to return?"

"I don't know such things," Teresa said. "You want me to open that for you?"

"No. I can manage."

"Good, because I'm tired." She pushed her walker out of the way and lay down on her side, curled up on her bed like a small child. One hand clawed the white afghan up on her shoulders.

With a thumbnail, Estelle popped the wax seal. She recognized the paper, selected from the display in Bianca Naranjo's upscale gift shop in Chihuahua. Estelle had met the captain's wife on two occasions, and had liked her instantly. At the same time, she could see that Bianca Naranjo had a complete hold on her husband's heart, despite his gallant and sometimes even seductive mannerisms. Perhaps she had even chosen this particular stationery.

Naranjo's handwriting was as old-fashioned as his courtly manner—broad black strokes with a fountain pen, perfectly straight and even, planned carefully to fit the small space. The message began on the inside, and then continued on the back of the card, entirely in formal English, never slipping into the familiar Spanish of their native tongue:

> *As you read this, know that Bianca and I wish for your prompt and complete recovery.*
>
> *With apology, but knowing that work will occupy your mind and speed your recovery, let me pass on this news to you: By the time you are able to read this, we will have secured permission to exhume the remains of Donnie Hansen, the brother of Chester. As you may be aware, his remains—and those of his wife—were not returned to the United States after the tragic "accident" two years past. That in itself is unusual. As soon as paperwork is complete, we will find the site near Quemada. Of course, I will let you know the results the moment they are made clear to me.*
>
> *If circumstances permit, I will call on you when you are well enough to receive casual visitors. If not, feel free to call me the moment that you are able.*
>
> *You should know that there is some relief in various quarters with the news that Manolo Tapia is no longer employed.*

Writing to that point in English, Captain Naranjo had reserved Spanish only for the salutation at the end: *Estoy a su disposición… I am at your disposal.* His signature was formal and reserved—it would have looked at home sealing a government document.

Estelle read the message again, then folded it neatly. If evidence had not been destroyed by fire during the violent car crash, or later during the hasty preparation for burial, the exhumation might yield something. Manolo Tapia's signature would be a 9mm bullet still rattling around inside Donnie Hansen's skull.

Had Chester Hansen paid to have his brother killed? It was a possibility. He had turned over his construction company to Donnie Hansen when he took the lieutenant governor's position. What Donnie had then done with the company—what direction he had tried to take it—would make for an interesting investigation in itself.

If Chester Hansen had paid to solve his problem with Donnie and then reneged on a portion of that payment to Tapia, as the killer himself had suggested, then the balance sheet was closed. The Hansens were dead, Tapia was dead. The three Salvadorans were dead, too, the link to their killers eliminated. If there was a connection between Hansen and the Salvadoran money, the attorney general might be interested in an examination of bank accounts.

But Estelle found that her thoughts kept circling back to the boy. There was nothing she could do to keep Hector Ocate within the jurisdiction of Posadas County. When federal authorities had exhausted their bag of tricks, Mexican officials would want their due, and there was nothing that the undersheriff of Posadas County could do about it.

All of his talent, all of his potential meant nothing now. Estelle tried a deep breath, drawing in to the point where the first stab threatened. If the boy had chosen to create a pastel of a leaping horse, or a portrait of his mother, or a thousand other subjects, he might never have been caught. But one soaring airplane had attracted admiring attention. He had wanted so badly to impress his father—and had managed to do it.

The door opened and her husband slipped into the room. For the first time, Estelle noticed the dark circles under his eyes. "We're going to have to start charging admission," he said, taking care to close the door securely.

"¿*Los dos?*"

"They're with *Padrino*. He said he'd keep 'em busy for a little while longer." Francis Guzman crossed to the bed, taking a moment to straighten Teresa's afghan. "You look cozy," he whispered to the old woman. He turned to Estelle.

"How's the pain?"

"None at the moment, *oso*," she replied. "You do good work."

"I wish I could take credit for every stitch," Francis said, and took her hand. "Two big events today, *querida*. They're going to see how you do on your feet for a few minutes, and a little later we're going to see how food tastes to you."

"Oh, joy. I already *know* how hospital food tastes." She squeezed his hand as hard as she could. "Can I see the boys before this hiking business?"

"You bet. And there's a couple of cops outside who keep pestering to talk with you."

"Bobby?"

"He said he was going to call you later. Maybe tomorrow. No, this is a couple of suit types. Feds. They're getting impatient."

"Ah. Let's get rid of them now, then," Estelle said. "First the suits, then the boys...and then the hike." She squeezed his hand again. "When does *home* fit into all of this?"

"We're lookin' at maybe Wednesday for a transfer."

"Just a maybe?" She noted his use of the word *transfer*, rather than *release*, but even a view of Posadas County through the hospital window on Bustos Avenue would be a relief.

"Yep." He turned at the shrill sound of a child's voice out in the hall. Estelle recognized Carlos' cackle, and her husband squeezed her hand again. "You sure you want to talk with the suits first?"

Estelle nodded. "Oh, *sí*. Let's get that over with," she said. "Once *hijos* take over the room, I won't have time for cops."

To receive a free catalog of Poisoned Pen Press titles, please contact us in one of the following ways:

Phone: 1-800-421-3976
Facsimile: 1-480-949-1707
Email: info@poisonedpenpress.com
Website: www.poisonedpenpress.com

Poisoned Pen Press
6962 E. First Ave. Ste. 103
Scottsdale, AZ 85251

8-11
14.95

T 565618

LaVergne, TN USA
05 April 2011
222910LV00002B/16/P